The Love of Friends

Also by Nancy Bond

A String in the Harp
(A 1977 Newbery Honor Book)

The Best of Enemies

Country of Broken Stone

The Voyage Begun

A Place to Come Back To

Another Shore

Truth to Tell

(Margaret K. McElderry Books)

The Love of Friends

NANCY BOND

Margaret K. McElderry Books

MARGARET K. McELDERRY BOOKS
25 YEARS • 1972–1997

Margaret K. McElderry Books
An imprint of Simon & Schuster Children's Publishing Division
1230 Avenue of the Americas
New York, New York 10020

Book design by Nina Barnett
The text of this book is set in 12-point Cochin.

Printed in the United States of America

First Edition

10 9 8 7 6 5 4 3 2 1

Library of Congress Cataloging-in-Publication Data
Bond, Nancy.
The love of friends / by Nancy Bond.—1st ed.
p. cm.
Sequel to: A place to come back to.
Summary: While visiting her friend Oliver in London, sixteen-year-old Charlotte reluctantly agrees to accompany him on an important trip to Scotland, during which she examines their relationship and tries to understand him better.
ISBN 0-689-81365-1
[1. Friendship—Fiction. 2. London (England)—Fiction.
3. Scotland—Fiction.] I. Title.
PZ7.B63684Lo 1997
[Fic]—dc21
96-38087
CIP AC

for all the friends who've given me support
during a difficult year, and especially for my family.
—N. B.

Epigraph:

From quiet homes and first beginning,
Out to the undiscovered ends,
There's nothing worth the wear of winning
But laughter and the love of friends.

—Hilaire Belloc

One

All around her the passengers from Charlotte Paige's transatlantic flight were reassembling their luggage, balancing their loads, and heading like pack animals toward the exit. Feeling rumpled and a little stiff, she gripped her suitcase in one hand and her duffel bag in the other and joined the flow, eager for her first glimpse of London. But when the automatic doors swung outward all she saw was the glare of artificial lights and a confusion of faces, a bedlam of heat and noise. She had no chance to stop and get her bearings. Passengers were crowding her from behind and she had to keep moving. Charlotte locked her fingers on the handles of her bags and thought this must be how an egg felt, dropped from its shell into the bowl of an electric mixer.

A hand closed lightly on her shoulder and she turned to find her seatmate from the plane giving her a questioning look. "You did say you were being met?" asked Barbara

Coburn. She had her bags stowed on a luggage cart; they were similar to Charlotte's, only more used-looking.

"Yes," said Charlotte. "He promised he'd be here. I'm sure he will, it's just—I hadn't thought—all these people!"

Barbara nodded. "It's worse every time I come. Anne's not due from Toronto for another hour. I could wait with you—?"

Charlotte almost said *Yes, please.* Barbara was in her fifties, a seasoned traveler who'd lost count of the times she'd been to Britain. She and Charlotte had passed the long, cramped night playing Travel Scrabble and telling each other where they'd come from and where they were going. Barbara's offer was tempting, but Charlotte stiffened her spine. "No, that's all right. Thanks. I know he's here somewhere, I just have to find him." And if she didn't, she had the Prestons' address and telephone number. She had the wad of British currency her father had pressed on her as a parting gift at Logan Airport in Boston, and all the travelers' checks zipped safely in the flap pocket of her L.L. Bean haversack along with her passport. She was sixteen, old enough to be responsible for herself.

"Well, have a grand time, Charlotte. Do all you can—you'll have time to catch up on your sleep when you get home!"

"And you. Scotland sounds so wonderful, if only—"

"You can't do it all in one trip," Barbara told her cheerfully. "I really envy you seeing London for the first time. It's never the same again."

Charlotte watched her disappear into the shifting

throng, then edged farther away from the doors and began to search the faces for one she recognized. The sooner she found Oliver and his parents, the sooner she could relax and let them take charge.

"Don't look so worried, here I am," said a voice that sounded not quite familiar. At the same instant she felt the suitcase handle whisked out of her fingers. She spun around and there was Oliver, looking down at her. He was a good two inches taller than her.

"I didn't see you!"

"You weren't looking in the right place. Doesn't matter, anyway, I saw *you*. No, don't put that down, let's get out of here. Why didn't you get a luggage cart?" Without waiting for an answer, he thrust her suitcase out in front of him like a snowplow and, grasping Charlotte firmly by the hand, towed her after him. Once they'd left the gate area, the mob thinned and Charlotte looked around for Oliver's mother and stepfather, but they were nowhere to be seen. In a quiet backwater behind a newsstand, Oliver put the suitcase down between his feet and brushed the wing of straight brown hair off his forehead. "That's better. What a scrum."

His hair was longer than Charlotte remembered, and his face had taken on a decidedly adult shape. He's eighteen, she thought with an odd little flutter. He's grown up. Somehow, in spite of months of anticipation, she didn't feel prepared.

"So you really came," he said, his expression almost challenging.

She gave a surprised gulp of laughter. "Didn't you

think I would? It's been arranged for *ages*. I only talked to you Monday, Oliver."

He gave a little shrug. "Unexpected things happen."

"Like what? You're not sorry I'm here, are you?"

The corners of his mouth twitched. "I'd have hated to make this trip for nothing, I promise you. Look, there's no point hanging around Heathrow. Do you need anything before we leave?"

"Like what?"

"The loo."

"The what?"

"Bathroom. WC. Rest room. Toilet. Bog. The loo."

"Oh." She shook her head. "Oliver, you sound different."

"It's not me. You sound different. *I* sound like everyone else. Eric says I've got an excellent BBC accent." He gave her the hint of a grin.

Eric. Again Charlotte glanced around. "Where are they? I mean"—she couldn't quite bring herself to say Eric and Paula—"I mean your parents. In her last letter, your mother said—"

The grin vanished. "Meetings," he said unspecifically. "Something came up."

"Unexpectedly?" she suggested, trying to bring it back.

But he didn't smile. "If you want, we can take a taxi from here. We'll have to queue and it'll cost a packet, but that doesn't matter. Or we could simply take the underground to Saint Pancras and get a taxi there. All right? Do you mind?"

He'd already decided, she realized. "All right." She tried not to feel overwhelmed. This wasn't exactly the welcome she'd braced for, but she supposed she ought to be grateful. She had been rather dreading having to face Paula and Eric Preston first thing in the morning after sitting up all night. She barely knew Eric, she'd only met him once, although she saw him often on the nightly national news broadcasts, reporting from London, where he was chief bureau correspondent. And though she knew Paula better, she didn't exactly like her. No matter how reasonably her mother explained about Paula Preston, why she'd done what she'd done, Charlotte couldn't help believing that Paula had abandoned her son. Oliver had been only eight when his parents had divorced; his father had cleared out and begun a whole new life with a new family on the West Coast, and Paula had packed Oliver off to a succession of boarding schools until she'd run out of places willing to accept him. Then she'd parked him on his elderly great-uncle in Concord, Massachusetts, while she continued her career at the National Endowment for the Humanities in Washington, D.C., and eventually married Eric Preston. When Oliver's uncle Sam had died suddenly, a year and a half ago, Paula had reclaimed Oliver, uprooting him from Concord and taking him to London.

Oliver picked up the suitcase again.

"Just don't lose me," Charlotte warned. "Not on my first morning. I'll take the next plane home if you do, Oliver."

He gave her an unreadable look. "Why don't I carry them both." Taking the duffel bag from her, he shouldered his way through the terminal. Charlotte followed, sticking to his heels. At least the extra inches made him easier to keep track of.

She let him do the fares without protest, grateful not to have to fumble with unfamiliar money, and once they were on the subway train, sitting side by side in a no-smoking car, she stopped concentrating and let her mind blur. It did seem anticlimactic to approach London through a series of tunnels. They looked like Boston tunnels: dim and grubby. If Paula had come to meet her with Oliver, Charlotte knew they'd be taking a taxi. She should have told Oliver that she *did* mind, that she wanted to stay aboveground where she could see something.

As if reading her mind, Oliver leaned next to her ear and said, "You're not missing anything. Really. Just lines of traffic on the motorway and acres of industrial park."

She squinted at the map above the sliding doors: a network of colored lines connecting black circles. She found Heathrow at the end of a dark blue one. There were a lot of circles between it and Saint Pancras; the names were very hard to read. She removed her glasses and polished them on a Kleenex. How they got so smudged sitting on her nose she could never fathom. But the smudginess wasn't all on the lenses. She was tired and there really was no point in struggling to read the names of places she was only passing underneath. She stifled a yawn and was overtaken by another, bigger one, and then . . . then a voice in her ear was telling her to wake up. "We're almost there, Charlotte. It's the next stop."

Sluggishly she swam upward through sleep, opened

her eyes, and yawned again. The car had magically filled with passengers in her absence. For just a second she was completely lost, then she remembered where she was.

"This is it." Oliver swung himself upright, balancing easily against the sway of the train. Charlotte unfolded rather more awkwardly and staggered. He reached out a hand and steadied her. "All right?" She nodded and swallowed. Her arm tingled under his fingers. The train stopped and he let go and hefted her luggage.

The air on the platform was stuffy and smelled of soot and hot metal. Oliver led the way to the end where there was an escalator. As she got on a step below him, he pulled her to the left so people could climb past.

"What *is* Saint Pancras?" she asked when they got to the top. "It sounds like a hospital."

"What? No, it's a railway station," he said as if she should have known. "You'll see."

They navigated an endless maze of tunnels up and down short flights of steps, around corners, past barricades and temporary walls plastered with signs apologizing for the inconvenience of construction, graffiti, and arrows to King's Cross, Saint Pancras, the Northern Line, the Metropolitan Line. Charlotte's head began to throb. She felt as if she were having a bad subterranean dream and didn't know how to wake up. Why hadn't anyone told her that England was underground?

Suddenly they were in the open air; she smelled wet pavement and diesel exhaust, and heard the hiss of tires on asphalt, the grinding of gears, the rumble of engines. A red double-decker bus loomed out of the traffic, and boxy black taxis wove in and out like dodgems. On the pavement she saw a dark-suited man wearing a bowler hat and carrying a furled umbrella. She felt a surge of delight: so there really were people who looked like that! But Oliver hustled her over a black and white crosswalk; she felt the hot breath of a truck on her face. On the far side he stopped. "There. Turn around. That's Saint Pancras."

It looked like something her architect brother, Max, and his five-year-old daughter, Hilary, might build out of red and white Legos, only multiplied by a hundred: spires and finials and towers and arches and buttresses. What a jigsaw puzzle it would make. "A railway station?"

Oliver gave her an almost-smile. "One of the best." He put her suitcase down and hailed a taxi as if he'd been doing it all his life.

"Where to, guv?" The driver looked like an African but sounded British.

"Highgate," said Oliver. "Ninety-two Summerson Gardens."

At last they were traveling aboveground. Charlotte sat back and waited for Oliver to explain where they were and what she was seeing, but he was silent, sitting forward on the seat, studying the road ahead as intently as if he were driving. She watched him for a while, trying to analyze the silence, until she realized all her muscles were tense. With an effort she relaxed and said, "I don't mind, you know."

"Mind? What don't you mind?" He turned his head, a frown between his brows.

"That they didn't come to the airport."

The frown deepened.

"I mean, unexpected things do come up."

"Oh, yes," he agreed. "They do."

It was her turn to frown. "Oliver—"

"There," he said, pointing out the window. "That's the Archway tube station. We're not far. This is Highgate Hill." The taxi was chugging up a long, steep incline. Outside, the dampness in the air was organizing itself into invisible drops; the driver turned on the wipers and people on the pavements began to put up umbrellas and coat collars. "Do you remember Dick Whittington?"

"Dick Whittington? You mean the guy with the cat?" He couldn't mean *that* Dick Whittington—

But, "Yes, the guy with the cat." Oliver's face lost some of its remoteness. "This is where he stopped. Where he heard the voice saying, 'Turn again, Whittington, Lord Mayor of London.'"

"You mean he was real?"

Near the top of the hill Oliver pointed out a big, green-domed Catholic church. "Holy Joe's. It's a good landmark—you can see it from a distance." The nickname sounded blasphemous to Charlotte, but he said everyone called it that. Beyond was a wet green park with puddles of bright flowers under its dripping trees, and across from it a row of little shops. The traffic had thinned, and the taxi turned right into a network of residential streets lined with parked cars and sober, stone-fronted houses.

"Ninety-four, you said?"

Oliver was leaning forward again. "Ninety-two. That's it, on the right, behind the horse chestnut." Ninety-two was the left side of a two-family house. A short flight of steps led up to the front door, and a longer one down to a little paved area outside the basement windows. "Connie got us the flat—it's the top two floors. Paula complains about the lack of mod cons—no elevator, no central heat, no dishwater—but it's so much better than the place we had in Holland Park. That was a hole. Peter and Inga live down there—" he gestured toward the basement. "It's called the garden flat to make it sound more attractive, but the garden's only a strip of grass and a sorry-looking tree at the back. Peter's the caretaker. They've got a baby," he added, as if it were contagious.

He ushered her through the front door into a dark, damp little hallway. Charlotte sniffed, wrinkling her nose involuntarily; there was a faint smell that reminded her of gym socks. "Inga's making cabbage soup," said Oliver. "Connie has the ground-floor flat. We go up." After his tense silence in the taxi, he seemed to be talking too much. Charlotte had trouble keeping up. "Who's Connie?"

"Connie Rinaldi." He unlocked the door at the top of the stairs. "I'm sure I wrote you about her. She and Paula were at school together ages ago. She runs a posh sort of tourist bureau in Hampstead, booking things for visiting dignitaries—hotels, special tours, theater tickets—money no object. Paula's working for her now. She hated the job at the Embassy. Keep going, the bedrooms are on the top floor. This one's yours. I think you've got everything you need, so I'll leave you to get settled." He deposited her bags on the pink-and-gray floral carpet and withdrew before she had her breath back from the climb. She heard his feet thud back down the stairs.

For a minute she stood still, then she took a deep breath and blew it up through her bangs. She remembered being twelve, cold and wet and abandoned in the middle of Commodore Shattuck's unfamiliar kitchen. Oliver had left her there and disappeared the first time they'd had anything to do with each other, one raw, wintry April afternoon, after they'd fallen into the Coolidges' pond. The memory was oddly reassuring; underneath his adult appearance, Oliver hadn't changed all that much.

The room was long and narrow, like a railway carriage, with a desk and electric typewriter at the far end, and a convertible couch made up as a bed in the middle. The single window looked out into the branches of the horse chestnut. Once she'd unpacked a few things and found the bathroom—it was next to a large double bedroom at the rear that she guessed belonged to Paula and Eric—she went to find Oliver. He was downstairs in the kitchen, sitting at a table by the window with his legs stretched out, looking very long, and a mug of something steaming in front of him. A radio played softly and he was staring into space, far away. Charlotte coughed diffidently and he actually jumped. "Why are you tiptoeing?"

"I'm not. You must have a guilty conscience."

"About what?" he asked sharply.

"Well, *I* don't know. What have you done to feel guilty about?" She'd meant it lightly, but Oliver glared at her and she blinked. For just a second she wondered if he was glad to see her. "I brought some photographs to show you," she said, changing the subject. "The farm, Amos and

Hilary, and a lot that were taken at the party for Skip and Deb after they eloped."

His face relaxed. He brushed the hair off his forehead, and pulled his legs under him. "Good. I hoped you would. Are you hungry?"

This was safe. "I think maybe I am. In fact, I guess I'm starving." She sat listening to Beethoven's *Emperor* Concerto while Oliver made her a cheese omelette and toast.

"Coffee?"

"Ugh. Is that what you're drinking? I thought everyone in England drank tea."

"Only in old novels. No, I lie. Lots of people do. Eric drinks tea. I'll make you some."

She would have preferred cocoa or even milk, but couldn't bring herself to say so. "When did you start listening to classical music?" Oliver was not the kind of person to use the radio for noise; if he had it on, he was listening.

"What? Oh, I don't know. We do a lot of music at school," he said offhandedly as he filled a blue-and-white teapot.

"Eliot says hello," said Charlotte, her mind making the logical jump from Beethoven to her favorite brother. "I talked to him just"—she paused, trying to straighten out her sense of time—"just the night before last. He called right after you."

"How is he?"

"He sounds fine. He's got a job this summer as a cook on rafting expeditions on the Snake River."

"Eliot? Your brother Eliot?" said Oliver, putting a paisley-print cozy over the pot. "The one who can't toast ready-made corn muffins without burning them?"

Charlotte grinned. "He says that people who are in constant danger of death by drowning pay very little attention to what they eat."

Oliver nodded. "That's Eliot." He'd made himself another cup of coffee and sat down across from her. "You were going to visit him this summer, weren't you? Are you still going?"

Charlotte shrugged her stiff shoulders; it felt good. Eliot, who'd started out to be a musician, was finishing graduate school in wildlife management in Montana. He'd been planning to take her backpacking in the Wind River Mountains in August, but then Oliver's stepfather had learned he was being reassigned to Washington in October. Instead of spending her own savings on a plane ticket to Billings, Charlotte had been given her high-school graduation present a year early: a plane ticket to London to visit Oliver. "Eliot's staying to do research for the Park Service," she said. "He promised I can fly out next summer." She didn't tell Oliver how torn she'd felt when she'd heard Eliot's voice, so cheerful and familiar, come bursting out of the telephone receiver, wishing her bon voyage. "The mountains'll keep, Chuck," he assured her. "I'll still be here and I'll be a much better cook."

Though not a match for Oliver, she thought, regretfully finishing her omelette. It had been pale golden and oozy with cheese and a hint of herbs. Barabara Coburn, who had strongly advised Charlotte against trying the airplane tea, would have approved of Oliver's. It was dark brown and had a few tiny leaves floating in it to prove he hadn't used bags. With plenty of milk and two heaping spoonfuls of sugar, Charlotte found it quite acceptable. The last year he'd lived in Concord, Oliver had done most of the cooking and shopping. His great-uncle had grumbled about being kept out of his own kitchen, but only as a matter of form. Oliver had approached cooking as he approached anything he decided to learn: single-mindedly. He had become quite proficient, much better than Charlotte.

"Hard work keeping a plane in the air for eight hours, isn't it?" he remarked, watching her eat the last corner of toast.

"I'll say." She was feeling much easier, relieved to have time to get comfortable with Oliver before she had to cope with Paula and Eric. Although they'd written frequently and even talked to each other on the phone now and then, she hadn't seen Oliver for a year and a half. "Max was explaining aerodynamics to Hilary at the airport, but I prefer the Tinker Bell Theory."

"Oh?"

"That's where you just clap a lot."

He smiled politely. "What about the photographs?"

The first few were of Charlotte's father and Oliver's dog, Amos: Mr. Paige looked benign, Amos as disorganized as ever, but clearly happy and well cared for. Oliver had had to leave him behind in Concord. "Dad's nuts about him," said Charlotte, still faintly surprised. "He says we ought to have gotten a dog years ago—they're very therapeutic—but Eliot had all those cats. Now there's only one cat left, Lap, and she doesn't pay any attention to Amos. Hu-Kwah stayed at the old house on Main Street. The Robinsons have adopted him." She handed Oliver another picture, this one of Amos by himself, gray and disheveled, his expression endearingly hopeful, gazing right into the camera. Oliver studied it in silence. At last he said, "I really miss him. I suppose he's forgotten me by now."

"Don't you believe it. He'd go crazy if you walked into the house. I brought you a frame for that—I thought you'd like to keep it. This one's the house from the back."

"Do you like it better now?"

"I've gotten used to it. Really, it's a nice house and Mom was right. With Deb and Eliot gone, the other one was much too big. And I'm far enough from school so I can take the bus instead of having to walk."

"Walking's good for you," he pointed out.

"Oh, Oliver, I used to *hate* it in the rain and snow!"

"You should learn to drive."

"I'm going to, in the fall. I've signed up for driver's ed, but I can still bike to the middle of town, and we're a lot closer to the Commodore's house." It was Oliver's house now, of course; his great-uncle had left it to him, but she still thought of it as Commodore Shattuck's. Oliver was only two years older than her; it didn't seem possible that he could own something as large and important as a house. "These are all of the farm last summer and fall—look at the sunflowers! They made the front page of the *Concord Journal*, and the *Globe* sent a photographer from Boston."

"The farm looks pretty good," said Oliver critically. "Andy's still serious about it?"

"Absolutely. He's going to restore the cider press this winter."

"But he hasn't got an orchard."

"He can buy apples wholesale. He's been reading about cider making for months. If he'd been studying it for school he'd've gotten an A, but if it was for school he wouldn't have studied it," said Charlotte dryly.

Their friend, Andy Schuyler, channeled all his time and energy into the Bullard Farm. It had been in his mother's family for 150 years, but when Andy and his twin sister, Kath, had been five, their father had stopped farming and gotten a job in the Concord Department of Public Works. Unlike farming, it paid a steady, reliable salary and had regular hours. But all Andy wanted to do with his life was farm. His parents, Pat and George, had leaned on him hard enough to keep him in high school until graduation, but after that they'd reluctantly agreed he could do what he chose. During the past three years he'd read everything he could get his hands on about organic farming. "More and more people are going to want vegetables grown without chemical fertilizer and pesticides," he had predicted, and it looked as if he was right. Charlotte's sister, Deb, bought his produce in quantity for her customers at the Magic Cupboard, her health food store. Last summer he'd enlarged the herb patches, growing several kinds of parsley and basil, as well as tarragon, dill, chives, and others Charlotte had never heard of. It was hard, intensive work, and Andy would never be rich—he acknowledged that himself—but he was doing what made him happy. In his own way, Charlotte often reflected, he was even more single-minded than Oliver.

"When you go home, will you work at the farm?"

"Mmm. Andy's short of help."

"No wonder. Does he pay anything?"

"Yes, of course he does. Not a lot, but—"

"Hmmm," said Oliver.

"He puts the money back into the farm, Oliver. He doesn't spend it on himself," she said defensively. "And he works harder than anyone."

"So you do it for love, not money."

She glanced at him, but his face gave nothing away. "You could say that. I like being outside all summer and watching things grow," she said carefully.

Oliver picked up another photograph. "Who's this?"

"Paul Watts." Charlotte was relieved to move on. "That's Andy's old tractor—the one from the barn? Paul got it running and he's going to help with the cider press. He hangs around the farm a lot now." She gave Oliver a thoughtful look. "That last year at school, did you know how Kath felt about you?"

For a minute Oliver didn't say anything, then, instead of answering, he said, "Paul and Kath go well together, don't they? When was this one taken?"

"At the party," said Charlotte, deciding not to push him. "Mrs. Watts said Paul would only have worn a suit to please Kath—*she* could never get him to do it." Paul Watts and Kath Schuyler had been caught by the photographer holding hands on the terrace beside the farmhouse.

Paul's expression was pleased and embarrassed; Kath's short curly red hair glowed like a nimbus around her face. She looked confident and happy.

"And here's the bride and groom," said Oliver. "I can't believe they kept it secret from all of you."

"They told Pat. She took care of the store while they were away and helped to plan the party. They went out to Nantucket for four days in September and when they came back they looked insufferably smug and they were both wearing wedding rings. It was a bit hard on Mom, I think—not that she wanted Deb to have a big formal wedding, but she would have liked to be in on it."

Regretfully, Oliver said, "It looks like a great party. I wish I'd been there."

"There's Eliot dancing with Pat."

"He got his hair cut."

"He claimed it was in protest because Skip hadn't asked him to be best man. The square dance was so much fun, no one wanted to leave and Andy's agreed to have another one in the barn this fall. Hilary went to sleep on the dog's bed under the dining room table and there was a terrible panic when no one could find her. Max was convinced she'd climbed into someone's car and been carried off. She was covered with dog hair, but otherwise—there she is, about to be taken home. This is the best one of Deb and Skip. He resigned from the bank last month and Deb's made him a partner in the Magic Cupboard. And Pat's got a regular part-time job there now. Eliot says it's incestuous."

Oliver grinned. "He would. Where was this taken? You and Kath and Andy and Paul. That's not the party, is it?"

"No," said Charlotte, wishing suddenly she hadn't put that photograph in with the others. "That's before the junior prom. We all went together."

"The four of you," said Oliver neutrally and Charlotte nodded, handing him a picture of the wedding cake. "Mom's friend, Sally Fenn, made it—those are real flowers. The top layer's in our freezer for their first anniversary. They loved the Scottish blankets your mother sent as a wedding present."

"Good." Full stop. He'd closed down at the mention of Paula. Charlotte searched for something else to say, but before she could find it, he got up and began to clear the table. "How do you feel? Shall we do something?"

She looked doubtfully out the window. "It's not a very nice day."

"It isn't actually raining. You don't want to take a nap, do you?"

"Deb said I shouldn't. She told me the best thing to do on the first day is to stay awake and go to bed early."

"Then we'll go for a walk. Come on, we can leave the dishes."

"What about your mother?"

"We'll be back before she is, don't worry. Do you have a mac?"

"A what?"

"A raincoat—mackintosh—mac," he translated impatiently. "You'll have to learn English, Charlotte."

Two

The route Oliver followed seemed very complicated. Charlotte quickly gave up trying to keep track of where they turned which direction; her brain felt too furry. Besides, she had no intention of going anywhere without Oliver, at least not until she was more familiar with her surroundings. The cool, damp air helped wake her up, however, and it did feel good to be walking.

"This is the High Street," said Oliver. "We came up it in the taxi."

"Where's your school?"

"On up that way." He waved his hand unspecifically.

"Will you show me?" Charlotte liked to be able to place the people she knew in their spaces so she could think of them with their feet on solid ground instead of floating in a vacuum.

"Later. Right now we're going somewhere really special."

They crossed the street and entered the park. The benches were empty and the paths practically deserted. Oliver went through and out the other side into a narrow, walled lane. "Here we are," he said, stopping in front of a stone archway. The heavy wrought-iron gate stood half open. Overhead, carved in the soot- and damp-stained stone, was LONDON CEMETERY.

"You don't mean this," objected Charlotte. "You haven't brought me to see a graveyard?"

Beyond the gate was a mysterious, secretive place, its narrow paths overhung with tangled tree branches. Ivy crawled up the memorials; weeds and grass and briars flourished unchecked, half burying obelisks and stone angels. Through ragged curtains of leaves, Charlotte glimpsed shrouded figures, broken columns, Celtic crosses. She followed Oliver down a roofless corridor of crypts, noticing with a kind of delicious horror that many of the doors were not securely shut; within lay an ominous, tented darkness. Hidden somewhere in the wild shrubbery, a bird sang, pouring out a disembodied stream of notes.

They had been wandering for about fifteen minutes when Charlotte asked curiously, "Do you come here often? You seem to know your way around."

Oliver stopped in front of a life-sized stone lion, lying nose on paws, asleep. "I wouldn't say *often.* One of the chaps from school—Timothy Harker—showed it to me. His father's a vicar and Harker likes cemeteries. He's compiling a guide, actually—where to find the best monuments and atmosphere. This is his favorite."

"It's very gothic," said Charlotte. "I wouldn't want to come after dark."

"Owls and foxes prowl in the dead of night."

"Foxes? In London? Oh, Oliver—dead of night," said Charlotte reproachfully, and he actually grinned.

"I thought we could walk across Hampstead Heath and take the bus back. All right?"

Obviously he knew where he was going, so Charlotte acquiesced without protest, although she realized afterward she ought to have questioned him about distances. It seemed to her like a very long walk from the cemetery to Hampstead Heath, through streets lined with expensive houses set back behind green and flowering front gardens. By the time they reached the Heath, the drizzle had turned to rain again. "Is this it?" said Charlotte, peering through the murk. All she could see was a great expanse of rough ground, trees, and grass, with here and there a dark figure hurrying along. "Wouldn't it be better to come when the sun's shining?"

"The choice," Oliver told her, "is to go on and get a bus from the Spaniards, or walk back the way we just came."

"Can't we get a bus from here?"

"There aren't any. We might as well go on."

Charlotte sighed. Rather than ask Oliver what the Spaniards was, or were, she decided to save her breath for walking. By the time they reached the Spaniards, which turned out to be a whitewashed pub on the top edge of the Heath, they were both wet, and Charlotte was beginning to feel as if she had swum the Atlantic.

"You said you wanted a walk," said Oliver, once they

were sitting in the dry interior of a number 210 bus, trundling toward Highgate.

"*You* said I wanted a walk," Charlotte corrected him. Her eyelids felt very heavy.

It was almost three o'clock when they reached the flat. Charlotte went up to change her clothes—her shoes and socks were sodden—while Oliver put some soup on the stove to heat. They sat in the kitchen with steaming bowls of it, cutting chunks off a block of cheese to eat with big round crackers. The soup was rich and very brown, like gravy. When Charlotte asked what it was, Oliver said, "Oxtail." "But what's in it?" "Oxtails." Experimentally, Charlotte tested another spoonful. "You don't really mean—?" Oliver nodded. "Of course." Charlotte tried to picture an oxtail *in situ*, but she had a little trouble conjuring up an ox. Like a cow with horns, that was the best she could do. She wasn't sure she ought to like the soup, but it was warm and, she had to admit, quite tasty. As the comforting stuff filled her stomach, her bones seemed to soften until she felt limp. "Now," said Oliver, regarding her speculatively. "Now," said Charlotte, "I think I *would* like a nap."

When she woke, the room had grown velvet dark. Through the tracery of leaves and branches outside the window, she glimpsed fragments of a rose-gray sky. Rolling onto her back, she stretched luxuriously. She had fallen onto the bed with just enough energy to pull the bedspread up; while she was unconscious, someone had covered her with a comforter. She had no idea how long she'd been asleep or what time it was. There was a digital clock on the desk by the window. She fumbled for her glasses and squinted at the square green numbers: eight-forty. Her nerve endings began to tingle slightly. She'd slept for more than four hours. . . .

Reluctant to move, she lay thinking about the events of the day, beginning with her arrival at Heathrow, the subway journey, the cemetery, the long, wet slog across Hampstead Heath. It seemed unreal, like a faintly nightmarish dream, but she knew it wasn't. Oliver really had dragged her miles and miles in the rain. Although it wasn't what she'd expected, reviewing it, she found she wasn't awfully surprised.

She considered getting undressed and going to bed properly. She was sorely tempted to put off Paula and Eric, who must certainly be home by now, until morning. But that was cowardly, and besides she had to go to the bathroom. There was a small washbasin the corner of her room beside the wardrobe where she'd hung her clothes. Peering at herself in the mirror above it, she sighed. There was a red wrinkle mark etched into her left cheek, and her hair looked flat and stringy except where she'd lain on it wrong and it stuck out over her ear. She washed her face with cold water and combed the hair down as best she could. The room was chilly—Oliver'd said no central heat. Her mother had been dubious when Charlotte packed the bulky Aran cardigan her sister-in-law, Jean, had knit her for Christmas—"It takes up so much room, darling"—but Charlotte pulled it on gratefully. People had told her England could be cold, and as the airplane had entered its descent pattern that morning, the captain had announced the weather in London was showery and the temperature was nineteen degrees. "Nineteen?" Charlotte had echoed in horror. "Centigrade," Barbara Coburn had said soothingly. "I can never remember how to turn it into Fahrenheit, but it's well above freezing."

Still, Charlotte had been right about the sweater; it warmed and comforted her as the soup had. Opening the door, she put her head out and listened. The silence was complete; no murmur of voices, no one moving around, not even the radio this time. The only light came up the stairwell from below. For a moment she wondered if everyone could have gone to bed. But it was too early.

Paula and Eric's room was empty and untouched; it looked just as it had when she'd arrived. So did the bathroom. The sound of the toilet flushing was unnervingly loud. At the top of the stairs she paused and took a couple of slow, deliberate breaths, pushing her rib cage apart and knitting it back together as Deb had taught her. Deb did yoga; she said deep breathing helped calm and center you, and Charlotte found it was true.

But five minutes later, breathing wasn't enough. By then she'd made a tour of the rooms on the floor below and found them empty. In case she'd missed something, she went back upstairs and tried Oliver's room, next to hers. It showed signs of recent occupation: Amos's photograph in the pewter frame she'd picked out had been placed prominently on his bureau, the bed had been sat on, the sweater and slacks Oliver'd been wearing were hung neatly over the desk chair, and a damp towel huddled on the floor under the basin where it had fallen. But Oliver was gone. She was alone in the apartment.

Downstairs again, Charlotte conducted a methodical search, but she could find no message in any of the obvious places. No note from Oliver to tell her where he'd gone and when he'd be back, and nothing from Paula, either, which struck Charlotte as peculiar. She and Eric must not have gotten back from their mysterious meetings. Ambivalent as Charlotte might feel about Oliver's mother, she was sure that Paula would have gone to great lengths to be on hand, if not when she arrived, then soon after. At the very least she would have left a note of welcome. Charlotte knew from Paula's frequent letters to her mother that she'd been organizing this visit for months: getting theater and concert tickets, planning a weekend in the Cotswolds, even arranging admission to Centre Court, Wimbledon. Paula was not careless about details and neither was her son.

Charlotte wished she'd never woken up; if she'd slept through until morning she wouldn't know she'd been abandoned. Unless, she thought hollowly, there was still no one there in the morning. For a moment she wondered if this was all—everything that had happened since she got off the airplane—one continuous unpleasant dream and she'd only *dreamed* she'd woken from it.

But she knew she was wide awake, so wide awake it would be useless to go back to bed, because she wouldn't sleep. Deciding that doing something was preferable to doing nothing, she went down to the first floor and knocked on Connie Rinaldi's door. There was a light on inside—she could see it shining underneath—but no one answered, and when she went out on the front steps she saw the other windows were dark. Connie Rinaldi was out, too. She hesitated for a moment. Peter and Inga were most definitely at home. From the flat below she could hear the robust wailing of an angry baby and the abrasive sound of a television turned up too loud. She felt too delicate to brave the noise and retreated.

It was almost ten-thirty when she heard a key in the lock. She had turned on all the lights in the living room and curled up on the squashy green sofa with a package of shortbread she'd scavenged from the kitchen and a month-old copy of the international edition of *Time*. She'd begun to feel hazy when she heard the click, and a moment later Oliver called, "Charlotte?" Instantly she was alert. She didn't answer; she waited for him to find her.

He was wearing a navy raincoat over navy slacks, a pale blue shirt, and a tie, and his hair was dark with rain. "I didn't think you'd wake up," he said, faintly aggrieved. Standing there, he looked like a stranger. It took Charlotte a minute to remember why she was angry with him. "Where did you *go*, Oliver?"

He shrugged out of his raincoat. "I had a meeting."

She spluttered, half laughing, half furious. "*Oliver!*"

He had the grace to look sheepish. "Don't shout. All right, I'm sorry. It was a rehearsal. We have a concert Friday night."

"A concert?" She was thrown off stride. "Who? What kind of concert?"

"It's a benefit for the concert hall at school. We're doing pieces from Gilbert and Sullivan with the Thurston Hall girls' chorus."

"Why didn't you tell me? Why didn't you wake me up? I could have gone with you."

"You were sound asleep, Charlotte. I looked in before I went—I didn't want to disturb you."

"You could at least have left a note. What was I supposed to think when I couldn't find anyone? I went downstairs to ask—"

"Connie?" His face went still. "What did she say?"

"Nothing. She wasn't there. I know what you told me, Oliver, but where exactly are Paula and Eric? Why haven't they come back?"

With an exaggerated sigh, he sat down in a frumpy, flowered easy chair beside the fireplace. It was faced with mustard-colored tile, and for the first time Charlotte noticed there was a molded-plastic coal fire in it. Oliver studied his hands for a minute; when he looked up, his face was a careful, unrevealing blank. "I didn't lie to you, Charlotte. They are at meetings. Don't snort. It's just that the meetings aren't here."

"The meetings aren't here," she echoed in bafflement. "What's that supposed to mean?"

"They're not in London."

"Look, Oliver—"

"I'm trying to tell you," he said irritably. "Paula and Eric are away. I was going to explain tomorrow."

She blinked at him. "But—wait a minute, I don't see—how could they be? They knew I was coming. You mean they won't be back tonight at all?"

"That's right. Or tomorrow, either."

"Why didn't your mother say anything?"

"It came up suddenly."

"But we only talked on the phone Monday night, Oliver. This is Wednesday. She must have known—"

"You had your ticket—all the arrangements had been made. It seemed pointless to disrupt everything."

"But not to even mention it—" Charlotte persisted.

"Look," said Oliver, "you're a big girl, Charlotte. Old enough to travel alone. Your parents obviously think so, and I was at Heathrow to meet you as promised. Here you are, safe and sound, so why make a fuss?"

"Well"—she wasn't entirely convinced—"I suppose if your mother thought it would be all right . . . how long will they be gone?"

He brushed the hair off his forehead. "Not all that long. A few days. It isn't as if you would have seen much of them, anyway. They're both extremely busy, hardly ever here these days. Ever since Paula started working for Con she's been run off her feet, even on weekends."

"But she made all these plans—"

"Yes, that's just what I've been saying. Nothing's changed because they aren't here right now. We've got lots to do—you won't miss anything. And now"—he stood up—"unless there's something you want, I think we ought to go to bed. I'm whacked. I'll show you how the hot water works so you can have a shower. It's not all that complicated when you know."

But Charlotte wasn't coping with unfamiliar plumbing

at that hour. She stopped outside her bedroom door and turned to face Oliver. "I want your word of honor that you won't disappear again without telling me."

"I promise."

"I don't even know how to use the telephone, Oliver, or who to call if I did. I'm not even sure where I *am*, for pete's sake."

"I was only out a couple of hours. I didn't desert you. I was sure you'd sleep until morning and you'd never know I'd gone. You should have—"

But, "The telephone," she exclaimed in dismay. "I said I'd call home when I got here. I don't know what to say."

"That you had a good flight and you're fine, what else would you say?" Oliver was calm and reasonable. "But why not wait till tomorrow. They'll expect you to be tired your first night, and you'll have more to tell them."

That was sensible; she didn't want to risk getting muddled and worrying her parents needlessly. Relieved, she agreed.

"We'll decide what to do when we get up," said Oliver. "Depends on the weather. Paula got us tickets to the Royal Shakespeare Company in the evening, and we'll go out to dinner first. Charlotte—"

About to close her door, she paused. Suddenly he smiled, his face lighting. "I'm glad you're here." It was like having a flashbulb go off at close range. Dazzled, she smiled back. "So'm I."

Over a late breakfast, they watched rain slide down the kitchen windows. "I should have brought boots," said

Charlotte. "My shoes aren't dry from yesterday."

Oliver sat down with a second mug of coffee. "More toast?"

Regretfully she shook her head and stifled a yawn. "I couldn't. I'm stuffed."

She had lain awake a long time after they'd gone to bed the night before, very aware of Oliver just the other side of the wall beyond her feet, and equally aware that Paula and Eric were not in their bedroom across the landing. She had never been alone in a house overnight with a male who was not related to her. Staring into the darkness, she replayed the conversation they'd just had. More important than what Oliver had said, she suspected, was what he hadn't said. In that regard he hadn't changed. She had chosen not to remember how stingy he could be with information when it suited him. He'd given her the impression that Paula had sanctioned this change in plan, but she couldn't recall Oliver actually saying so. Her own parents, she knew perfectly well, would not be happy with the new arrangements. She doubted they would have let her come if Paula had explained that she and Eric would be away when Charlotte arrived. But Paula had not been the one to telephone Monday night. Oliver had. He was the only person she and her mother had spoken to. It was possible that Paula had already gone, but then why hadn't she called earlier? Could she have been so busy, it slipped her mind? Or did she really think it made no difference?

When Charlotte woke, the room was full of gray rain light, and although she remembered the disturbing questions, they seemed much less urgent. Whatever the answers, there she was in London; she couldn't seriously consider taking the next flight home. She was almost a senior in high school, intelligent, responsible, and capable of looking after herself. To prove it, she bent her mind to figuring out the shower. It was a flexible metal hose with a head that could be attached to the wall over the bathtub. When she twiddled the knobs, it dribbled water down on her that was hot on one side and cold on the other. High up on the wall, across the room, was an electric bar heater that Oliver had thoughtfully left switched on. However, since even Charlotte knew from elementary physics that hot air rose, she didn't see how it could make much difference in the large, chilly cube of air. What, she wondered, rubbing herself down vigorously, must the temperature be in the depths of winter?

She hadn't known what to wear. Oliver said the theater, but not until evening, and there was a whole rainy day first, so she put on a pair of dark green jeans, a jersey, and her sweatshirt. As long as she and Oliver were on their own—she frowned at her reflection. Her parents would most definitely not be pleased to know that. She decided to assume that Oliver's mother had confidence in their maturity. But did she feel mature? And Oliver—he looked grown up, certainly, but was that the same thing?

After breakfast, she washed the dishes while Oliver dried them and put them away. As he hung up his dish towel, he said, "All right," as if they'd been discussing something and had made a decision.

"All right what?" said Charlotte.

"Museums. As long as it's raining we might as well be

indoors. We'll walk down to Archway and take the bus."

"Is it far?" asked Charlotte suspiciously.

Oliver gave her a little grin. "It's all downhill, Charlotte. Walking's the best way to see things."

"It's also the best way to get wet."

"You're drip-dry," he said unmoved.

"Which museums?" she asked, giving in. Mentally she reviewed the list she'd been making in the back of the journal the Schuylers had given her as a going-away present. It was a handsome bound book with a batik cover. Pat had lettered the title page TRAVELS WITH CHARLOTTE, and the younger twins, Cindy and Carl, had done a decorative border of clouds and airplanes in blue and pink, using potato stamps. If she didn't start using the journal right away, Charlotte knew it would intimidate her, so she'd begun writing down on the last pages all the things people told her she must not miss. Everyone had suggestions.

"Wait and see," said Oliver irritatingly. He eyed her sweatshirt. "Are you going to wear that?"

"Why shouldn't I? Is it too casual? Do I need to dress up?"

"No, it's only—well, it labels you."

"What do you mean, it labels me? It says University of Montana. What's wrong with that? Eliot sent it to me."

"Forget it. It's fine."

"Oliver—"

"Do you want an umbrella? Here—put this in your bag." Handing her a small, neatly rolled black sausage, he told her to wait while he went downstairs first. He was gone before she could ask why. A minute later he called up to her. She found him standing on the front steps.

"What was that about?"

"Hmm? The rain's supposed to stop late this afternoon. We can go on the river tomorrow." They walked down to Holy Joe's and turned left onto Hornsey Lane. Charlotte paid attention to street signs this time. "I need a map so I can figure out where I am."

"Not as long as you're with me."

"But what if—"

"This is the Archway," he said, interrupting. "There's central London, down there." They stood in the middle of a bridge; beneath their feet roared a smelly torrent of traffic, half of it churning south into the heart of the city, the other half grinding north, up the hill. Charlotte gazed into the gray, furry distance and strained to see Saint Paul's Cathedral and the Houses of Parliament, Kensington Gardens, and the Thames as Oliver pointed them out. On a really clear day, he said, you could see the hills of Surrey. Charlotte felt a tingling in the soles of her feet: all the places she'd been hearing and reading about were *real* and she was going to see them. The rain didn't matter—everyone said it was supposed to rain in England. "Oh, Oliver, there's so *much!* How will I ever see it all? Jean said—oh, nuts! I forgot my camera. We'll have to go back."

"Too late. The morning's practically gone already. Anyway, it's not a good day to take photographs, and we'll be inside most of the time. You can buy postcards." She was about to protest when he caught her by the hand; she let him pull her down the long flight of steps to the

Archway Road, enjoying the sensation of his fingers around hers. It had been a very long time since they were together.

Jean's favorite museum was the Victoria and Albert. If you got tired of looking at paintings, you could wander off in search of costumes, armor, clocks, or illuminated manuscripts. Deb had told her she mustn't miss Turner's watercolors at the Tate. On the plane, Barbara Coburn had added the National Portrait Gallery to her list. And her father had said, "Of course you'll see the British Museum. . . ."

Oliver disregarded the lot; he had his own, very definite ideas and didn't invite suggestions. Their first stop was Sir John Soane's Museum, of which Charlotte had never heard. It was an eighteenth-century town house facing a green square. Sir John had been an architect, and he'd filled his house with a vast collection of paintings, chunks of ancient masonry, bits of statuary, drawings, and funerary urns. At the bottom of the house was a room called the Sepulchral Chamber, where he'd installed an Egyptian sarcophagus from the Valley of Kings. "He seems rather preoccupied with death, don't you think?" observed Charlotte. "It's interesting, but I wouldn't want one in my basement. I'll bet he had trouble keeping housekeepers—and think of all the dusting." Oliver gave her a an odd sideways look. "I hadn't considered it quite that way before."

After a hurried and unmemorable lunch in a crowded little sandwich bar, he took her to the Silver Vaults, another place no one had mentioned. They descended in an elevator to a subterranean world of brightly lit, glittering little shops, each with its own heavy safelike door. The shops were filled with silver objects: candlesticks, flatware, toast-racks, pitchers, napkin rings, coffee services, soup tureens. It was like walking through a fairy tale, except for the price tags on everything. And the hawk-eyed security guards who made sure you paid before you took home your ivory-and-silver-backed bureau set, or your twelve-branched candelabra, or your engraved epergne.

Charlotte surfaced in a daze, feeling as if she had a kind of visual indigestion, and allowed Oliver to steer her down Chancery Lane to their last stop, the Public Record Office. There, in a small display room, he showed her Lord Nelson's logbook from the Battle of Trafalgar; Magna Carta, signed by King John at Runnymede in 1215; and the Domesday Book, written on sheepskin, which was a detailed census of the lands and people of England ordered by William the Conqueror in 1086. "These are the *originals*," Oliver stressed, "not copies." She did her best to understand what she was seeing, because he wanted her to be impressed, but she found it difficult, and the ancient handwriting impossible to decipher because her head was stuffed by that time with such a jumble of queer things she couldn't focus properly.

Outside, the light was draining from the gray-smudged sky, and Charlotte realized she was exhausted. "There's lots more," said Oliver as they started to walk, "like the Inns of Court and the Guildhall, but we'll see them later.

I've been planning what I wanted you to see for weeks. Tourists miss the really special stuff—they haven't a clue."

"No, I suppose they haven't," said Charlotte. "But Oliver—"

"It's getting late. We'd better take the underground to Highgate—it's quicker."

It was also crowded and they had to stand the whole way. Jerked about like a marionette, Charlotte clung to a pole for support. This had not been at all as she'd envisioned her first day in London; although it had been interesting, she had a feeling of anticlimax. Opposite her, Oliver balanced easily, feet apart, the hair falling over his forehead. He was gazing with abstract concentration past her left ear at a poster for a temporary employment agency. Communication was clearly out of the question, which, Charlotte realized, was a good thing. She was much too tired and muddled to straighten out her thoughts and explain to Oliver in a forceful yet diplomatic way that while he might prefer the esoteric and unusual to the traditional tourist sights, *she* was the tourist, and they'd have to work out a compromise.

Three

"There's no one in there, Oliver. I don't think it's open." Charlotte peered dubiously through the window into the dim, narrow space that stretched back from the restaurant door. It was lined with a double row of empty tables covered with white cloths.

"Of course it is," replied Oliver, opening the door and ushering her inside. "Europeans generally dine later." He nodded to a small, stout woman in black who sat where she could keep an eye on the street while she knitted. She had a faint mustache on her upper lip, and her hair looked as if it had been woven out of the same coarse gray wool on her needles. She smiled, showing a gold tooth, and out of thin air a waiter appeared. His mustache was luxuriant and his hair black and curly, but there was a strong family resemblance. He greeted Oliver as if he knew him, and called him "sir," and Oliver called him Spiro.

Charlotte saw there was another couple in the restaurant, sitting near the back conversing quietly over bowls of soup. Spiro took her coat—the new rust-brown London Fog trench coat bought especially for this trip—and hung it with Oliver's on a metal rack, and Charlotte looked up to find Oliver studying her. She blushed, she couldn't help it, feeling the heat rise up her neck and flood her cheeks. He pulled out her chair for her.

They had gotten back to the flat in Highgate with, by Oliver's precise reckoning, only forty-five minutes to make themselves presentable before setting out for the middle of London again. After toiling up the hill from the subway station, Charlotte had been hoping for at least half an hour's nap before getting dressed, but she was tired enough to be afraid that if she allowed herself to lie down and close her eyes she would have a terrible time waking up and a headache for the rest of the evening. Besides, if they were going out to dinner and the theater, well, that would take some preparation. She was determined to show Oliver that she, too, had changed since they'd last been together.

During the past winter, Charlotte's sister, Deb, had taken her in hand, pushing her to see beyond the self-image she had of a slightly pudgy, defensively unobtrusive, awkward adolescent, to what actually appeared in the mirror. Charlotte still found it hard to see herself as she was becoming, instead of as she'd always been, but Deb kept nudging her. Deb was fourteen years older than Charlotte; she had passed through adolescence before Charlotte had any idea there was such a trial awaiting her.

By the time Charlotte needed her sister most, she and Deb had gotten over their sibling hostilities and become friends; Charlotte was immensely grateful for Deb's help.

Deb was largely responsible for Charlotte sitting there, in the Philadelphia Restaurant in London, across the table from Oliver Shattuck, wearing her new glasses with the square, amber-tinted frames; a simple dark green and brown paisley dress; her hair—Deb said it was honey blond with highlights, rather than mousy brown, as Charlotte had always believed—in a French braid; a hint of warm brown eyeshadow artfully applied to make her hazel eyes seem larger. The effect was good, Charlotte knew it. She'd checked herself over carefully in the full-length mirror in Paula's room. The dress was a jersey and fell softly from her hips; it bloused a little at her waist, emphasizing rather than concealing it, and showed the gentle curve of her breasts. Her father had given her a thin gold chain for her sixteenth birthday. She had smiled at herself as she hooked it: a satisfied, expectant smile.

And then Oliver didn't notice. He was waiting for her by the door, his raincoat on, holding hers. "Right," he said as soon as she appeared, and thrust the coat at her. Deflated, she slid her arms into the sleeves while he vanished down the stairs, telling her to wait.

"Oliver—" she began when they were outside in the street.

"What?" He sounded preoccupied.

"Nothing." She couldn't very well say, "Don't you think I look nice?"

"We haven't much time. We'll get a taxi from the High Street. Come on."

By the time she climbed into the cab, she was feeling ill-used and cross. The pretty shoes with their little heels she had bought to go with the dress felt at least a size too small. Clearly they weren't intended for walking very far very fast. All that effort wasted, she thought glumly as they wound their way through snarls of rush-hour traffic. She might just as well have kept her jeans and sweatshirt on—except that Oliver would have noticed then. He'd have objected, probably made her go and change. In an obscure way, this was all Deb's fault.

She remembered Andy's reaction when he had arrived at the Paige house to escort her to the Junior Prom. *He* had noticed, right away, and it had taken him a large part of the evening to get over it, to stop being awkward and stiff and to loosen up with her. He'd treated her as if she were a stranger and he hadn't any idea what to say to her. Poor Andy, social occasions were his notion of purgatory.

But finally, there in the restaurant, came the moment of recognition, when Oliver actually *saw* her, and his expression changed. Spiro returned and handed them menus, and Charlotte was glad of the distraction. Now that she had Oliver's attention, she wasn't quite sure what she wanted to do with it. She fumbled with her menu, but once safely behind it she watched Oliver as he gravely studied his. This was the Oliver she remembered from his great-uncle's memorial service a year and a half earlier: the Oliver who had taken a sudden giant step away, not so much from her, as from being young. By some optical illusion he seemed much older than her grown-up brothers. His eyes caught hers. "I—I don't know about Greek food," she apologized quickly to cover her confusion. "Baklava, that's Greek, isn't it?"

Unexpectedly he grinned, reminding her in a flash of the boy she'd gone to school with. "That's *dessert*, Charlotte. But then you always have liked dessert best, haven't you?"

Her sweet tooth had been a sore point for so long that she teetered on the brink of offense before remembering that it didn't matter anymore. Her figure had mysteriously changed. Oliver looked as if he felt grown up; Charlotte didn't feel grown up, but she was working on it.

"Do you like lamb?"

"Lamb? Yes, I do."

He gave a nod. Spiro glided over. "Are you ready to order, sir?" Attentively, he wrote as Oliver spoke, and Charlotte observed in bemusement. Spiro said, "Thank you, sir," and took the menus, and Charlotte half swallowed a giggle, choked, and had to take a hasty sip of her water.

Oliver frowned. "What's funny?"

"You are," she said, not thinking, and the frown deepened. Oliver did not like criticism. "I was just thinking—" she coughed. "Thinking about the time you knocked me into the Coolidges' duck pond."

"*I* knocked *you?*"

"Yes, you did. You know you did. That was the first time I'd ever been inside Commodore Shattuck's house, when we went to get dry."

For a moment his face looked broody, then slowly he smiled. "Uncle Sam gave me quite a scolding about that after you'd gone. For leaving you in the kitchen while I went to change my clothes. He said that was no way to treat a friend."

"We weren't friends."

"Uncle Sam knew that. And he knew that if I was going to stay with him we would be. He decided we would be."

"I wonder what he'd think now, if he could see us."

Oliver was silent, the grin gone. "Anyway, he can't," he said flatly. "Uncle Sam's dead."

Spiro brought bowls of egg-lemon soup, and instead of pursuing the subject of the Commodore, Charlotte asked Oliver how he knew about the restaurant. "I'd never have guessed it was Greek from the name."

"Philadelphia's a Greek word, Charlotte. It means 'brotherly love'—didn't you know that?" She hadn't; she'd thought it was simply a city in Pennsylvania. "I was taking Greek last year," he went on. "This is where Connie sends homesick Greek diplomats. She went to school with the owner's daughter-in-law. Spiro's a grandson, and that's his grandmother, Mrs. Lemonakis, by the door."

In the middle of the souvlakia and rice pilaf, which Charlotte found herself enjoying very much, Oliver suddenly said, "You look very pretty, Charlotte. Those are good colors on you."

She stared at him, forgetting to chew. Then she swallowed and said, "Thank you," in a kind of croak.

They had baklava for dessert, and little cups of thick,

dark coffee. Charlotte gave up on the coffee after a taste, but relished every morsel of the honey-drenched pastry. "That was wonderful," she said, regarding her empty plate.

Spiro brought the bill and placed it discreetly at Oliver's elbow. Charlotte realized she had absolutely no idea how much her dinner had cost. There had been prices on the menu, but they'd been in pounds sterling, which meant nothing to her yet, and, anyway, Oliver had made the decisions and done the ordering. She leaned toward him across the table. "Oliver, I don't have any money—I mean English money. I've got to get some tomorrow—Dad said I should cash my traveler's checks at a bank—" The extra he'd given her at the airport was for something special, he'd said, something she didn't need, or really wanted to do, not ordinary expenses.

Oliver nodded. "We'll do it in the morning."

"Keep track of what I owe and I'll pay you back. You bought lunch, too, and there are all the fares."

"They were my treat," he said magnanimously, "and this"—he took a plastic card out of his wallet—"is Eric's."

"Oh, but—"

"He'd be paying if they were here, Charlotte. He's getting off cheaply. You needn't worry, it's my card. I have it under his name. He gave it to me to use, so I am."

"Well, if you're sure—"

"Absolutely. You're our guest, remember." He signed the slip Spiro gave him as if he'd done it often before.

This time he helped her into her coat, settling it on her shoulders in a way that made her feel as if she'd stood up too fast. On the pavement, he linked her arm through his, holding her close beside him, and she almost forgot how uncomfortable her shoes were. It was a long walk to the theater; Oliver seemed accustomed to walking great distances. She decided it would be a good idea to keep that piece of information well in mind.

At the theater, Oliver checked their coats and guided her through the door marked DRESS CIRCLE. Their seats were in the center, near the front, and the play was wonderful. Charlotte was unfamiliar with Shakespeare's *A Comedy of Errors*; they'd struggled through *A Midsummer Night's Dream* in English class last winter and she hadn't liked it much. Bottom and the rustics had gone on and on at tedious length, and the lovers chasing each other in endless circles through the wood had seemed silly rather than romantic.

This play, about two sets of twins getting hopelessly mixed up, was equally silly, but as she watched, it dawned on her that it was *supposed* to be silly. It was supposed to make the audience laugh. The red-haired Dromios somersaulted about the stage; Antipholus from Ephesus gazed blankly at the woman who believed she was his wife, while her sister fell in love with him against all reason. They tied themselves in impossible knots and then, somehow, at the end, everything came out right and Charlotte was left feeling satisfied and happy rather than educated and bored.

Only one thing bothered her. It had nothing to do with the play; it was the two empty seats on Oliver's left. As far as she could see at the intermission, the theater was full, except for those two seats. Two people had evidently planned on coming and found at the last moment they couldn't make it after all. Oliver seemed not to notice. In the intermission he bought them each a little tub of pink and white ice cream, which they ate with small wooden paddles. "It's different when you see a play like this," he said. "Then you realize that you're not supposed to read it out of a book, you're supposed to watch it happen and listen to it."

"I didn't expect Shakespeare to be funny," said Charlotte, digging away at her ice cream. "Or easy to understand. Mrs. Wolitzer made it sound like a foreign language. We're doing *Macbeth* with Mr. Harvey next year. I wish we could just see it instead of spending weeks plodding through the text."

"Isn't Mr. Harvey the track coach?"

"Mmm. He also teaches honors English. Eliot had him twelve years ago and he hasn't changed a bit. He wears sweat socks to class and blows his whistle at the end of the period."

She didn't ask Oliver about the empty seats. She was enjoying herself too much to risk spoiling the evening, but they lurked at the edge of her consciousness. The tickets, she felt sure, were back in Highgate, probably on Paula's dressing table, or the mantlepiece, or the hall table—wherever the Prestons kept things like that. Paula had bought them before she realized she and Eric would be away. Oliver had made it sound as if she had gotten the tickets just for him and Charlotte; he'd made it sound like his mother's blessing was on Charlotte's visit in spite of her and Eric's absence.

"You're very quiet," said Oliver in the taxi on the way back.

"What? Oh, my feet hurt," she said, surprised at her glibness. "I never should have brought these shoes. Deb warned me. But then," she added with some spirit, "I didn't expect to walk so far in them."

She could almost hear him shrug. "Sorry," he said, but only for form's sake.

The driver pulled in to the curb and stopped and Oliver got out and paid him. He held the door for her. They weren't in front of Ninety-two Summerson Gardens.

"Where are we?"

"Just around the corner," said Oliver.

"My feet are killing me, Oliver. Weren't you listening?"

"It's not far. You can take off your shoes as soon as we get inside."

At the front steps he said, "Wait here a minute, will you?" He went up stealthily and unlocked and opened the door before motioning her to join him. She opened her mouth, but he put his finger to his lips. "Baby's asleep. Take off your shoes," he whispered. She wanted some answers, but it felt so good to get out of the heels. She wriggled her toes and gave a long sigh of relief. He scooped up her shoes and thrust them at her. "Go on up," he said in her ear. "Just keep going."

She heard noises behind the door on their left. Oliver gave her a little push. "Go *on*. Quick!"

Pausing on the landing, she heard the door below open, and light pooled in the hall. "Oliver?" said a woman's voice. "It is you—I thought it must be."

"Hello, Con."

"I was going to ask you to come down and have supper with me tonight." Her accent was decidedly English. "We went to the theater—the Aldwych. A *Comedy of Errors*. Have you seen it?"

"Not yet, but I've heard it's good. Didn't Paula get tickets for—"

"You'd like it. They've added music, but it really works."

"Maybe she'll go with me when she gets back. Everything all right upstairs, is it? Isn't your concert tomorrow night?"

"Yes."

"Can I get a ticket at the door, d'you think?"

Oliver didn't answer right away, then he said, "I'm not sure. Probably. It's only Gilbert and Sullivan, you know."

"Not highbrow enough for me, you mean? I often slum on Friday nights, Oliver." The voice had a teasing note in it.

Charlotte would have liked to look at its owner. She sounded as if she knew Oliver pretty well.

"I suppose you'll be too busy for supper tomorrow, but what about Sunday? I've got Arabs Saturday—they want to go to Canterbury. I warned them it'll be an absolute zoo on the weekend, but their hearts are set on it. All I'll want when I get home is a hot bath and a stiff drink. So Sunday?"

"Yes, all right. Thanks, Con."

Oliver came pounding up the steps and the light vanished. He ran into Charlotte on the landing. "Ouch!" she said, more annoyed than hurt.

"I thought you'd gone up."

"You have the key," she pointed out. "Anyway, why didn't you introduce me?"

"I was afraid she'd invite us in if I did and I know you're tired. And you still have to call your parents. Connie's very nice, but she does go on." Oliver breezed past her to unlock the door to the flat.

Charlotte followed, groaning. "I wish you hadn't reminded me."

Oliver made a thing of hanging up their coats, rattling hangers in the closet. "I don't suppose you want anything before bed?" Clearly she was supposed to say no. When she didn't answer right away, he said, "If it's a nice day and we can get an early start, we'll go on the river tomorrow. You'll like that."

"What about your concert?"

"Not to worry. It doesn't start until half-past seven. There'll be plenty of time."

"No," said Charlotte. "I mean, do I get to go?"

"Do you want to?"

"Oliver!"

He gave an impatient little sigh. "Yes, well, of course you can. Why not?"

"I could go with Connie," she said, watching him.

He didn't turn a hair. "That's a good idea."

Four

At seven twenty-five, Charlotte slid into her seat on the left side of the balcony. If Connie Rinaldi was in the audience, she had no idea where—she still didn't know what Connie looked like. Oliver had been peculiarly slow about moving that evening, taking forever to wash and dress, assuring her that the concert hall was only around the corner and it would take no time at all to walk there—no need to hurry. By the time they left, Connie's ground-floor flat was empty. She'd gone, whether to the concert or somewhere else. "Too bad," said Oliver.

Charlotte had dressed with care, wearing her other good dress: a two-piece coral-colored polo. This time she wore comfortable shoes with flat heels and crepe soles. She wasn't surprised to find that it actually took them almost ten minutes at a quick jog to reach the hall "around the corner."

At the door, Oliver was collared by a lanky dark-haired boy. "Collins is going bonkers out back, Shattuck. Where have you been? You were supposed to be here at seven. Come on!" Away they went, disappearing into the crowds. Charlotte, abandoned once again, surrendered the ticket Oliver had given her, and went to find her seat.

During the year and a half they'd been apart, Oliver had written with gratifying frequency. His blue English air letters were easy to spot among the usual mail. Charlotte remembered the queasy lurch her stomach had given the first few times she'd slit open the flaps. On the one hand, she'd been enormously relieved that he'd written at all; on the other, she'd been extremely apprehensive about what he'd written.

She still couldn't think calmly about their stolen day at Plum Island. All those months later the memory of it triggered an instant, searing embarrassment that prevented sensible thought. Oliver's great-uncle had just died. His mother and stepfather, whom he barely knew, were about to arrive. His fate was already sealed; both he and Charlotte knew that. He was about to leave the place that had become his home after a difficult settling-in period, to leave the friends he'd made, the dog he was devoted to, the school he was successful at. His mother was finally prepared to assume responsibility for him, even though that meant wrenching Oliver away from Concord. The few days after the Commodore's death had been intense and emotional, confusing and exhausting. When Oliver had carried Charlotte off to the beach in the dead of winter in his great-uncle's car without telling anyone—even Charlotte herself—where they were going, he had been desperate. He'd demanded assurances and a commitment from her that she had been unable to give him right then, at that exact moment. She protested that she needed time; he countered that he didn't have any.

They managed, barely, to come to an understanding the night before he left, but it was so complicated, so fraught, that as soon as he was gone, Charlotte had begun to be afraid her response had been inadequate. She was afraid she might have lost Oliver as a close friend and would never have the chance to find out what more he might have become. Then the letters had started to arrive and she began to relax.

Oliver's letters were always entertaining and conversational. There was nothing in them she couldn't share with her parents or sister, or her friends Andy and Kath. He described London and the impossibly tiny, dark flat in Holland Park they'd first been provided with; he told about visiting the BBC studios in Bush House with Eric, and Paula's dissatisfaction with her largely secretarial job at the Embassy, and the private boys' school in North London to which he'd been admitted.

But mostly he asked questions. How had the spring play at the high school gone? Had Todd Jasper gotten a good enough English grade to stay on the tennis team? And who had replaced Oliver? What about the tenants in the Commodore's house? His great-uncle Sam had left it to him in his will and Oliver had refused to let his mother sell it, so he was a landlord. Were the tenants keeping up the garden and feeding the Canada geese as agreed? Had Charlotte remembered Amos's rabies shot and heartworm test? What new crops was Andy planning for the farm? What was the news from Eliot in Montana? As the year progressed, he wanted to know all about the Paiges' move from the big Victorian house on Elm Street to the smaller, modern one on Esterbrook Road. And Kath's budding romance with Paul Watts. And Deb's wedding. He even asked about Charlotte's niece, Hilary, and the new baby Jean was expecting in August, although he'd never been interested in small children. What was Charlotte reading? What movies had she seen? Charlotte was never at a loss for things to write back about.

He was clearly starved for news of Concord. Although he didn't sound miserable or maladjusted, Charlotte diagnosed homesickness. Occasionally in his letters he'd mention someone from his new school, but only in passing. He never said much about any of them. Oliver was not easy to make friends with; she knew that as well as anyone.

She also knew that Oliver was a master at hiding his feelings and thoughts. It had taken her a long time to learn how to get below the carefully poised surface he presented to the world to where the currents ran deep and turbulent. With his letters, she figured it was a matter of reading between the lines. By the time she'd set out for London she prided herself at having gotten quite good at it.

But sitting in the middle of an audience of strangers, waiting for the chorus to come out and the conductor to begin a concert she'd known nothing about, Charlotte realized how much she had conveniently allowed herself to forget. Distance had softened the focus, and eighteen months was a long time. Oliver was much more complicated than his letters—

A swelling of applause pulled her out of these disturbing thoughts. She gathered herself while the headmaster welcomed them, explaining that the concert was a benefit for the repair and renovation of the concert hall. As everyone knew, the school had a long and proud history of musical excellence. In 1967, Yehudi Menuhin had conducted the first concert in the new hall, and since then it had hosted a distinguished legion of visiting musicians, composers, and conductors, as well as provided an acoustically outstanding space for the school's own students. Oliver had never mentioned a word of this in his letters. To the best of Charlotte's knowledge he'd never paid particular attention to music. But perhaps it was mandatory at the school and he hadn't told her because he didn't care.

The chorus came out in an orderly line, girls first in black skirts and white blouses, boys in white shirts, dark suits, and ties. They arranged themselves according to parts on the risers in a shallow semicircle. Charlotte found Oliver in the third row, left of center, just in front of the dark-haired boy. Oliver's expression was absorbed; he didn't look out at the audience. After a minute or two, a young man and a young woman appeared and settled themselves facing each other at two grand pianos. Then the conductor, a lean, athletic man with a long face—Collins, Charlotte supposed—strode out and gave a quick, neat bow.

Thanks to her family, her brother Eliot in particular, Charlotte had an excellent working knowledge of Gilbert and Sullivan, even the more obscure operettas like *Utopia Limited* and *Princess Ida.* The pianists began with a spirited rendition of the overture from *The Mikado*, and she settled back, feeling that at least for the present she knew where she was. The boys sang, "If you want to know who we are, we are gentlemen of Japan . . ." and as soon as they finished, three girls stepped forward to identify themselves as "Three little maids from school." They were good, and the audience was appreciative.

When the applause faded, however, Oliver detached himself from the chorus and began to sing in a pleasing, confident tenor, "A wand'ring minstrel I, a thing of shreds and patches . . ." At the first note he uttered, Charlotte felt the skin down the back of her neck prickle, and by the end, while the people around her clapped warmly, she discovered she was sitting on the uncomfortable edge of her seat with her fingers clenched tightly together in her lap. She hadn't even thought to ask him whether he was a tenor or a bass.

She knew Oliver well enough to be sure he would never have agreed to perform alone if he hadn't been certain he could do it, not adequately, but well. He hadn't said a word to her about having a solo, but perhaps it accounted for some of the tension between them since she'd arrived, the knowledge he harbored that this loomed on his horizon. If only he'd told her—but how like Oliver that he hadn't.

By the time they'd left the flat that morning, the sun, tentative at first, was growing more sure of itself. Oliver was ready to set out at once for the middle of London, but Charlotte reminded him that she needed to visit a bank and a post office so she could start sending cards home. "Oh, all right," he said with rather bad grace, and he took her to a branch of Lloyd's on Highgate High Street. She wasn't used to handling large amounts of money and thought fifty dollars would surely do to begin with, but impatiently Oliver pointed out that it was Friday and the banks wouldn't open again until Monday. He suggested two hundred dollars, which seemed like a fortune to Charlotte. "It has to last me two weeks, you know, Oliver."

"You don't need to spend it all, it won't spoil." Reluctantly, she agreed to one hundred and fifty; in pounds sterling it was a lot less, but still. Feeling nervous, she zipped most of it into the secret pocket in the flap of her canvas shoulder bag, glancing about to be sure no one was watching as she did it.

This time they took the underground from the Archway Road Station. As they stood waiting for the train, Charlotte asked precisely where they were going and Oliver explained that it was a straightforward journey on the Northern Line to The Embankment, where they'd change and go one stop to Westminster. But at breakfast Charlotte had been studying the map she'd made Oliver dig out for her, and consulting the back of her journal. Frowning at the diagram of colored lines on the sooty wall, she said, "If we get out at Charing Cross instead, wouldn't we be right at Trafalgar Square? We can walk to the river and see things on the way."

"I thought you didn't want to walk," replied Oliver as they found seats.

"Of course I do," exclaimed Charlotte. "Especially when I'm wearing the right shoes and it's not raining."

"It'll take longer."

"I'm on vacation."

He gave up the argument and eventually they emerged into the dazzle and frenzy of Trafalgar Square. In the middle of the whirlpool of traffic stood Lord Nelson on his column, attended by four large, benign lions, pigeons swirling about him like a blizzard. Dizzily enchanted, Charlotte stood and tried to absorb it all. Oliver pointedly consulted his watch.

"That must be Admiralty Arch," said Charlotte. "So Buckingham Palace is down there, at the end of Pall Mall. Oh, Oliver, couldn't we just—"

"Mall," corrected Oliver. "Rhymes with pal, not hall."

"Seriously?"

"Of course, seriously."

"But that sounds all wrong," she protested.

He shrugged. "I can't help that, can I? Come on, Charlotte, the light's changing. We go this way."

"But—"

This time she'd remembered her camera; in spite of Oliver's impatience, she kept stopping to use it. Outside the Horse Guards' was a crowd of tourists admiring the scarlet-coated guards on their gleaming, patient horses. Small children gazed up in wonder and adoration while their parents immortalized them on yards of color film. In a fit of shyness, one little Japanese boy attached himself anxiously to Oliver's trousers by mistake. Oliver looked down just as the boy looked up, and Charlotte wished she'd been fast enough to capture their mutual expressions of astonishment and horror.

Oliver wouldn't wait for the guard to change, but he allowed her a quick detour at Downing Street to see Number 10. He fidgeted outside camera range while she paused to take a picture of Big Ben with a red double-decker bus passing in front. "You know, you can get postcards," he told her.

"Not the same," said Charlotte. "You can buy postcards in the airport. I want my own photographs."

"You look like a tourist."

"Oliver, I *am* a tourist."

"You don't need to advertise it."

Beneath the bulky, invincible statue of Winston Churchill in Parliament Square they had a brief, energetic argument. Charlotte wanted to go into Westminster Abbey.

"No you don't. Not really," Oliver told her firmly. "It'll be packed with tourists, Charlotte. Just look at all the coaches outside."

"But we're right *here*, Oliver. How can I go past without seeing it? Just give me twenty minutes."

"The point is," he said with exaggerated patience, "you *won't* be able to see it. It'll be like a railway station at rush hour in there. It'll be a complete waste."

"I don't believe that," declared Charlotte, but he hadn't waited for her answer. Sorely tempted to mutiny, she watched him walk away from her. She had a map and plenty of money; she had no key to the flat, but as long as the sun was shining, that didn't matter. She was confident that she could find her way to Highgate. She could always—the pedestrian signal blinked. Oliver stepped off the curb without looking back and disappeared into the crowds surging across the street. Charlotte's confidence wobbled. "Oh, all *right!*" she said crossly to Winston Churchill.

The fact that Oliver was waiting for her on the other side did nothing to moderate her temper; he'd assumed she would follow him. That really annoyed her. Not speaking, they crossed again to the pavement above the Thames where steps led down to the excursion boat piers tucked in beside Westminster Bridge. A sightseeing launch, its decks cluttered with people, came into view, plowing through the glittering water. Charlotte stopped and made a protracted business of getting her camera out, then waited until the boat got close enough to look like a boat rather than a speck. She ignored Oliver, who, after a minute or so, said, "I'll go and queue for tickets."

When she joined him she felt slightly calmer. He hustled her up a ramp marked GREENWICH, saying, "We want seats on the top deck by the rail." Deftly he slid past slower passengers and outmaneuvered a large family of Americans to take possession of two places at the end of one of the benches in the bow. They looked surprised at finding their seats suddenly occupied, but moved on in search of others.

"We could have made room for them," objected Charlotte. "They were here first."

"They were indecisive," replied Oliver. "And, anyway,

you didn't come all the way to Britain to surround yourself with Americans."

"You're American," she pointed out. "So are Paula and Eric. I *am* surrounded by Americans."

"Don't be so literal, Charlotte. We aren't tourists, we're living here. That's entirely different." The boat gave a blast of its horn, and the mooring lines were cast off. The pier slid away from them. "I told you we had to hurry. We only just made it."

"We could have taken that one," said Charlotte. As they circled under Westminster Bridge and started down the river, people were boarding another boat.

"It's not going to Greenwich, only as far as the Tower."

"The Tower? What Tower?" She gave him a suspicious look.

"The Tower of London, of course. You'll see it—we go right past. You can take a photograph of Traitors' Gate from the river, the way the traitors saw it. It's quite grim."

"But we don't stop there," she said, wanting to be sure she had it straight.

He shook his head. "Greenwich is a lot farther downriver."

She digested this information in silence. She had a vision of herself as the only American ever to visit London without seeing any of the major sights: the Tower, Westminster Abbey, Buckingham Palace. . . . She'd go home and people would ask where she'd been and look blank when she told them. Sitting very still, she practiced deep breathing.

It was a beautiful day to be on the river. They chugged

down the wide, gray-green Thames in the windy sunshine while gulls seesawed on invisible air currents overhead and the city flowed past on either bank. All around them people laughed and chattered in a dizzying variety of languages and accents, and somewhere behind them a guide pointed out the sights and made terrible, sometimes incomprehensible jokes over a crackly loudspeaker. Gradually the knot in Charlotte's chest eased and she felt she might be able to look at Oliver without bursting into argument. Although he'd behaved as if he hadn't noticed anything wrong, Oliver must have felt her relax, because he laid an arm along the back of her seat and said quietly, "I've been waiting a very long time to do this with you." Making a determined effort, she let go of her regrets and resolved to enjoy the day. But as they passed the Tower of London she vowed silently she'd return. Oliver had not heard the end of it.

It was midday by the time they docked at Greenwich. The elegant, colonnaded buildings of the Royal Naval College shone like bleached bone in the brilliant light, a lawn so perfect it might have been broadloom carpet stretched between them.

Oliver proposed they have lunch before exploring and Charlotte was happy to agree; whether because of their argument or the salt air, or both, she was hungry. She expected another sandwich bar for expediency's sake, but instead Oliver took her to a pub called The Yacht. "Can I really go in?" she asked, filled with curiosity and doubt. She'd never been in a bar in her life, but Deb said pubs were different. "I wouldn't have brought you otherwise," said Oliver. He did not go where he felt unsure of himself.

After the brightness of the sun on the water, The Yacht was dark. The ceilings were low and the space inside thick with noise and appetizing smells. All the visible chairs, stools, and benches seemed to be filled; the horseshoe-shaped bar in the middle was lined two- and three-deep with people waiting to order, or ordering, or paying, or trying to extricate themselves without spilling from hands full of brimming glasses. Oliver steered her through the good-natured fray, out onto a small terrace overlooking the river, and instructed her to snag the first two chairs that became vacant while he went back inside.

After five minutes or so, two women left and Charlotte appropriated their table. She felt conspicuous and inexperienced until she realized that no one was paying any attention to her. A light breeze came off the musty-smelling water, but the sun warmed her comfortably. She watched the gulls dip and lift against the mild blue sky and listened to the mutter of conversation and chink of glasses around her. She supposed Oliver would come back sometime; she wasn't worried, she was ravenous and otherwise very happy.

At last he reappeared with lunch on a tin tray: two plates laden with thick crusty slices of French bread, slabs of butter, chunks of orange cheese, and two glistening brown globes the size of Ping-Pong balls. He passed her a small mug of amber liquid; his was darker. "What is it?" she asked dubiously. She didn't like beer; from time to time her father let her try it at home to see if she'd changed her mind, but so far she hadn't.

"It's cider," said Oliver. She took an experimental mouthful and spluttered. Instead of the rich, sweet taste of fresh-pressed apples, this was dry and fizzed on her tongue. "It's very mild." Oliver was watching her. "You can buy it in supermarkets." Charlotte wasn't sure she liked it any better than beer, but something in his expression made her determined to drink it.

The bread and cheese were delicious. She eyed the Ping-Pong ball, but didn't ask. Instead she waited to see what Oliver did with his. Casually he picked it up and put it whole in his mouth. Charlotte copied him, trying not think about oxtails. It was a pickled onion, sharp and vinegary but good, and the cider washed it down very well. "All right, is it?" asked Oliver, a glint in his green eyes. "Of course," she said, as if it weren't the first pickled onion she'd ever eaten. "Why wouldn't it be?"

After lunch they walked up the tree-stippled green hillside behind the National Maritime Museum. Somewhere between the bottom of the hill and the top, Oliver laced his fingers through Charlotte's in a familiar way, and their shoulders brushed. Everything flew out of Charlotte's head except that moment in that place with that person.

Perched on the crest of the park was an odd and attractive little house: the Old Royal Observatory. Through its courtyard ran the Greenwich Meridian; when Charlotte discovered that she could stand astride it with a foot in each hemisphere, she bullied Oliver into taking her photograph. He grumbled about light and focus and not knowing which button to push. "The only button there is,"

Charlotte told him. "It's an idiot camera—everything's automatic. Wait a minute—we could ask that man to take a picture of both of us—" But Oliver had the camera up and she heard the electronic whir of the shutter. "Too late, it's done." He handed it back.

The house was full of a collection of early scientific instruments. Charlotte quickly lost interest in chronometers and astrolabes, but she was enchanted by the view, reaching back into the hazy depths of London, past the Queen's House and the towers of the Royal Naval College, with the Thames glinting like a pathway of crumpled foil, stapled in place by its bridges. "What a lovely place to live," she said dreamily, leaning her elbows on a windowsill and propping her chin on her hands. She felt Oliver come to stand behind her. Even though they didn't touch, she knew he was there. It was a thoroughly satisfactory day, as he had promised, and he never once said, "See, I told you you'd like it," though perhaps that was because he couldn't believe she hadn't.

And now, to end the day, another wonder. Bemused, Charlotte made herself sit back in her seat, although she couldn't entirely relax. The songs flowed gracefully into one another, allowing only briefly for applause: choruses, solos, duets. Oliver and the dark-haired boy sang in a quintet from *The Gondoliers* about the impossibility of straightening out life's tangled skein, which seemed particularly apt. Just before intermission they were joined in a trio by a sultry blonde whose left eye was hidden behind a shining cascade of hair. At astonishing speed and with great clarity they sang a patter song that so delighted the audience, the conductor made them repeat it. When they finished, the dark-haired boy—Timothy Harker, Charlotte learned from the program—grinned self-consciously, Oliver gave a composed little bow, and the girl, whose name was Maeve McGraw, tossed her head with a practiced, theatrical gesture that momentarily exposed her missing eye.

Charlotte stayed where she was during intermission, meditating on Oliver's secretiveness. The second half of the concert went very quickly, and ended with one of Charlotte's favorite songs: "I Have a Song To Sing-O." Oliver performed it with a very small Chinese girl who had a pure, fluting soprano, and the chorus came in behind them at the end, voices swelling to fill the hall. As the last notes died the headmaster reappeared, leading the enthusiastic applause. The soloists bowed; the chorus bowed; the pianists stood and bowed, then sat and played the cachucha from *The Gondoliers* while the performers filed out.

Halfway down the staircase, Charlotte paused and scanned the faces in the lobby. Oliver and Timothy Harker stood near the door, deep in conversation.

Five

"—when we get back," Oliver was saying.

"You're bonkers, Shattuck. She'll have your guts for garters—she'll absolutely *murder* you. My father'll do a moving eulogy—hopes blighted, so young, so full of promise, all that. There won't be a dry eye. Pity you won't be around to hear it, but—hullo. You must be *the* Charlotte."

"Well, I'm *a* Charlotte," she said, joining them. "Who'll have your guts for garters, Oliver?"

"It's just a vulgar expression," he said, choosing not to answer. "Charlotte Paige, Timothy Harker."

Timothy reached out a long-fingered hand and shook hers firmly. "He was born shaking hands," said Oliver. "His father's a clergyman."

"You're the one who collects cemeteries," said Charlotte.

"Shattuck, what have you been telling her?" Timothy sounded embarrassed.

"I thought she should know the worst," said Oliver.

"You were wonderful in the concert," Charlotte told Timothy warmly. In the second half he had sung "I Am the Very Model of a Modern Major-general," earning cheers from the house. "My brother says anyone can sing the ballads, but it takes real talent to do the patter songs well."

"Thanks," said Oliver dryly. "Never mind that Eliot can't carry a tune."

"Not true," said Charlotte. "You never said a word about singing solos."

"Didn't I?"

She glared at Oliver. There was a brief silence, then Timothy said, "It's rather an obscure talent, actually. Patter songs, I mean. Useful as a party piece, but not much call otherwise. Speaking of parties—"

"I told you, Harker. We can't. We have to be off early tomorrow."

"We do?" said Charlotte.

"Yes, we do." From Oliver's tone, she gathered she was not supposed to ask why. She was about to, anyway, when Timothy said, "Look, it's not that late, Shattuck. Just come for an hour."

"Not possible. Sorry."

"Where can't we go?" asked Charlotte.

"Didn't he tell you that, either?" Timothy's face wore an expression of great innocence. "One of the chaps is having a party. Members of the chorus—that's us—and hangers-on—that's you. Steven lives up beyond Pond Square—not far. His father's governmental. It's a posh house—you really ought to see it."

"It must have slipped Oliver's mind," said Charlotte, feeling perverse. "I think it would be fun."

"Really?" Timothy gave her a hopeful smile. "You seem to be outvoted, Shattuck. Don't be a sore loser."

Oliver scowled at them both. "Oh, all right. But just half an hour." As they set out up the street, he said, "Harker only wants us to go because he's too much of a coward to show up by himself. He's terrified of Mad Margaret."

Timothy grimmaced.

"Is she the one with the hair?" asked Charlotte.

He nodded. "I simply cannot understand it. What can she possibly see in me, Charlotte? Be honest. Do I look like a sex object?"

She couldn't suppress a giggle, then bit her lip, afraid she might have hurt his feelings.

"Precisely!" he exclaimed, unbruised. "Why doesn't she go after you, Shattuck? You're much sexier."

"It's because your father's a vicar," replied Oliver. "That's fatally attractive."

"Rubbish. There's nothing attractive about it. Mostly it's a dead bore."

The house was a big one, not divided into flats like Oliver's. It sat back behind trees and a stone wall; light from the windows splashed its dark garden, and Charlotte could hear the sounds of music and voices. Timothy rang the bell, but the door was open and Oliver led the way inside. Steven turned out to be the tall, handsome black student who had sung with great emotion in a resonant bass, "A policeman's lot is not an 'appy one." When Oliver introduced Charlotte as his friend from the States, Steven gave her a broad, hospitable smile. "Another former colonial! Welcome, welcome, Charlotte, so glad you could come." Charlotte was aware of Timothy peering nervously around her shoulder. Steven's grin grew broader. "She's looking for you, too, Harker."

"Yes, but she wants to *find* me. She's terrifying!"

Other people came up the steps behind them. Steven waved toward the back of the house. "There's plenty of food in the kitchen. Go help yourselves."

The kitchen was enormous; virtually every surface was covered with pizzas still in their cardboard boxes, and trays of pastries. "What about you?" said Charlotte to Oliver as they made their way through the madhouse.

"What about me what?" Oliver secured a couple of paper plates. "Do you care what kind?"

"Anything but anchovy. I just wondered if there's a Mad Margaret stalking you."

Surprise flickered across his face and was gone in an instant. "Not that I'm aware of. Do you want a lemonade? Let's get out of here."

They found a small untenanted couch in one of the front rooms. "Of course," said Oliver as they sat down, "there's still Harker's sister, Gillian."

"Oh?" Charlotte coughed a little on her lemonade.

"She's a real knockout—and she's only ten."

"Oh. Look out, Oliver, you're going to drop that—" Too late. A large lump of tomato fell off Oliver's slice of pizza and landed juicily on the beige carpet. He muttered under his breath and bent to pick it up.

"That looks like blood," said Charlotte. "You need a sponge."

He gave her his plate and went off to see what he could find while she sat back, nibbling her pizza and observing the ebb and flow. Somewhere there was music playing, but it couldn't compete with the jumble of voices and fell through the cracks, a few notes now and then. The adrenaline that had gotten her that far was disappearing like water down a drain and she was beginning to drift, but there was something very comforting about being in a room full of people she didn't know and was unlikely to see again. She didn't have to worry about what any of them thought.

The couch creaked and shifted. She turned her head to find one of the strangers had taken Oliver's place beside her. He crossed his legs negligently and gave her an assessing look. He had thick, slightly shaggy black hair and deep-set brown eyes. "Do I know you?" he asked, and she shook her head. "I probably should, though, shouldn't I?"

"I doubt it."

"Why? Aren't you very interesting?"

She blinked at him. "Excuse me?"

"Oh, don't apologize."

"I wasn't," said Charlotte. "I wouldn't dream of apologizing."

"Good." He gave her a sudden smile, so infectious she couldn't help smiling back. "So who are you?"

"I'm Charlotte. Who are you?"

He cocked his head at her. "My name's Daniel Kelly. Bass. Third in, second row from the back. I'm told I sing powerfully. I think it's kindly meant. I take it you aren't from Thurston Hall?"

"Concord-Carlisle Regional District High School."

"Aha." He considered her a moment. "You're a Yank. I can tell by the color of your eyes. Dead giveaway, eye color. If you don't mind my asking, how did you get here?"

"We walked," said Charlotte.

Daniel Kelly leaned back and folded his arms. "Just happened by and thought it looked like fun, so you crashed? Or are you a friend of Steven's?"

"I've never met him before, actually." Out of the corner of her eye she caught a glimpse of Maeve and Timothy in the doorway; his back was against the jamb and she was standing very close. Charlotte couldn't see her face, but Timothy's expression was a comic mixture of apprehension and delight. Then bodies got in the way.

"Look, Charlotte," said Daniel. "I don't believe in beating around the bush. I find you utterly fascinating. Has our relationship got a chance?" His sudden volley caught her wrong-footed and she couldn't think of a quick answer. "No!" he cried, putting his finger lightly on her lips. "Don't answer that! I can see it in your eyes—I'll throw myself off the Archway."

"You'll live to regret it," she replied, lobbing back.

"Well, how about this. Term's over, you could run away with me. We'll find a grotty little bed-sitter in Islington over a fish-and-chip shop and live in blissful squalor—"

"Charlotte?"

Bemused, she looked up to find Oliver standing in front of them, a frown hovering between his eyes.

"Do you know this person?" asked Daniel, addressing them both.

"Yes, he's—"

"Yes, Kelly, she's with me," said Oliver, "and we're just going. It's getting late, Charlotte."

"If you wait long enough, Shattuck, it'll start getting early," advised Daniel helpfully.

"The squalor sounds attractive," said Charlotte with regret, "but I'm afraid there's no future for us. I've enjoyed meeting you, Daniel Kelly."

His face twisted in extreme distress. "Was it something I said?"

"Probably. But I can't remember exactly what."

"Look, I'll give you my telephone number—I'll write it in indelible ink on the inside of your wrist if you like. Ring me if you think of it, no matter what time night or day."

"When you two are quite finished," said Oliver.

"I don't think that's what he means," said Charlotte to Daniel.

"No, it isn't," Oliver agreed. "I mean now."

"I'll never look at another Charlotte as long as I live," vowed Daniel as Charlotte stood up. Timothy and Maeve had disappeared—together? Charlotte wondered hazily. "Should we say thank you?" she asked, following Oliver into the front hall.

"I have," he replied. "Steven's in the kitchen making coffee."

"What about the rug?"

"They can move the couch over the spot." He ushered her through the front gate. "What were you talking about in there?"

"Oh," said Charlotte, "this and that. Mostly nonsense." Talking to Daniel, once she'd got her balance, had been like talking to one of her brothers. She had a sudden picture of Eliot somewhere in the Montana wilderness. He was probably sitting beside a campfire playing his guitar—except that the time would be wrong, she reminded herself. He was how many zones away? She gave up and asked Oliver, "Is he a friend of yours?"

"Kelly? I know him. We're in the same form at school. He's very bright but he doesn't take anything seriously. You seemed to be having a good time." His voice was carefully neutral.

"Yes," said Charlotte. "I did have a good time. I'm glad we went. But Oliver"—she was reminded of an earlier question—"what do we need an early start for tomorrow? You haven't said what we're doing."

"No. I haven't. I'll explain when we get back."

Connie's windows were dark, but there were lights in the garden flat. As she waited on the front steps for Oliver to unlock the door, Charlotte could hear underneath her feet Tom Jones singing faintly, "It's Not Unusual." There was a note taped to the banister with Oliver's name on it.

"Do you want a cup of hot chocolate?" he asked at the top of the stairs.

What Charlotte wanted was to go to bed. The day stretched behind her, its beginnings lost to sight. Was it really only that morning that she'd cashed her travelers' checks? She hunched her shoulders and yawned. "Yes, I suppose so."

The note was from Connie; Oliver left it on the kitchen table where Charlotte could see it: "Super concert—sorry I missed you. Don't forget supper Sunday. Love, Con." She rubbed her eyes and yawned again. "What I don't understand, Oliver, is why you didn't tell me about singing. You never once mentioned it in your letters."

"It's no big thing," he said, filling a saucepan with milk, getting mugs out.

"But when did you start?"

"Last autumn. I was playing tennis and I got tendonitis so I had to drop out for the term. Harker said why didn't I try out for the chorus, so I did. Just for something to do."

"You don't have tendonitis now, though—"

"Of course not. But I couldn't just quit the chorus. We were working on the Bach B-minor, and Collins needed tenors—"

"And you're good," she finished for him.

He didn't deny it, merely shrugged and poured cocoa into the mugs. He brought them to the table and sat down across from her. She braced herself. There was something on his mind besides singing. He sat staring into his mug for several minutes, then looked up at her, his eyes calculating. "Do you remember Captain MacPherson?"

She blinked stupidly. "Who?"

His mouth tightened.

She scrabbled around in the back of her mind—the name had to be there somewhere. "MacPherson? Wasn't he—he was your uncle Sam's friend—the one from England?" She felt triumphant.

Oliver's expression eased slightly. "Scotland," he corrected.

"Who came to reenact the battle at the Old North Bridge four years ago in April. You'd just come to Concord yourself."

He nodded approvingly as if she'd just given the right answer to an exam question. "I'd hoped you'd remember him."

Another silence. "Well?" prodded Charlotte.

"I want to go see him. I thought we'd go tomorrow."

"All right. Is he here in London?"

"No, not exactly."

"Look, Oliver. Just tell me. I'm too tired to play twenty questions."

"He's in Scotland. We have to go to Scotland to see him."

It was Charlotte's turn to be silent. This conversation was proving much more difficult to keep track of than the one she'd had earlier with Daniel Kelly. Of course that had been largely nonsense—it really didn't matter what she said so long as she hit the ball back over the net. This was serious. She sighed, blowing on her cocoa, and noticed a skin forming on it. She hated cocoa skin. She didn't really want the cocoa, anyway; her digestive system had closed down after the pizza. Finally she ventured, "I'm a little hazy about the geography here, but isn't

Scotland quite a long way away?"

"It'll take several days."

"But you're having supper with Connie Sunday night."

"Oh, Charlotte. Not if we're going to Scotland."

"But her note—and I heard you tell her—"

"I'll leave a message." He sounded exasperated. "That's not a problem."

"*We're* going to Scotland?" She was still trying to get hold of this idea.

"Yes. At least I hope we are. It's up to you."

"Now wait a minute, Oliver. I'm confused. And don't look at me like that." She glared back at him defiantly. "You'll have to explain better if you want me to agree."

"It's not that complicated. Jamie MacPherson was one of Uncle Sam's closest friends, right? They were together in World War II on the same convoy ship in the Atlantic. When Uncle Sam died, I wrote to him to let him know. And I told him that I'd be coming to London with Paula and Eric. There wasn't time for him to write back before we left, so I sent him my address once we got here." He looked into his mug, swirling the liquid around in it gently. "He wrote me a long letter about Uncle Sam—a lot of things I hadn't heard. Paula didn't know Uncle Sam at all, not really. She just shipped me off to him when she ran out of choices, and Eric had never met him. It was pointless to talk to either of them about him."

I knew him, thought Charlotte, a little hurt. Oliver hadn't written to her about his great-uncle.

As if guessing what was in her mind, he said, "Jamie knew Uncle Sam when he was young. He could tell me what he'd been like before I was born. I wanted to know—I think it's important to know," he added almost angrily. "No one else does."

"So you want to talk to him in person," said Charlotte. "I can understand that. But why have you waited so long?"

This time he looked straight at her. "I wanted you to come with me."

She felt herself melt. Before she dissolved completely, she said, "Would they have let us go? Paula and Eric, I mean?"

He shrugged. "That doesn't matter. They aren't here. Look, Charlotte, I was furious when Paula said—she just announced—that she was going to Germany with Eric, so you'd have to postpone your trip. She said Eric needed her with him this time."

"Postpone?" echoed Charlotte. "But you never said—"

"No. I didn't see why you should have to change your plans at the last minute so Paula could have a holiday in Germany. I thought we'd have a better time with them away. We could do whatever we wanted—we could go to Scotland, just the two of us. There's no one to interfere."

"She doesn't know I'm here."

Oliver shook his head.

"But she'll find out. And then—that's what Timothy was talking about, isn't it? What *will* she do—have you thought about that?"

"Of course I have."

And she knew that, being Oliver, of course he had. Her skin prickled. "When do they come back?"

"Late Sunday night."

"*Sunday?* Oh, Oliver." What had he done? She stared blindly at him. Only a few hours ago she'd been remembering the day he'd absconded with her to Plum Island without telling anyone. She'd known then, and she knew now, that her mother was not entirely convinced of Oliver's trustworthiness. Mrs. Paige had made generous allowances for him; he'd had a pretty miserable childhood, and it was obvious that once he'd settled down, he'd made a real effort with his uncle. Charlotte's mother was genuinely fond of Oliver, but Charlotte was her youngest child, and her protective instincts were strong.

"Are you saying you won't go." It wasn't a question.

Was she? She tried to imagine what Paula Preston would do when she arrived back in Highgate Sunday and discovered that not only had Oliver not told Charlotte she'd have to put off her trip, but that the two of them, both underage, had gone off to some unknown destination in Scotland.

"Don't say anything for a minute, just listen," said Oliver. "I've worked it out—it's not that hard. You pack what you need for the trip—say four or five days, not much—and I'll put the rest of your gear in my room. She won't find it, she leaves my things alone. One of the chaps in the chorus is going to North Wales tomorrow for a week. His family's got a cottage on the edge of some bog in the middle of nowhere—no electricity, no phone. I'll leave a note saying I've gone with him. She won't like it, but she won't fuss—she's always after me to do something with my friends from school"—he made a face—"and it'll make her feel less guilty for going with Eric. I can ring from a public phone somewhere, just to say I'm all right. She won't know a thing until we get back."

"And then what?"

"All hell will break loose. This is my fault, Charlotte, the whole thing. No one can blame you for any part of it. I was supposed to tell you not to come. Paula was going to talk to your mother, but I said no, I'd do it. She can't punish you, neither can your parents. You didn't know. By the time any of them find out, we'll have done it." He leaned back in his chair, his expression suddenly remote. "Or we can just sit here like ducks, waiting to be potted Sunday night when they get back. It's up to you."

"Gee, thanks, Oliver. What an attractive choice you've given me," said Charlotte crossly. "I've got half a mind to call up Daniel Kelly and see what he has to offer."

"You could do that. Are you finished with your cocoa?" Oliver stood up and took the mugs to the sink without waiting for an answer. He turned his back and made a production of rinsing them out.

Charlotte watched him. Thoughts churned in her head like clothes in a washing machine. "Where in Scotland?"

"North of Aberdeen."

"How far is Aberdeen from here?"

"About five hundred miles."

"And how do we get there?"

"By train." Oliver's voice was level; he kept his back to her, scrubbing the saucepan. "We go to Edinburgh tomorrow and spend the night. You'd like Edinburgh, we went last summer. Aberdeen's farther north, and beyond that is

Cullen, where Captain MacPherson lives. It's a fishing village."

"That's why you wanted me to cash all those travelers' checks."

"I thought the money might be useful."

"What time did you mean to leave?"

"Early. There's a train from King's Cross at seven-forty-five. Connie should still be asleep."

Charlotte rubbed the back of her neck. "Oliver, I'm exhausted. I'm going to bed."

He turned around. "Are you going to Scotland?"

She heaved an enormous sigh. "Yes, well, why not?" Which was a dumb answer, she knew as soon as she gave it. There were compelling reasons why not, but she doubted she was capable of thinking straight just then. Oliver's face relaxed and she saw that he hadn't been certain she'd agree, in spite of his careful calculations.

Alone in her room, lying in bed, she wondered if it had occurred to Oliver as it had to her that Paula, or her parents, or all three, were liable to forbid the two of them from seeing—maybe even from writing to—each other. In a few years that wouldn't matter, at least not technically, once she and Oliver were old enough to do what they wanted, but the immediate future looked pretty bleak.

Six

At King's Cross Station the next morning, Charlotte and Oliver got caught behind a large Indian family with limited English, struggling to extract tickets from an indifferent clerk. Controlling himself with effort, Oliver finally managed to work out that the Indians had come to the wrong place; they wanted Charing Cross, not King's Cross. When at last he succeeded in explaining this to them, they were effusively grateful. They thanked him so thoroughly, in fact, that by the time they'd hurried off to the underground, the seven-forty-five train to Edinburgh had gone, and Oliver and Charlotte were in danger of missing the eight o'clock if they didn't sprint for it. Most of the compartments were already full. They took the first two seats they found together, facing backward and inside. Oliver hoisted their knapsacks into the overhead rack and offered Charlotte one of the newspapers he'd bought at the Archway newsstand, but she shook her head. "How long's the trip?"

Oliver unfolded the *Guardian*. "About six hours."

"All the way up England and into Scotland?" she said disbelievingly.

"It's a small island, Charlotte."

"At least that will give us time to discuss a few things."

"Later." Oliver glanced significantly at the other four people in the compartment. The woman by the window opposite plucked a cigarette out of her capacious leather handbag and lit it, blowing a thin stream of translucent smoke into the communal air. Oliver shot her an irritated look, raised his paper like a shield, and disappeared behind it. She paid no attention. She had perfect mauve fingernails, long legs, and a very short suede skirt. The small, neatly dressed man next to her was absorbed in a sheaf of papers on which he was making notes. He sat very precisely in the middle, taking up only his allotment of space, but every now and then, Charlotte noticed his eyes flicker sideways, toward the legs.

Sprawled across from her was a boy about Oliver's age, jeans out at the knees, black leather boots with silver chains over the insteps, hair falling raggedly over his jacket collar. His eyes were shut, his lips moving silently, a small transistor radio glued to his ear. On the far side of Oliver, the sixth seat was occupied by a stout woman with permed gray hair, wearing sensible shoes, who went to sleep as soon as the train began to move, and snored audibly. Charlotte chewed her lower lip, thinking it was a waste of a good window seat. If Oliver wasn't going to talk to her, at least she'd have a better view of the landscape. None of their fellow passengers, she was sure, would have the slightest interest in their conversation, but arguing with Oliver was useless.

London straggled out messily behind them. She glimpsed rows of drearily identical houses, on drearily identical streets, strung together like beads on an abacus. If it was late and dark, did people ever forget which one was theirs? She tried to imagine how it would be to live in a house that looked like everyone else's—suddenly she sat up straight. "My towels! Oliver, what about my towels?"

The paper jerked. "What?"

"My towels. Did you remember? I didn't."

Mentally she had leaped from the anonymous suburbs to the flat in Highgate and begun reviewing it, room by room, wondering what she had left out for Paula and Eric to find. She and Oliver had washed the dishes from breakfast, putting them away, and she'd thoroughly gone over her bedroom twice to be sure she hadn't missed a book or a pair of shoes. Oliver had stowed her suitcase and duffel under his bed where they couldn't be seen, even from the doorway. He'd left the envelope for his mother on the hall table, and she'd watched him slide another one under Connie Rinaldi's door on their way out.

"I folded them and put them away," said Oliver.

"But they were damp."

"I put them on the bottom. Stop worrying, Charlotte, will you?" He shook out his paper again.

She looked up at her knapsack—its straps dangling over the rack—and pictured its contents: underwear, toothbrush, nightgown, two jerseys, sweatshirt robe, journal in which she'd scarcely had a chance to write yet, socks—she'd packed in a hurry that morning, distracted by Oliver's impatience. The knapsack was Eliot's day-pack: not intended to hold that much. He had sent it to her in Concord as a going-away present, by UPS. She'd opened the box and recognized the stained green nylon immediately; it was covered with cloth badges he'd picked up on his travels: Mount Katahdin, the Marlborough Chamber Music Festival, Yosemite, Tanglewood. Her mother had gently suggested that she might not need a day-pack in London, but there was no way Charlotte could leave it behind, although she'd had no idea how useful it would turn out to be. "I hope I've brought the right clothes," she said after a while. "You weren't much help."

Lowering the paper, Oliver gave her an exasperated look. "We're only going for a few days, not the indefinite future. And if you've forgotten anything vital, you can replace it in Scotland. They have shops, you know, and they speak quite good English."

"Thanks." Jean's college roommate, Betsy, had gone off to France for six weeks one summer with a small suitcase filled with Tampax, just in case. Everyone laughed when Jean told the story, but how did you know, Charlotte wondered.

"What now?" said Oliver, who'd been watching her.

She was too embarrassed to tell him. "I didn't know I'd be going to Scotland, Oliver. This trip isn't turning to be at all what I expected."

"And you're sorry you came."

The edge in his voice surprised her. Under the confidence he was not completely sure of himself. "I didn't say that. I just might have packed differently. Look, I think I'm being a really good sport, considering."

"Considering?"

"Considering what we have to look forward to when we get back."

"There's no point stewing about that now, it'll only spoil the trip."

"Do you really know where we're going, or are you inventing it as we go?"

"Cullen is about seventy miles northwest of Aberdeen on the Moray Firth. Is that specific enough?"

"How do we get there from Edinburgh?"

"We go to Aberdeen and ask. I expect there's a coach."

"A coach? That sounds like Wells Fargo." She saw he wasn't amused. "Does Captain MacPherson know we're coming?"

"In my last letter I wrote that I was hoping to visit in July. I'll ring him from Edinburgh. I have his phone number."

"But didn't he write back? What if he's not home?"

"He'll be home."

"Oliver, how can you be sure?"

"If I weren't sure, we wouldn't be doing this. All right?" He glanced self-consciously around the compartment, then raised his paper.

No, it wasn't all right. She wanted to ask him what he wasn't telling her. She wanted him to talk to her, but she saw that he wouldn't, not then. So she sat in silence, staring out the window until her thoughts had calmed enough to let her see what she was looking at. Then she settled back to watch England roll by.

After a while, she said, "Oliver, do you know what that yellow stuff is? We've passed fields and fields of it—look, over there."

He glanced out and shrugged. "Haven't any idea."

"It must be some kind of crop. I bet Andy would know."

"Andy isn't here."

"No, but—"

"Andy's in Concord, picking beetles off his tomato plants and counting beans, and you're on your way to Scotland with me, and who cares what they grow in the fields out there?"

Far away on the horizon she glimpsed a cloud forming. "I'd like to know. I'm interested."

"Oh, come off it, Charlotte. Are you really? You don't have to pretend with me, you know."

"What do you mean?"

This time he put the paper down. "I mean you're not going to dedicate your life to agriculture."

"Well, maybe not, but Andy—"

"Andy. Andy's a hard case, we both know that. You don't feel the way he does about farming. How could you? It's plain hard, physical labor, that's all, and what do you get to show for it? Blisters, sunburn, and mosquito bites."

Stung by his dismissiveness, she said, "You spent three years working at the farm yourself, Oliver. If you didn't like it—"

"I did it for the same reason you did. It was expedient. If I hadn't found something constructive to do with my time, Paula would have shipped me off to some character-building camp, or made me spend the summers in Washington taking accelerated math classes. Your parents would have done the same."

She couldn't deny the truth in what he said. As long as she had something genuine to occupy her summer, her parents didn't try to organize her vacation for her. At first they were mildly surprised by her sudden interest in growing vegetables, but they accepted it, as they accepted most of the unexpected things their children took notions to.

"And, anyway, I didn't say I didn't like it," Oliver went on. "The marketing and the advertising were all right, so long as I didn't have to spend my days doubled up weeding carrots or heaving baskets of squash around. I learned a lot about business, but I'm not making a career in agriculture. Three years was plenty. It was time to move on."

He expected her to agree, she could hear it in his voice, and on the one hand she knew what he meant. The farm was a summer job; she'd never really thought of it as extending into her future beyond, say, high school. But at the same time, she found reassurance in thinking of the Bullard Farm as permanent. It had been in Andy Schuyler's family for four generations, and except for the seven years when his father had stopped farming, the land had been under continuous cultivation. The farm should be there simply because it had always been there, a productive, essential part of the landscape. Charlotte might not love farming as Andy did, but she discovered she was coming to love the farm as his mother, Pat, did.

"They're talking about selling some of the land," she said after a few minutes.

"Who?"

"Andy's parents, Pat and George. They've had an offer from a developer." It made her slightly ill just to think about it. Houses marching across the cornfield beyond the pond: blocky imitation colonials painted fake colonial colors, each with a two-car garage and blacktopped driveway, weed-free lawn, regulation rhododendrons and azaleas mulched with bark chips, a basketball hoop, a grapevine wreath on the door. How shabby the Bullard farmhouse would look by comparison, but it had an honest dignity that the new houses would never achieve because it was what it had been built to be.

"I'm not surprised," said Oliver calmly. "That land must be worth a lot. Acreage in Concord is highly desirable."

"But it's part of the farm," Charlotte protested. "Andy's growing corn on it."

Oliver gave a little shrug. "So he can grow corn somewhere else. They'd be stupid not to sell, Charlotte. They'd have money in the bank for a change—a cushion in case something happens. Pat could get a new car—"

"That's not the point."

"Why isn't it? Anyway, it's still their land, not Andy's. Why shouldn't they be able to sell part of it? Face it, Charlotte, that kind of farm is an anachronism. A few fields and some worn-out machinery? You can't make a living that way—you can't support a family. Andy's father realized that. If Andy isn't too boneheaded, eventually he'll realize it, too."

"I can't believe you're saying this!" Charlotte burst out. "I thought you'd be sympathetic."

He frowned. "I'm being practical, Charlotte. Keep your voice down. There's no future in the kind of farming Andy's doing."

"That's just not true. Andy isn't trying to do what his father did—he's doing new things, and every year he's more successful. This business with organic vegetables, for instance. Deb can't buy enough of them for the Magic Cupboard—she sells out every day in the summer. And the herbs? Last year he tried a cutting garden—zinnias and marigolds, snapdragons, that kind of thing? The customers loved it. They were willing to go out and cut their own flowers. He knows how to adapt what he's got to what people want—"

"And at the end of the summer, how much profit has he made? Have you ever stopped to figure out how much it costs to grow, say, *one* organic tomato? It can't possibly be cost-effective."

"Oliver, you sound so cold-blooded. Money isn't the whole thing."

"Maybe not, but it's a lot of the whole thing. Did Andy tell you about selling the house lots?"

"No, Pat did. Andy hasn't said anything, he just went ahead and plowed the field this spring and put corn in." Attempting to prove to Oliver that she wasn't being purely emotional, she said, "As long as the land's being farmed, the taxes are lower." Taxes were not normally part of Charlotte's vocabulary, any more than were benefits, deficits, profit margins, and budgets. Those were words that belonged to the adult world, a world, however, that she was beginning to feel press uncomfortably close.

Oliver was obviously not impressed. He merely said, "Andy's being stubborn. I feel sorry for his parents."

"Pat doesn't want to sell, either," replied Charlotte. "After all, it's her family's farm."

"Look, Charlotte, there's no point in us arguing about this, is there? It's nothing to do with either of us, really—we're well out of it. I can't remember how we even got on to the subject." Once again he picked up his newspaper and withdrew, terminating the conversation, leaving Charlotte dissatisfied.

She wasn't at all sure the business of the farm was nothing to do with her. She remembered clearly the day Pat had told her about the developer's offer. They'd been sitting together on the low, flat stone wall beside the farmhouse in the soft September afternoon, putting rubber bands around bunches of fresh-cut green and opal basil. The spicy-pungent smell had clung to Charlotte's fingers like invisible gloves. With the beginning of school, summer had officially ended, but the farm was still producing quantities of corn, spinach, and tomatoes, herbs and late-variety raspberries, tons of summer squash, onions, and potatoes. The stand was busy with customers and Andy trucked vegetables to Deb's store in the middle of town on his way to school every morning.

In spite of the bustle and urgency, there were still

afternoons like that one, when the sun lay thick on the fields below the house where the cicadas—hot-bugs, Pat called them—buzzed endlessly and catbirds mewed from the elderberry bushes. When there were quiet tasks to do, providing the chance to sit and absorb the little world. Pat was barefoot, wearing an ancient denim wraparound skirt and a wrinkled shirt the color of tomato juice. Often when she was with her, Charlotte forgot Pat was old enough to be her mother. They talked as if they were the same age. "You know," Pat said after a while, "we've been thinking of selling off a piece of land down there—on the other side of the pond."

"Selling it?" echoed Charlotte in disbelief. "What for?"

"Houses. There's been a developer pestering George for more than a year now. He reckons he could put six or seven houses on it and we'd hardly see them. He's offered George a fortune—well, I suppose it isn't a fortune, really, but it sounds like one to me. All those years put together when George worked and worked and worked getting crops out of it, he never made that much. We could have the house painted and fix the bathroom and still have money to save in case any of the kids actually decides to go to college. . . ." Her voice trailed away. Charlotte watched her look around, her eyes lingering on each detail of the landscape with affection. A chipmunk appeared suddenly on the wall six feet away, gave them a beady stare, then vanished into a crack.

"But you can't be considering it, not really," Charlotte almost pleaded, caught off guard by the force of her feelings.

Pat blinked. "We'd be foolish not to. We aren't going

to do anything immediately, Charlie. The land won't decrease in value, but—oh, I *hate* money! Let's talk about something else. I'm going to try to make opal basil jelly Sunday, will you help? It ought to be a lovely color."

Time to move on, Oliver said, but Charlotte wondered how easy that would be for her. She was only just realizing that she'd begun to put down roots.

Seven

"We'll try that one across the street first. There's no point lugging our gear all over the city."

"But it looks so—big," said Charlotte faintly. "Big" wasn't the right word, "real" was closer, but she doubted that Oliver would understand what she meant. They'd come up the steps from Waverly Station, which was below street level, to find themselves in the middle of Edinburgh with the sun shining between banks of fierce cloud, a chill breeze blowing, and torrents of traffic whizzing past.

"Of course it's big, it's a hotel, Charlotte," Oliver replied snappishly.

"Won't it cost an awful lot?" It wasn't until they'd gotten off the train that it had dawned on her that they were going to have to find a place to spend the night. She'd never had to do it for herself before.

"Yes, it probably will. But it's convenient and no one will pay any attention to us."

"Why would they?"

"Well, look at us. If we try a guest house or a bed-and-breakfast, people are much more likely to wonder what we're doing. Even if we pretend you're my sister they'll be suspicious. In a large hotel no one will notice."

The enormity of what they were doing hit her like a cold shower, but before she could say anything, Oliver was crossing the street while cars throbbed with impatience at a red light. Without hesitating, he pushed through the glass-and-chrome doors of the Royal Castle Hotel. On the ground level there was a narrow beige lobby with a bank of elevators and a wide carpeted staircase. The reception area was on the next floor, landscaped with potted foliage plants and conversational clusters of chairs. Along the front of the hotel, through more glass doors, Charlotte saw a formal dining room: tables with starched white cloths and vases of flowers, and picture windows that opened on the city. Oliver dumped his knapsack on the floor at her feet. "You stay here while I get us a room."

A little wildly she caught his arm. "A room, Oliver?"

"Yes. We'll share it. We don't need to spend the money on two."

"Now wait a minute—"

"For heaven's sake, Charlotte. It's purely practical. I'll get a room with twin beds. You can sit up fully clothed all night if it makes you happy."

Suddenly Charlotte refused to be steamrollered. Oliver was pushing her again and she wasn't going to be pushed. Whatever he had in mind, if she didn't like it, she wasn't going to accept it meekly. "I'll get my own room, then. If it's only for one night, I'm sure I have enough money." She hadn't the faintest idea what a hotel room in the middle of Edinburgh would cost—it could be as much as a hundred pounds, she supposed.

Oliver's face went blank. He stood perfectly still for a moment, regarding her. Her nerve almost cracked, then she met his gaze defiantly, flattening her mouth into its stubbornest line. "Wait here," he said coldly. He unzipped his jacket and smoothed down his pullover before approaching the reservation desk. The clerk behind it greeted him with an inquiring smile, and although Charlotte couldn't hear what she said, she knew the clerk called Oliver "sir." In spite of her good slacks and cardigan, Charlotte felt like a rumpled little girl, not someone old enough and responsible enough to go racketing around a foreign country on her own, staying in hotels. Of course if her parents knew what she was doing, they wouldn't think she was old enough and responsible enough, either. She hoped Oliver wasn't giving their real names.

She half expected him to return and say the clerk had refused on the grounds they were too young to register. Instead he brought two keys. "Yours," he said expressionlessly, giving her one. Swinging his knapsack onto one shoulder, he stalked to the elevators. The plastic tag on her key said 329; she closed her fingers around it so hard, the edges cut into her hand. A cross-looking couple got on with them, wrapped in discontent. The woman pulled out a roll of Tums and ground two between her teeth. When the elevator stopped on the third floor, they and Oliver turned right, and Charlotte, following the arrow that pointed to rooms 320–338, turned left. Oliver hadn't told her his room number and she hadn't asked.

She fumbled with her key in the lock, got the door open, and shut herself safely inside before the pressure building between her ears exploded. She took a gulping breath, and hot, furious tears burned her eyes. Oliver had done this to her before: made her feel wrong and inadequate and immature. She ought to have seen it coming, discussed it with him, gotten the details straight before she'd agreed to leave London. Instead she'd chosen not to think about them; she realized that now.

Gradually the roar in her ears faded and her sense of self returned. Why should it be her fault? She smudged the tears away angrily with her fingers and took stock. Room 329 was small, decorated in dull shades of green, probably meant to be restful. Over the single bed was a vivid painting of purple mountains reflected in a lake, the sky violent with sunrise or sunset. Otherwise the furniture was utilitarian: a night table with a lamp bolted to it, a chair, a dressing table, and a large cabinet whose doors concealed a television, a couple of glasses, and an empty ice bucket. Half a dozen warped coat hangers dangled from a railing to her left, and through the door on the right was a bathroom the size of a coat closet. From the window she had a view of a narrow service alley and the back of an expressionless building. The room was clean, but the curtains smelled of ghostly cigarettes.

She certainly hoped the room wasn't costing a hundred pounds a night. Oliver had probably asked the clerk for the pokiest one in the hotel out of spite. Well, it would do overnight; she wouldn't give him the satisfaction of complaining. After rooting out her toilet kit, she went into the bathroom and spent a good long time washing her hands and face, brushing her teeth, combing out her hair, and braiding it. No makeup was Deb's advice, but a little blusher when you feel stressed and pale does wonders. It did. Charlotte's reflection gazed back from the mirror, gratifyingly calm and self-possessed.

Action was what she needed. She'd be a jerk to spend the afternoon shut in her room waiting for Oliver to knock on the door. She checked through her L.L. Bean haversack: passport, travelers' checks, wallet and cash, camera. Feeling bold and determined, she locked her door and set off to explore Edinburgh.

Through the windows in the reception area she studied the view: in the foreground the wide main street, the zigzag glassed-in roof of the railway station, and the steps they'd climbed an hour ago. Beyond lay a swath of rich green mounded with trees and splashed with flower beds. There was an ornate stone monument near the street, and rising behind, spiky and sharp, like the spine of a dinosaur, a long ridge of dark buildings ending in a rocky outcrop ringed with walls and battlements: a castle. She'd never seen a real castle before. Less than a week ago she'd been playing Travel Scrabble with Barbara Coburn, listening to her talk about Scotland, never dreaming she'd set foot there herself.

"That's Edinburgh Castle," said Oliver conversationally.

"Oh, really." She hoped he hadn't noticed her jump.

"We can walk to it. There's a good view from up there," he went on as if there'd been no disagreement between them earlier. "If you aren't too tired?"

"I'm not a bit tired." He must have been sitting there waiting for her. She wondered what he would have done if she hadn't appeared. Would he have gone to get her, or would he have set out by himself, as she was prepared to do? Descending the stairs, she felt a whisper of regret—not so much that he was with her, but that she wouldn't have the chance to prove she could have gone alone.

"How's your room?" he asked, the question sounding innocently polite.

"Fine. How's yours?"

"Small."

"Oliver, it's incredible!" Across the city the sun flared in swift, brilliant spots of light; the sky seethed with tumbled masses of black cloud, gilt-edged as they swept across the sun. Edinburgh spread below, somber gray and brown, spiked with towers. Charlotte and Oliver stood on the parapet of the castle, beside a row of cannons. "Why didn't you tell me you'd been here?"

Deliberately Oliver turned his back on the view and leaned on his elbows. "I did."

"You did not. When?"

"Last summer. Paula and Eric and I came up in August for four days during the Festival, just before Paula started working for Connie. I thought I sent you a postcard."

"Well, you didn't. Did you stay at the Royal Castle Hotel?"

"You've got to be joking. It's not posh enough. Connie used her connections and got us into the Caledonian—that big one, over there. It cost a packet, that's how Paula knew it was good. We didn't see anything much except the performances; the place was packed. You could hardly move. They have a Tattoo up here on the Esplanade at night—massed bands, kilts everywhere, 'Scotland the

Brave,' and a lone piper spotlit on the battlements. They lay it on with a trowel."

"It sounds wonderful!"

Oliver hunched a shoulder. "It's a spectacle put on for all the tourists to gawk at. If you like that sort of thing, that's the sort of thing you like."

"Honestly, Oliver," said Charlotte in exasperation. "What else did you do?"

"Con got tickets to two concerts, a piano recital, a really depressing Russian play, and *La Bohème*. Paula was over the moon—she collects culture. Afterward she could say to people, 'Well, when I heard Alfred Brendel at the Edinburgh Festival—'"

The edge in his voice when he mentioned his mother disturbed Charlotte. Reluctantly she said, "I thought you were getting along with her."

"Did you? I expect that's what she thinks, too, so I must be. Anyway, I don't want to talk about Paula. Let's go somewhere. What do you want to see?"

"I don't know what there is," said Charlotte. "I don't know anything about Edinburgh."

"We'll walk down the Royal Mile," Oliver decided. Leaving the castle, they started down the long sloping street that followed the dinosaur's spine.

"I wish I could send Hilary a postcard," said Charlotte, looking at a rackful outside a souvenir shop.

"Why can't you?"

"I'm not supposed to be here, Oliver."

"What difference does that make? By the time she gets it, everyone will know."

He was right. "I've only got English stamps—"

"Doesn't matter, they'll do. What about this one? Greyfriars Bobby." She'd been thinking of a picture of the castle, or a piper in a kilt, but the card he handed her showed the statue of a little dog on a pedestal. "I must have been about ten when I read the story," he said.

"What story?"

"Do you mean Jean never made you read *Greyfriars Bobby?* It's about a Skye terrier. His master was a shepherd who died here in Edinburgh and Bobby refused to leave his grave."

Charlotte made a face. "Jean knows I don't like animal stories. I hated *The Yearling* and I couldn't finish *Black Beauty*. I think they're morbid."

"Bobby was faithful, not pathetic. He lived in the kirkyard and went across the street to a pub for dinner every day. As I remember, he had a lot of friends."

"Did you read Albert Payson Terhune, too?" This was a side of him she didn't know.

"Some. It was a phase," he said dismissively. "I haven't thought of Greyfriars Bobby in years."

"The statue's not far from here," said Charlotte when she emerged from the shop with her postcards. "The woman told me how to find it, and I bought a guidebook with a map. She called him 'the bonnie wee dog.'"

"I'm sure she did," said Oliver dryly.

"Well, I can't send the card unless I've seen the statue, so let's find it."

Greyfriars Bobby wasn't hard to find. He sat alert on his pedestal, a former drinking fountain, outside Greyfriars kirkyard. "It says he stayed here for fourteen years." Charlotte studied her guidebook.

"The story's a real tearjerker. Walt Disney turned it into a movie."

"Wait a minute. Oliver, stay there—just like that. Don't move."

"What? Oh, Charlotte—" He scowled as she stepped hastily backward, pulling out her camera.

"Don't glare at me. It's for Amos. I'll tack it over his supper dish when I get home. Try smiling."

He didn't exactly smile, but he stopped frowning and she snapped the shutter before he could think better of it, not sure what she'd see when the photograph was developed.

After a short digression into the kirkyard to see the grave Bobby had guarded—"This is one you can tell Timothy Harker about," said Charlotte—they returned to the Royal Mile and continued down it, Charlotte pausing frequently to read bits out of her guide, while Oliver demonstrated monumental patience. She ignored him, mostly successfully. If only they had more time. All along the street were museums and houses with historic markers, interesting shops and narrow alleys that invited exploration, but Oliver kept her moving. They found the heart-shaped pattern in the paving stones that marked the old tollbooth, and admired the crown tower on Saint Giles Cathedral without going inside.

At the bottom of the Mile stood the tall ornamental gates of Holyroodhouse. "It's so hard to look and read at the same time," lamented Charlotte. "If only I'd known we were coming. I had no idea—let's go sit on one of those benches by the fountain." She hunted for the right page in her guide. "This is where the Queen stays when she's in Edinburgh. She has a garden party here every summer."

"I wonder what they do if it rains," said Oliver, stretching his legs out.

"I'll bet it never does," she said dreamily, and he snorted. She gazed enraptured at the butterscotch-colored palace with its round towers and billiard-table lawns. The late afternoon sun glazed the rock hills beyond with golden light; people strolled leisurely across the wide gravel forecourt. "I can't imagine actually *living* there."

"Cold and damp most of the time. The heating bill must be staggering."

"Mary Queen of Scots lived in it for six years in the sixteenth century. Her secretary, David Rizzio, was murdered in front of her. It says you can see the spot."

"Why on earth would you want to? Charlotte, I never realized you were a compulsive sightseer."

"Well, I didn't know you read dog stories, so we're even. As long as the Queen isn't here, you can go inside. Oliver, I've never been in a palace before—oh, shoot!" She frowned at her watch. "We've missed the last tour—it started at three forty-five."

"Pity," said Oliver insincerely.

"What about tomorrow morning? You said it's not far to Aberdeen, and Captain MacPherson doesn't know we're coming. We could even"—she paused as the idea blossomed—"we could even stay another night. Why not? We'd have the whole day, and there's so much—"

"Tomorrow's Sunday," said Oliver. "Nothing will be open and I only booked the rooms for tonight."

"That's easy—we'll ask when we go back. Holyroodhouse opens at eleven on Sundays and there are lots of other things to do. We could climb Arthur's Seat. It's an extinct volcano and it says the views—"

"Charlotte." Something in his voice stopped her. "That's not why we're doing this."

"I know, but—"

"The train to Aberdeen is at ten, and we still have to get to Cullen."

She sighed and closed the guidebook. She was tempted to remind him that this was her vacation, but his mind was fixed on Captain MacPherson, and to argue with him now would only lead to lost tempers. There was always the return journey, she reminded herself. Once Oliver had accomplished his mission, she was sure she could persuade him to play a little. She glanced at him, but he was gazing into the distance, deep in thought.

On the next bench was a couple, heads bent together, talking intently. Charlotte hadn't paid them any attention when they sat down, but suddenly the woman pulled away from the man and stood up. She was striking: her clear, creamy skin was set off by a tumble of glossy auburn hair, and she wore a long skirt and soft green tunic that gave her an exotic, gypsyish look. "Well, that's it, then," she said, and started toward the gate.

"Deirdre, wait!" Springing to his feet, the man went after her. He caught her by the arm, turning her to face him. They were well matched: He was slightly taller, lean and wide-shouldered, with thick blond hair, attractively tousled. He was quite beautiful, Charlotte thought, trying not to stare.

"Of course I mean it!" His voice was urgent. "I just need a little more time, that's all."

She gave her hair a rippling shake. "I can't wait, Ewen. I've told you. I won't miss this chance. If you can't go with me, I'll find someone who can."

"And I've told you, I'll go. I swear I'll tell them."

"That's what you've been saying—"

"I will, Deirdre. I promise." He gathered her into his arms, right there in front of Holyroodhouse and all the tourists, and kissed her. For a moment she seemed to resist, then twined her arms around his neck and kissed him back.

"Charlotte," said Oliver, "close your mouth."

Blushing hotly, she tore her gaze away.

"I was just saying we should start back if we're going to be in time for dinner. It's a long way and I expect they're crowded on a Saturday night."

"They? They who?"

"The hotel, of course."

"Oh, no, Oliver. We can't."

"What do you mean? Why can't we?"

"Did you see the dining room? I didn't even bring a skirt with me—you told me not to bother. I can't go to dinner there looking like this."

He just stared at her for a moment as if she were speaking Swahili, then gave his head a brief shake. "All right, there's room service."

It was her turn to feel exasperated. "Oliver, there must

be hundreds of places to eat in Edinburgh. I'm sure we can find something else."

"How?"

"We could ask."

"We don't know anyone to ask."

"I'll find someone," she declared, accepting his challenge. There were moments when it seemed to her they hadn't gotten much beyond that bitter April day when they'd fallen in the Coolidges' pond. She'd noticed a small craft shop outside the gates, its windows full of handmade things: sweaters, scarves, pottery, silver jewelry. If it hadn't been for Holyroodhouse basking in the sunshine she would have gone in. Now she had a reason.

When she came out again fifteen minutes later, she was triumphant. She had also rashly spent quite a lot of her money on two pairs of genuine Argyle socks for her father and Max, a silver pin woven into a Celtic knot for her mother, and a knitted lamb for Hilary.

Oliver had been hanging around outside. "What took you so long? I thought you were asking about a restaurant."

"I did. But I couldn't ask without buying something, Oliver. That would have been tacky. She says we should go to The Cottage. It's not very far and it sounds perfect, but she says it fills up, especially on the weekends. She marked it on my map."

Eight

"The Cottage?" said Oliver skeptically when they found it a short time later. On the pavement halfway down a block of undistinguished office-looking buildings stood a sandwich board with THE COTTAGE printed on it. Underneath, in chalked capitals, someone had written TRAVELLERS! HERE—TONIGHT! and scrunched below that was an illegible list of dinner specials. Behind the sign was an open door that gave on a narrow flight of steps, and wafting down came a tangle of voices and gusts of laughter. "The woman in the store said it's cheap, the food's good, and there are folksingers on the weekends," said Charlotte.

Oliver gave an unhelpful grunt.

She wished she could see what it looked like before committing herself, but the woman in the store had reminded her of Jean, and she had unhesitatingly recommended The Cottage. "It's an adventure, Oliver. It'll be fun."

"All right," he said reluctantly, "but this is your choice." He was making it clear that whatever happened, he was not responsible.

She led the way up, through the warm air in the stairwell, thick with cigarette smoke and the brown, viscous smell of gravy. At the top was a big, low-ceilinged room with a plain planking floor and virtually nothing in the way of decor, just a hodgepodge of tables of various sizes packed so close, it was hard to tell which were occupied and which weren't. A large, red-faced girl with an enormous dish towel tucked into the top of her jeans greeted them. "Just the two of you, is it?"

"Janet, you seen Graham?" asked a man behind Charlotte. She was aware of Oliver standing close, giving off negative vibrations. Deliberately she blocked them out.

The girl shook her head, pushing the frizzy bangs out of her eyes. "Not me, but ask Alec—he's in the kitchen." To Charlotte she said, "Do you mind sharing, or would you be wanting a table to yourselves?"

Charlotte almost said they'd be willing to share; she wouldn't have minded, but she knew Oliver would loathe sitting with strangers. "Well, let me see." Janet surveyed the room for a minute, then said, "Got it," and led them in a kind of line dance in and out of the tables to the far side. As she went, she exchanged words with customers, speaking to many of them by name. It was a very mixed group, not just young people, informally dressed in jeans, sweaters, cotton skirts, and rumpled tweedy jackets. Charlotte felt immediately at ease. The Cottage was a Scottish version of the folk club Eliot liked to frequent near Harvard Square: nothing fancy, just a place to meet friends, eat, and listen to live music. He'd taken Charlotte, when he was home last Christmas, to hear a friend of his from conservatory days.

Janet put Charlotte and Oliver at a narrow table beside a low platform. They had to sit side by side on a bench, leaning back against the wall. "You're in luck," she told them cheerfully. "Two of the best seats in the house. Did you see the specials on the way in? No? Here—I'm running short of menus, so can you look on? The soused herring's off." She handed Charlotte a well-fingered sheet of paper on which was a handwritten menu, barely clearer than the board downstairs. "Pete'll be along for your order. No hurry. Enjoy yourselves."

"They ought to open some windows," muttered Oliver.

"It's part of the atmosphere," said Charlotte, stowing her bag on the floor behind her feet.

"It seems to be the *entire* atmosphere. It's a wonder people don't pass out from the smoke." He leaned over and squinted at the menu. "What're you supposed to do—close your eyes and point? Can you read that? It looks like 'neeps.'"

"We can ask Pete, he'll know."

"If there really is a Pete."

Like a conjuring trick, Pete suddenly appeared out of the smoke at Oliver's elbow. At least Charlotte assumed he was Pete since he was wearing a dish towel around his middle like Janet's, and he pulled a pad and a much-bitten pencil out of his back pocket. He had wispy brown hair and pockmarked cheeks and was almost as hard to understand as the menu. On his recommendation, Charlotte ordered something called cock-a-leekie. When she asked what it was, he refused to tell her; he gave her a wicked grin and told her to "live dangerous!" Oliver ordered shepherd's pie. "It'll be overcooked and stodgy," he predicted when Pete had gone.

"Then why did you order it?"

"I know what it is." He sat back, looking remote. She wanted to give him a jab in the ribs and tell him to loosen up. He couldn't always be in control of every situation; but she realized he was protecting himself against the unknown. Had they gone back to the hotel, he would have relaxed and she would have been uncomfortable.

The room was filling rapidly—there was scarcely an empty seat that Charlotte could see—and the noise level had risen. She was filled with a sense of happy anticipation. Her cock-a-leekie arrived eventually in a vast basin-like bowl with a basket of dense brown bread and a pot of butter. In front of Oliver, Pete set a plate on which was a whole small pie in a crockery dish. Its lid was golden mashed potato sprinkled with cheese, and beside it was a heap of cooked cabbage. "Now," said Pete, "what you'll be wanting to wash that down is a pint." He was gone before Charlotte could ask, "A pint of what?"

She inhaled the damp, savory steam rising from her bowl. The contents were a rich chicken stew: chunks of meat, rice, leeks, and several large black objects like giant olives. Remembering the pickled onion, she took a bite of one and found it was a prune; odd, but good. "How's your shepherd's pie?" she asked Oliver.

"It's not bad," he said rather grudgingly. He seemed to find the cabbage acceptable as well, although he didn't mention it, he simply ate it.

Pete came back soon with two brimming glasses, said something that sounded to Charlotte like "*Slange!*" and vanished again. Cautiously she tried hers; it had a dark, dankish flavor and was cool rather than cold. She could tell it was beer, although it wasn't like the stuff her father bought. It was an acquired taste, she decided, like avocado. She wondered if the Edinburgh police ever checked for underage customers in a place like The Cottage, especially on a Saturday night, then chose not to worry. Oliver clearly wasn't.

While they'd been occupied with their food, two men had come up on the platform to arrange chairs and mess around with guitars, a fiddle, and a couple of odd-looking flat drums. Setting up for the performers, Charlotte assumed, but after a bit, they sat down and quietly, as if filling in time, began to noodle on the guitars. Gradually the chatter in the room thinned out and bits of melody came through. One of the men looked up and around and grinned. He was large and a little pouchy; his sandy hair was starting to retreat from his round, flat-cheeked face. The other man was smaller and darker, with an unruly beard and a dour expression. He had big, long-fingered hands, out of proportion to the rest of him—good hands for a musician, Eliot would have said. He muttered something to his companion, who gave a shrug, bent to listen to his guitar, and gave one of the pegs a half turn. The dark man nodded.

"You do realize that once they really start, we'll have a hard time leaving," warned Oliver.

"I don't want to leave," said Charlotte. "I want to hear them."

Oliver took a long swallow of his beer, and she could feel him retreat into himself. She wished he could just relax; she didn't want to worry about whether he was enjoying himself or not.

There was a sudden scattering of applause and someone called out, "Ewen, you're late. What you been up to, man?" Making his way through the tables, Charlotte saw the man she'd noticed earlier at Holyroodhouse—there was no mistaking him. "Oliver, look!"

"What?"

"He's the one we saw down at the palace. The one—"

"So?"

"That's not the same woman with him."

This one was younger, with a wild bush of brown hair largely obscuring her face. She wore a long, shapeless brown dress over a lace-edged petticoat, and a sort of rusty riding jacket with a black velvet collar, and black lace-up boots. Charlotte had seen photographs of some of Max's college friends looking like that in the beginning of the seventies, as if they were still playing dress-up out of trunks in the attic. Ewen leaped athletically onto the platform, leaned down, and cupped the girl's head lightly with his hand and gave her a quick, proprietary kiss. She smiled, her face lighting, and sat down at his feet. The bearded man thrust a guitar at Ewen and took a mouth organ out of his pocket. Without any sort of introduction, they plunged headlong into a loud, fast tune. The effect was immediate: heads came round, cups and glasses went down, people stopped eating and became an audience. After half a dozen bars, the room pulsed with clapping and stamping. Under the table, Charlotte's foot tapped in rhythm. The unfamiliar music poured into her, seized her, and swept her along at breakneck speed before hurtling at last to a breathless stop. The clapping turned to cheers.

Hardly pausing, they were off again, singing: "Oh, my love she's but a lassie yet! Oh, my love she's but a lassie yet! Let her stand a year or twa, she'll no be half sae saucy yet!" This time Charlotte joined the clapping. There were yelps and whoops from the tables and the floor vibrated through the soles of her shoes.

After the third song, Ewen introduced the group: himself; his brother, Graham Robertson; and Nick Stewart, the dark-haired man. "Hey, Ewen! Where's Deidre, then?" someone called out. Nick Stewart's thick brows drew down fiercely toward his beard and he said something inaudible to Graham, but Ewen smiled. "She'll be along, don't you fret. She's waiting for us to warm you up. You've been getting a free ride till now. Let's hear you sing!"

Everyone knew the chorus of the next song; after the third verse, Charlotte had picked up most of the words—"For it's up wi' the bonnets of Bonnie Dundee," she sang with the rest of them. The hairs on her neck prickled and for a painful moment she wished it was Eliot sitting beside her instead of Oliver. Eliot would have been singing at the top of his lungs; Oliver did not participate.

As the last notes rang out, a woman joined them on the platform: Deirdre, the same Deirdre Charlotte had seen kissing Ewen by the fountain. She'd changed into a loosely belted green and gold dress that shimmered softly as she moved. She smiled and bowed in response to the clapping; her hair rippled and shone. Then she turned and said something to Ewen. He hesitated, gave a nod, and went over to whisper to the other girl. Without answering, she got up and drifted to the back corner of the platform, where she sat next to Charlotte.

"I'm sorry I'm late," said Deirdre, expecting no one to hold it against her. "We'll just have to make up for it, won't we?"

"You can make up for it with me after the show," offered someone.

She laughed. "You'll be under the table by the time we've done with you!" She had a rich, flutey soprano that rose like cream over the men's voices. She sang several songs alone, accompanied by Nick and Ewen, one of them in a language Charlotte guessed was Gaelic.

At the next break Oliver gave Charlotte a nudge. "It's getting late."

She'd forgotten about time. She had no idea how long they'd been there; she was too wrapped up in the music and the undercurrent of drama she sensed among the performers. "But they aren't through."

"We don't *have* to stay until the bitter end, Charlotte."

"I know, but why can't we? No one's sitting up waiting for us. No one even knows where we are. What does it matter how late it is? We can sleep on the train tomorrow."

"All right," said Oliver. "I won't argue with you."

"Good."

No one seemed to want to stop, but finally the songs began to run down. "We'll send you all home singing a nice song, shall we?" said Graham finally, his face red and shiny. "'Wild Mountain Thyme' to finish us up." There was a mutter of approval.

"But before we go," said Deirdre smoothly as Nick played the opening chord, "Ewen and I have an announcement to make." Nick's fingers froze on the strings, Graham's eyebrows shot up, and Ewen looked as if he were waiting for a balloon to burst in his face. Deirdre smiled her warm, beautiful smile. "Ewen and I"—she paused for effect and the room was quiet—"Ewen and I have been offered a recording contract. We'll be away off to London, the two of us, in the morning. So you see, this is a farewell concert we've been singing you. It's an ending and a new beginning! Wish us good luck, will you?" The audience complied willingly, but underneath the clapping and cheering, Charlotte could hear murmurs. No one had expected this, not Nick or Graham by the look of them, or the girl sitting on the edge of the platform near Charlotte. She was absolutely still, her fingers gripping the boards, her face pale, her eyes wide.

Nick pulled everyone back together, beginning the song again, and the applause and rumbling subsided. He sang the first verse alone in an unpolished, slightly rough voice, a sweet, lilting tune: "Oh, the summertime has come, and the hills are sweetly blooming, and the wild mountain thyme grows around the blooming heather. Will you go, lassie, go?" It wrapped itself around Charlotte's heart and squeezed. Everyone joined the chorus and she felt tears rise up in her throat. At the end, they repeated the chorus one last time, and she turned to look at the girl, but she was gone.

The walk back to the Royal Castle Hotel was long and chilly, but as Oliver pointed out, there was no choice. Although there were buses, they had no idea which ones went where, and the streets near The Cottage were empty of taxis.

As soon as The Travellers left the stage, Oliver hustled Charlotte out of the milling, in-no-hurry-to-go-home crowd. "We're paying all this money for *two* hotel rooms," he reminded her. "We ought to use them for a few hours, anyway. Otherwise we could simply have spent the night on a bench in the station."

As they left, Charlotte kept looking around for the girl with all the hair, but she had vanished. Almost, Charlotte thought, she could have imagined her. She was desperately tired and her head was bursting with everything she'd seen and all the songs she'd heard. Suddenly The Cottage was so stuffy she could hardly breathe, and she was grateful for Oliver's firm, steadying grip on her shoulder as he propelled her down the stairs and out onto the damp, cool street. Greedily she sucked in a huge lungful of city-smelling air.

"You're not going to faint, are you?" asked Oliver suspiciously, keeping hold of her arm. "It'll be midnight by the time we get back to the hotel."

She shook her head. "Just give me a minute. I'm all right. Can you find it?"

"Of course."

They walked in silence through streets that threw unfamiliar shadows on the pavement. Charlotte's thoughts were full of The Cottage. The evening had been better than anything she'd imagined, but it was incomplete. She felt as if she'd picked up a magazine in a waiting room and found the middle part of a story: the beginning unknown, the end unwritten. Who was the girl and where had she gone? Would Deirdre and Ewen be successful in London? What would happen to Nick and Graham without them? She'd never know.

"What?" said Oliver. "Why did you sigh?"

"Frustration. I was thinking about The Travellers and wondering what they'll do next."

"You mean the singers?" He shrugged. "I expect they'll go on singing. Why?"

"But two of them are leaving. That'll change everything."

"So?"

"Oliver," she said after a minute, curious, "did you enjoy that at all?"

"What? The music?"

"Everything. The whole evening."

"Yes. It was all right." He sounded faintly surprised.

"I thought it was much better than all right. The songs were terrific. I'd love to find a tape—maybe I could in Aberdeen—"

"It'll be Sunday, Charlotte. Nothing will be open and

we won't have time to shop, anyway. The point is to get to Cullen, have you forgotten?"

"How could I? You keep reminding me."

"I should never have let you come."

"Let me come?" She stopped dead on the pavement, her voice rising. "What do you mean, let me come, Oliver Shattuck? You *asked* me to come."

"I mean in the first place, to London. I should have done what Paula wanted." He kept walking, his shoulders hunched, his hands in his pockets.

All the stuff in her head was churning around and she'd begun to feel the day had gone on much too long. "Oh, nuts!" she said crossly, and went after him.

When they reached Princes Street, she temporarily forgot her exhaustion at the sight of the floodlit castle, high above them on its rock. A shiver traveled down her spine; she wondered if there were any Scots among her Paige ancestors.

Even though it was a bit after midnight, the hotel was brightly lit and seemed surprisingly busy. Charlotte and Oliver waited for the elevator with a couple in evening clothes—he in a dark suit and ruffled pink shirt, she in a slinky black dress, beaded jacket, and heels so thin they looked like drill bits. When the doors slid open, a noisy, glittery group swept out and gusted away into the darkness. Two more couples crowded in behind so that at the third floor Charlotte and Oliver had to edge their way out; everyone else was going up.

Charlotte fished for her key in her bag, overtaken by an enormous yawn.

"Good night." Oliver sounded politely formal.

"Um, wait. What about tomorrow—I mean today? I don't have an alarm clock."

"I'll call you. Breakfast starts at eight. If we don't get the ten o'clock train, there isn't another until five-thirty."

The dining room made her anxious. "We could buy something on the train."

"We're paying for breakfast with the rooms," he told her.

Nine

All she wanted to do was strip off her clothes and fall into bed, but she caught a whiff of herself and grimaced: she smelled like a dirty ashtray. Not just her clothing; her hair stank, too. Hoping her things would air out overnight, she hung them up and sluiced herself under the shower, shampooing vigorously. Washed clean and rubbed pink, she climbed into bed and realized that she was tired but not sleepy. Before she turned out the light, she needed a little time to slow down, so she dug around in her pack for her journal. She'd barely managed to write a few hasty notes in it so far, nothing remotely reflective. She riffled the pages, trying to decide whether to begin at the beginning with London, or start with Edinburgh and leave the early part for later. A piece of paper fell out; it had been stuck somewhere in the middle. It was a Bullard Farm receipt for spinach, dated last September and signed by her sister, Deb. She picked it up and saw that someone had written on the back. Andy. She knew his handwriting. "Dear Charlotte, When you find this I know you will be having a wonderful time, and I will be missing you. Love, Andy." She stared at it.

Andy, she remembered, hadn't said good-bye to her. He'd been off buying manure from a dairy in Stow the last time she'd gone to the farm. Kath and Paul had been there, and Pat and all the younger kids, and they'd given her the journal. She hadn't thought much about Andy's absence at the time; his name was on the card, and she was only going away for two weeks. He could have bought his manure on another day, but she was used to his preoccupation with the farm.

With his note in her hand, she understood it was more than that. He didn't like good-byes. He found it extremely difficult to cope with leave-taking, whether temporary or permanent. She remembered how hard he'd taken Commodore Shattuck's death and Oliver's departure. Unlike Oliver, he wasn't about to conceal his feelings. Even Kath, his twin, was better at self-protection. But he'd wanted Charlotte to know. She stared hard at the note. What had he wanted her to know? Something he couldn't bring himself to say outright, but he was afraid to leave unsaid.

Suddenly Charlotte was overwhelmed with a longing for home: for Concord, her family, the farm, the Schuylers. What on earth was she doing in Scotland? By the time she got back the asparagus and strawberries would be over and the peas would have gotten big and mealy, no longer the tiny sweet ones she ate straight out of their pods. She was missing things. Somehow she hadn't reckoned with the fact that life would continue while she was away, and when she got back, people would have moved on. Without thinking, she had assumed that everything would remain fixed, frozen in place, like a game of statues in reverse. She had considered the trip an adventure, not a choice.

By choosing to visit Oliver, she had chosen to miss the Fourth of July picnic. It was happening at that very moment, she realized, stricken. People were eating grilled hamburgers and salad made with lettuce just picked from the field, Pat Schuyler's fresh strawberry pie mounded with whipped cream. All her family would be there, sitting on the grass under the big trees beside the farmhouse, watching lightning bugs wink in the dusk, and bats hawk for insects across the road. In a short time, a bunch of them—Deb and Skip, maybe Pat, Max, Jean, and Hilary, Kath and Paul, Dan and Andy—would pile into a couple of cars and drive to Cambridge to park in front of Max and Jean's house and hike to the river, where they'd sit on the bank and watch the fireworks shatter the dark sky. Last year she and Andy had held hands walking back. This year he would have put his arm around her and he would have kissed her. . . .

He'd kissed her after the Junior Prom, a slightly awkward, earnest kiss that had filled her with enormous affection. She kissed him back and felt him relax, then they looked at each other and smiled, understanding something without words—the same thing that was there in his note.

Kath had approached her first about the Junior Prom.

"It makes sense for the four of us to go together, don't you think?" she had said forthrightly after school one day. It was the beginning of May. "It would be easier for Paul because he knows you and Andy." Paul had graduated from high school two years earlier and had been working for Vinnie Terrasi, who owned a garage in Bedford specializing in foreign car repair. In the fall he was going to be a freshman at Boston University. Aside from Kath, Andy, and Charlotte, he didn't know anyone in the junior class.

"That's fine with me," said Charlotte, "but I haven't been invited to the prom yet."

"Well, you know you will be. It's the farm, of course. He spends every waking minute on it, and I expect he dreams about it at night, too. He's specially anxious about the peas—remember last year when we got hardly any?"

Kath was right. It was a terrible time of year to expect Andy to think about anything but crops. And she was right as well about Charlotte knowing she'd be invited. Even though Andy said nothing, she assumed he knew she knew he'd invite her. After talking to Kath, she went ahead and bought a dress, under Deb's supervision: pale yellow with a scoop neck and softly gathered skirt. It didn't look like anything much on its hanger, but with Charlotte inside it was transformed. She stared at herself in the mirror, scarcely able to believe what she saw.

As the prom got closer, Charlotte set aside her vague feeling of disappointment that Andy hadn't formally asked her, leaving it instead to his sister to make the arrangements. In fact she allowed herself to forget he hadn't asked. She saw very little of Andy—just glimpses at school, where he was physically present, and slightly longer glimpses at the farm, where his mind was thoroughly engaged with questions of irrigation and mulch, probable yield, and the new pick-your-own strawberry field.

So, when he actually *did* ask her, a little more than a week before the prom, she was momentarily at a loss for an answer. He had offered to drive her home from the farm in Pat's car late Thursday afternoon. He was going to stop at the Magic Cupboard on the way and pick up the sign Deb had made for the strawberry patch: a big, grinning strawberry with stick arms and legs, saying PICK ME HERE! Deb was particularly pleased with the strawberry color she had achieved. "I hope people will understand what it means," said Andy a little doubtfully. "'Pick-your-own' is more obvious."

"Take my advice," said Charlotte, "and don't mess with the artist. Especially not *that* artist. Anyway, if people are too dumb to know what you're advertising, you don't want them as customers."

"Well, we can try it," said Andy, still doubtful. As he pulled into Charlotte's driveway, he stopped the car. They were quite a distance from the house. "Charlotte, there's something I want to ask you."

"I know. Can I pick spinach tomorrow," she said resignedly.

"No. It's nothing to do with the farm." His voice was serious.

"You're kidding."

"Look, Charlotte. It's about the prom."

He had her full attention. "You can't go."

"What?" She'd thrown him off his stride. "Do you mean you don't want to?"

"Me? Andy, I've already got my dress."

"But—who are you going with?"

"Well, you, of course."

"But, I haven't—I mean I didn't—"

"Weren't you going to?"

"Yes."

"Well, all right. We're going with Kath and Paul, aren't we? Kath and I have been talking about it for weeks."

"She told you."

It was the first time since they'd become friends that she'd known one of the twins to be angry with the other. She could hear it distinctly in Andy's voice.

"You didn't say anything, and Kath just assumed—and it's a good thing she did, Andy Schuyler. The prom's next Friday."

"I know." He sounded unhappy as well as angry. "It's just—there's been so much going on and I—I wasn't sure—"

"Oh, Andy." Charlotte sat still a moment, looking out the window, then she turned to him and said, "Let's pretend that you just asked me, and I just said yes. All right? My dress is yellow, by the way."

"Yellow? That's nice."

"In case you're thinking of a corsage?" she prompted gently.

"Oh, yes. Of course."

When she saw Kath the next morning, Kath looked somewhat chagrined, but only somewhat. She told Charlotte that Andy had informed her that it was none of her business to invite his date to the prom. But Pat had overheard and had told Andy that *he* had no business leaving it until the last moment—among other things, it wasn't fair to Charlotte, and he ought to be grateful to his sister for acting on his behalf. "Anyway," Kath finished, "It's all come out right, and Andy won't stay mad. He never does."

But suppose, thought Charlotte, still clutching Andy's note, just suppose Oliver hadn't gone to London. Suppose he'd still been living in Concord? Suppose she'd had to make a choice between the two of them? At that moment her brain simply shut down; she had overloaded the circuit and a fuse had blown, and she couldn't think about any of it anymore. Shaking herself, she slipped the note carefully back into the journal, turned out the light, and dug under the covers, eager for unconsciousness.

It didn't come. Lying in the darkness, she was immediately aware of a deep, rhythmic pulsing, like a gigantic heartbeat. On and on it throbbed, insistent, hypnotic, intensely irritating. Abruptly it stopped. There was a jangly blat of noise, then the beat recommenced, a different rhythm: boomba-boomba-boom-BOOM boomba-boomba-boom-BOOM. At first she thought it was coming in through the open window, but when she shut it, there was no difference. All those people in the elevator—they were going to a dance, and the dance was right over Charlotte's head. Any minute those stiletto heels would punch right through her ceiling.

She threw herself onto the bed and covered her head with a pillow, knowing it was useless. Her watch said ten to one—all the coaches should have turned back to pumpkins and the bands should have played "Goodnight, Ladies" half an hour or more ago. But the people in the elevator had just been arriving. . . .

This was Oliver's fault. His room was probably at the front of the hotel, with a panoramic view of the castle and no ballroom overhead. At that very moment he was probably sound asleep—

The telephone rang. Charlotte's heart shot up, hit the back of her throat, and ricocheted wildly around her chest. She managed to pick up the receiver after the second ring. Her voice was a croak; she cleared her throat and tried again.

"Did I wake you?" said Oliver.

Equal parts of relief and fury seized her. "Oliver Shattuck—"

"She didn't mention the ballroom, Charlotte."

Charlotte was silent. Oliver said, "If you can't sleep, either, I thought—look, why not come to my room until it's over. I've got a deck of cards."

"Cards? In the middle of the night?"

"Have you got a better suggestion?"

She hadn't. "I don't know your room number."

"Three-fifteen."

"What if someone sees me sneaking along the halls? Oliver?" But he'd hung up. She sat there considering; the pulse overhead began to race and she made up her mind. She thrust her feet into her Reeboks and pulled her green sweatshirt robe over her head. It was warm and all-concealing. With the hood up, no one would see her face. Checking to be sure the hall was deserted, she sprinted along it to room 315 and knocked furtively.

Oliver opened it immediately and looked her up and down. "You ought to say trick or treat. You look like a runner bean."

"If I were you, I wouldn't make wisecracks," she advised him.

"I called the night clerk. He says it should be over by two." He was wearing dark red pajamas and a short navy cotton robe. His hair was smooth and water-dark.

Room 315 was just like Charlotte's; the painting over the bed, though not identical, was clearly by the same artist: lurid purple mountains and an agitated sky the color of a bad bruise. She wondered if you could order them in bulk, like television cabinets: "I'll take a gross of the Scottish Highlands. . . ."

"Suppose I'd been asleep. Would you have apologized for waking me up?"

"I might have. Actually, I was hoping you were on the other side of the hotel where it's quieter. I'd've come and slept on your floor."

"There's always benches in the railway station," she reminded him. "How much are we paying for this?"

"You aren't paying anything. Don't worry."

"What do you mean?"

"I put it on Eric's credit card. Don't look shocked—it

was the practical thing to do. I decided we should save our cash."

"But won't he be furious when he gets the bill?"

"In the grand scheme of things it's not going to make much difference," Oliver pointed out dryly. "I've got two decks of cards, as it turns out. What do you want to play? Gin rummy? Russian bank? Canasta?"

Most recently the game of choice in the Paiges' household was Go Fish. Aunt Charlotte was frequently called upon to play with Hilary. The challenge lay in not winning against someone who laid all her cards face up on the table.

Charlotte yawned, she couldn't help herself. Her eyelids were lined with sandpaper. "Sorry. My brain's numb. You'd better pick something mindless."

He smoothed the spread over his rumpled sheets and they sat on the bed to play Old Maid. Overhead the dance rumbled and crashed like breakers against a cliff. After Oliver won the fourth hand, Charlotte leaned back against the headboard, locking her arms around her green-robed knees. "Tell me, why exactly are we doing this?"

He gave her an uncomprehending look.

"I mean going to see Captain MacPherson."

"I have told you." He shuffled the deck, bending the cards so they interleaved with a lisping sound.

"Yes, all right. So you can talk to him about the Commodore. But why does it have to be now, this way? Couldn't you have waited? Suppose you'd told Paula what you wanted to do—"

"No. Are you going to pick up your hand?"

She shook her head. "I can't tell a four from an eight at this point. Does Paula know about Captain MacPherson?"

"She knows he exists, yes." There was a silence while he reshuffled and began to lay out solitaire, positioning the cards with exactness. "I told her that I'd been writing to a friend of Uncle Sam's, someone he knew during the war. Look, Charlotte, if I'd told her I wanted to visit him in Scotland while you were here, she'd have made a family holiday out of it. We'd be touring castles and museums and gardens all along the way and staying in four-star hotels—"

"Would that be so awful?" asked Charlotte. "As long as we got to see Captain MacPherson as well?"

He laid a black seven on a red eight and moved a red six over, squaring the edges carefully. "I'm sorry I got you into this," he said finally. "I hadn't realized you'd be so worried about it. I thought—I hoped—you'd just understand why I had to do it this way."

"Oh, Oliver, how can I understand if you won't explain?" she burst out. "If we'd just stayed in London we'd be in trouble, but this will turn everything into an international incident. You made it sound like an adventure, but it's more than that—it has to be."

"More how?" He turned another card.

"I don't know. You haven't told me. You are so hard to talk to sometimes! I'd forgotten—"

He looked up, meeting her eyes squarely. "That's it precisely. You'd forgotten."

She stared back, troubled, wishing she could look inside his skull and see what was there; lay it out like the cards he was laying out on the bed in front of him. With Andy the problem was words; he didn't hide what he felt, he just had trouble articulating it. Oliver's emotions lay buried under a protective layer like a callus, thick and hard, almost impossible to penetrate.

She ought to have guessed that was what she was seeing, had been seeing since she arrived at Heathrow Airport: not the feelings, but the callus. "I want to understand, Oliver, honestly I do," she said softly. "A year and a half is longer than I'd realized when we've only had letters."

"I'm forgetting him, Charlotte. I'm forgetting Uncle Sam. He's growing hazy and I can't—I've got to find out everything I can about him so I can hold on to him. I can't afford to lose him." His voice was low and rough. "It scares me. That's the truth, it terrifies me. A year and a half shouldn't be that long. Uncle Sam gave me something I'd never had before and I may not have again—I ought to remember every detail. You have no idea how lucky you are, Charlotte. Having no idea is part of your luck."

"Is it Paula? Is she really so awful?"

He sighed and put down the cards. "That's too easy. No, she isn't awful. If everything had gone the way it was supposed to—if she hadn't flown to Germany with Eric—by the end of your two weeks you'd have thought she was all right. You'd have liked her. She had all kinds of things planned for us, special things. She was determined she'd give you a wonderful time, to show you how grateful she was to you for being my friend."

"Oh, Oliver—" Charlotte was genuinely distressed.

But he gave his head an impatient shake; that wasn't what he wanted. "Not just you—your family and even the Schuylers, though heaven knows she has nothing in common with them. You're proof, all of you, that I'm not really abnormal. Not emotionally disturbed. If you're willing to be my friends, she doesn't have to be overwhelmed with guilt about the past. We function by not talking about what happened before, by dealing with now. And that's fine—it suits both of us. As far as I'm concerned, Concord has nothing to do with Paula. I don't want her there. Once I'm through school she'll have done her duty, we can shake hands and go our separate ways. That's what we're working toward."

"But isn't that one more reason why we shouldn't be doing this?" asked Charlotte. "When she finds out, isn't it going to destroy that?"

Oliver didn't answer. He got up and went to his knapsack, which stood neatly on a folding luggage rack against the wall. Unzipping a pocket inside the top flap, he took out a blue envelope. For a moment he stood looking at it, then he handed it to Charlotte. The stamp was Scottish: the Queen's head and a thistle, and it was addressed to Mr. Oliver Shattuck, 92 Summerson Gardens, London, N6, in small, neat letters. She looked at him doubtfully. "Go on, read it," he said, and took himself over to the chair by the window.

The note inside was dated *7* June.

Dear Mr. Shattuck,

I regret to inform you that my brother-in-law, James, has been quite ill this spring. He has only just returned home from hospital in Aberdeen, where he has been undergoing treatments. Fortunately, I have been able to arrange my affairs so that I can look after him, for the summer at least.

I am taking the liberty of answering your letter since he is at present unable to answer it himself. I do not think, at this time, it would be advisable for you to visit him, but I am sure he would welcome another letter from you.

I am yours sincerely, (Mrs.) Una McCaig.

In the emptiness, Charlotte became aware of the dance band again, pounding away, relentlessly gay.

"He's dying," said Oliver.

"The letter doesn't say that. You don't know."

"Read it again, Charlotte. He's been quite ill. He's been having treatments. He's unable to answer my letter." He knew the words by heart. "He's the same age as Uncle Sam."

"She doesn't want you to visit."

"I have to."

Charlotte bit her lip, frowning at the note. "If you'd

told Paula—that he'd been sick, I mean—surely she'd have let you go."

"She'd have felt she had to go with me. If I'd argued hard enough, she might have let me go by myself."

But she'd never have allowed Oliver and Charlotte to make the trip alone together, that's what he was saying. And he was saying he couldn't do it on his own.

She opened her eyes to find a whispery light creeping into the room through the window; overhead there was a blissful silence. Charlotte found she was lying on the very edge of the bed, wrapped like a mummy in the bedspread, her robe bunched uncomfortably under her thighs. Cautiously she turned her head and found Oliver sound asleep beside her, lying on his stomach, his face half buried in a pillow. Hers had fallen onto the floor. She wondered what time it was; the light looked early, but it also looked damp. She wondered where her glasses were. Last she knew, they'd been on the bridge of her nose. . . .

Hoping that Oliver was as unconscious as he seemed, she raised herself gingerly on one arm and eased her legs over the side. Something hard jabbed her in the stomach: her key. She'd put in the front pouch of her sweatshirt. Her glasses were on the table, folded on top of the letter. Echoes of the night before rolled around in her head and her eyes felt sore. She stood up and peeled off the spread. It was six-fifty, and the scrap of morning she could see out the window was gray and vague. Oliver gave a soft snort and rearranged himself, spreading out. She froze. Whatever came next, she wasn't ready to face him at that moment; she needed to organize herself a little first, inside and out.

On her return journey along the corridor, she ran smack into a sleepy-looking man carrying a laden breakfast tray. She hunched herself together as small as possible and scurried past him, pretending she hadn't seen the speculative glint in his eyes. Why should it make her feel crawly? she asked herself crossly. What did it matter, anyway? She'd never see him again.

There was no point in lying down. Best thing, she decided, was another shower. This time she mixed the water only lukewarm and shuddered as it hit her skin. Then she dressed, rashly allowing herself a clean jersey, and repacked her belongings. She wished she had resisted the lamb; the socks and the pin could be scrunched in, but there wasn't room for Hilary's lamb no matter how she squeezed, so she stuffed it into her haversack. All the while her mind worked over what Oliver had told her, eating away at it, chewing and chewing and chewing, swallowing, trying to digest it.

She went back to that winter day on the beach at Plum Island, remembering how shocked she'd been by Oliver's anger. He'd been angry at his uncle for dying. Commodore Shattuck hadn't wanted to die, she'd protested. How could Oliver blame him? He wasn't being rational. But he'd needed the anger, she understood now, in order to keep functioning, in the grip of grief and loss. He'd let the anger show and hidden the rest.

At five minutes to eight, she shouldered her pack and her bag, glanced around to make sure she hadn't forgotten anything, and went back to room 315. There was no answer to her first knock, so she knocked harder. If all else failed, she could telephone him from her room or ask the desk clerk—

The door opened about a foot. Oliver's hair stood up in spikes; he squinted at her as if his eyes hurt. He was still wearing his robe, but it had had a rough night. "What time is it?"

"Eight."

He rubbed his face with his hands, yawning painfully. "I didn't hear you leave. How can you look so revoltingly awake?"

"I took another shower. When did the band stop, do you know?"

"It was after two. You were out cold by then." He groaned. "Look, Charlotte, go away, will you? Just go somewhere. I'll be down in fifteen minutes."

"All right, but I'm leaving my knapsack. And you can find room for Hilary's lamb." She pulled it out of her bag and thrust it at him.

"What?"

Princes Street was filled with milky fog. The pavement was wet and the castle had disappeared as if enchanted. Early Sunday morning, and there was almost no traffic in the middle of the city, and only a few people in the dining room. Oliver made it by twenty minutes past eight, looking shadowy around the eyes, but otherwise pulled together. "Did you pack the lamb?" she asked.

"Why on earth did you buy it?" He sounded irritable.

"I told you, for Hilary."

"It should have been an albatross."

A wiry little waitress with gray hair seated them by the windows, her pale blue eyes scrutinizing them. Oliver gave his room number and she wrote it on her pad impassively. "Why didn't you give her *both* numbers," whispered Charlotte when she'd gone.

"What difference does it make? It's all the same bill."

"Yes, I know, but—" The waitress was back, with tea for Charlotte and coffee for Oliver.

The set breakfast was scrambled eggs, bacon, and fried tomatoes. "Do you suppose," said Charlotte as she ate her way appreciatively through it, "they have a dance here every Saturday night, or were we just lucky?"

"Probably," said Oliver absently.

The grayish brown square of bread on her plate next to the tomatoes proved unexpectedly resistant. She chiseled it to fragments with her knife and tried one, crunching it in her back teeth. "It's wonderful. I think it's been fried in bacon fat. Deb would have a fit."

"Mmm."

She looked at him. He was holding his cup in both hands, staring out at the foggy street. He'd barely touched anything, only eaten a slice of toast and a forkful of egg. She was about to ask for his piece of fried bread when he registered her attention and put his cup down in the saucer. "This is a mistake," he said abruptly.

"What?"

"No. Not a mistake. *My* mistake. I checked with the station, there's a train back to London at ten-thirty."

Cautiously, Charlotte said, "Ten-thirty? This morning?"

"Of course this morning. When else? We'll be back in Highgate before anyone knows we left. We won't have to tell them."

Never mind that Paula believed Charlotte was still in Concord. "My family will know when they get the postcards," she pointed out. "I sent one to Hilary and one to Mom and Dad. I put them in the box before you came down."

"We'll worry about that in ten days."

"But Oliver, you said—"

"Look, Charlotte, it was a lousy idea. I wasn't thinking straight. When we get back, I'll talk Connie into helping us—I know she will. She'll let you stay with her tonight, so Paula won't know until tomorrow. She'll be furious, but she'll see it's not your fault and she'll make sure the rest of your holiday is what you expected. She won't express herself until you've gone home."

"Do you mean you're giving up?"

His mouth tightened. For a moment he didn't speak, then he said, "You read Mrs. McCaig's note."

"That was nearly a month ago. I'm sure he's better by now."

"Or maybe he's taken a turn for the worse. Maybe he's dead." Oliver's voice was unemotional. "In any case, as you said, she doesn't want me to visit."

"But if you show up on the doorstep, she'll have to let you see him."

Oliver shrugged. "The point is, I shouldn't have gotten

you into this to begin with," he said, not looking at her.

The fried bread settled heavily in Charlotte's stomach; she had lost her appetite for his. "Oh nuts, Oliver! You are the most exasperating person I've ever known. We've already gone too far. No matter what we decide, we're in trouble. Now you say we should turn around and go back without finishing what we set out to do, which I personally think is really dumb. Is that what you want?"

"*You* didn't want to come in the first place."

"That's irrelevant. You're using me as an excuse."

"What do you mean by that?"

"You're losing your nerve. You're afraid of what you'll find when you get to Cullen, but you won't admit it. Instead, you claim you're thinking of me."

For a moment she thought he was going to explode; she braced herself. He took a long, slow breath, looked her in the eye, and nodded. "All right. We'll go."

Ten

Their arrival in Aberdeen was not auspicious. By the time they reached the city, they were both tired, and what had been fog in Edinburgh got wetter the farther north they went. In Dundee it was etching thin slanted lines across the train's windows, and in Aberdeen a steady, discouraging rain fell. The station was damp and chilly. When Charlotte eventually managed to dig her jacket out of the bottom of her knapsack, it looked as slept-in as Oliver's bathrobe. "Why didn't you pack it on top?" he asked her unhelpfully. His midthigh-length waterproof shell was neatly folded and ready to hand. He left Charlotte muttering under her breath as she stuffed her belongings away, and went to ask about getting to Cullen.

She was tying the cord when he came back, urging her to hurry up.

"Why?"

"The bus leaves in less than ten minutes."

"Without me, then," declared Charlotte. "I'm not going anywhere until I've found the ladies'."

"We'll miss it."

"Then we'll get the next one. No one's expecting us, so it doesn't matter when we turn up, does it? And I'm not sitting on my heel all the way to Cullen."

"There isn't another bus until seven this evening."

"That's too late."

"Exactly!" he exclaimed irritably. "But by this time I don't suppose we have any choice."

"Why can't we stay here tonight—there must be lots of places—and take the bus tomorrow? We don't know how big Cullen is or what it's like, Oliver. I don't want to get there after dark in the rain and have to find somewhere to sleep." It was a practical plan, even Oliver could see that, although he didn't want to say so outright. Not actually agreeing, he said, "There's a hotel across the street."

But Charlotte, having won the first round, was ready for the second. "Not another hotel," she said firmly.

"Why not? There won't be a dance on Sunday."

"I don't care. We can't go on using Eric's credit card—at least *I* can't. It'll have to be somewhere cheaper. The woman next to me on the plane said they always stay at bed-and-breakfasts."

Oliver argued about convenience and anonymity, but Charlotte dug her heels in, and finally, ungraciously, he gave up. The man at the ticket counter sent them off toward the seafront, which, on a mild, sunny afternoon, would have sounded inviting. But as they trudged out into the rain and wind, it merely sounded bleak.

The city had a closed-down, unwelcoming feel: evidently nothing was open on a Sunday. Charlotte was conscious of being very far from home and in a foreign country. Rain splattered her glasses and dripped off the brim of her hat, and she hoped grimly that Eliot's pack was still waterproof. Her pants stuck wetly to the tops of her knees where her jacket ended.

After what seemed like ages, they left the commercial part of the city with its monumental granite civic buildings and office blocks, and entered a residential area. They passed several private houses with BED-AND-BREAKFAST—FULL signs in their front windows, and Charlotte felt her resolve slipping. If they had to go all the way back again—

"There's one," said Oliver. It was a square house with tall windows, set back from the street behind a wall, with a sign that said VACANCY. They stood on the corner across from it and looked, while the rain fell. Charlotte waited for him to say, "All right, this is your idea." She wasn't sure she could walk up and ring the bell by herself. "If we stand here staring much longer, they'll think we're too thick to come in out of the rain," he said.

The doorbell was answered by a frenzy of barking at ankle height, followed by an indistinct male voice, which turned out to belong to a boy about Oliver's age, with a foam of reddish-blond curls on top of his triangular face, like froth on a pint of beer. With practiced skill, he held a small, fierce-sounding cairn terrier imprisoned behind his legs. "Hold your whisht, Flora!" he commanded, but the dog was evidently stone deaf. "Would you be wanting a room? Mum's out, but I can show you what we've got." He bent and scooped the dog up; it stopped barking, but peered belligerently at them through a haze of fur.

"We're very wet—" said Charlotte apologetically.

The boy grinned. "Be a wonder if you weren't. Close the door, will you?" From a room on the right came the tinny, excited sounds of spectators at some televised sporting event. Oliver cocked his head. "Wimbledon?"

"Yeah. Men's quarters," he said over his shoulder, starting up the staircase. "Can't say I like your McEnroe much. He's a good enough player, but so bloody-minded. Here's the bath—" He indicated a large, chilly-looking room at the top of the stairs with a bathtub in it. "The loo's there—" a second room, narrow as a closet, containing only a toilet. "If you want a bath, you'll have to let Mum know. It's extra for hot water. We've got a room at the front with a double bed, and one at the back with twin beds."

"Both," said Charlotte. "With twin beds," said Oliver. They regarded each other for a moment, then Charlotte gave in.

"Right you are. It's thirteen pounds the two of you, bed and breakfast. All right?" With Flora clamped firmly under one arm, he opened the door on a bedroom.

"We'll take it," she said without bothering to look.

He nodded. "I'll leave you to it, then. Will you sign the book when you come down? It's on the hall table." And he was gone, thumping back downstairs to his tennis match.

"Well, that was easy," said Charlotte. "He didn't ask anything about us."

"His mother would have. We're just lucky she's out. We'd better put the same last name in the guest book."

The room was furnished with mismatched pieces: a massive wardrobe of some dark wood that made Charlotte think of fur coats and fauns; a dresser that was too big for the space between the windows; a sink in one corner; and two high, narrow beds separated by a wobbly night table. Someone had put a matchbook under one of its legs to make it a little steadier. On the foot of each bed were two well-worn towels in assorted colors. Still, it was much cheaper than the hotel had been, and it was scrupulously clean.

Charlotte sat experimentally on one of the beds; it dipped in the middle. "What do we do now?"

"Don't know about you," said Oliver, peeling off his wet jacket and hanging it over the single chair, "but I'm going to watch tennis."

"Can you? Isn't it private?"

"The television'll be in the lounge where guests can watch. There's no point sitting up here all afternoon. Are you coming?"

Patting her damp braid, she said, "I must look like a drowned rat. You go ahead."

To her disappointment, he did, without contradicting her or trying to persuade her to come with him. As soon as he'd gone, she wished she had. What did it matter how she looked, anyway? Both boys would be glued to the tube.

Standing at the window, she gazed moodily into the sodden back garden. It was jumbled with flowers, and at the end, by a high fence, there was a vegetable patch. She could spot vegetable patches anywhere now. Wimbledon was one of the treats she'd been looking forward to. Someone had promised Eric a pair of tickets to the women's semifinals, and she and Oliver were to have had them. The prospect of actually sitting in the stands, overlooking the increasingly worn, scruffy turf of Centre Court had filled her with excitement. She'd see the royal box with genuine royalty in it—maybe the Duke and Duchess of Kent, or Princess Anne or Margaret, or even the bride-to-be, Lady Diana Spencer. She wondered if anyone in the royal family actually *liked* tennis, or was it simply a public duty to appear so someone like Charlotte Paige, from Concord, Massachusetts, could go home and say, "I saw Princess Margaret at Wimbledon."

She knew something about tennis herself. She and her brother Eliot had often batted a ball back and forth on the town courts at Emerson Playground. Oliver had been on the high school tennis team. He was very good, but then he never committed himself to anything in public unless he was very good, like singing solo in the concert. He hated the idea of embarrassing himself by being less than proficient, and held himself to very high standards. At first Charlotte suspected him of showing off, but she came to realize that it was something far more complicated. He was afraid of being found wanting, of being seen to make mistakes for which he was sure he would not be forgiven. If he wasn't convinced of his ability, he wouldn't try; he'd pretend indifference. He was not good at criticism, either. He took it as condemnation, proof that he didn't measure up. Not surprisingly, he was better at singles than doubles because he could never bring himself to trust his partner. "It's easier if it's just me, win or lose," he told Charlotte once. "No excuses, no false modesty. Either I'm good enough, or I'm not." He had no interest in team sports like basketball or football. Too much was beyond his control, and he didn't like rough physical contact.

The second time Charlotte had played tennis with Oliver had been the last time. She was mildly competitive herself, but he was dead serious. Charlotte doubted that he was capable of simply fooling around on the court; he couldn't shift gears. She'd begun by trying to keep up with him, but when he wasn't smashing the ball directly at her, or lobbing over her head, or passing her, he was instructing her. "No, don't hold your racket like that, Charlotte. Watch the ball—don't look at me. Bend your knees more. Don't run around your backhand."

Red in the face, sticky all over, out of breath and raw from his criticism, she had finally paused long enough to ask why she was putting herself through it. "Look, Oliver," she announced, "I'm finished. Love–forty. You win. Game, set, match."

"You're quitting?" he asked, incredulous.

"That's right. I'll watch you, but I won't play with you."

"How are you going to improve your game? I'm trying to help you." He hadn't understood.

She just shook her head. "Let's stay friends," she said firmly. In the unlikely event that she ever improved enough to beat him, she realized he'd hate it. And if she didn't, *she'd* hate it. In either case it would put a strain on their relationship, and that was too high a price.

She thought about going downstairs and joining Oliver and whatever-his-name-was, watching the court made tiny on a flat, garish screen, and felt no enthusiasm. It was the spectacle of Wimbledon, the sensation of actually being there—sunshine, champagne and strawberries, the crowds—not just seeing the tennis, that she was being cheated out of. She could be home in Concord watching it on television. But there was no point in brooding, she needed a distraction. Leaving her wet pants on, she stowed her haversack inside the wardrobe, put some money in her pocket, and shrugged back into her damp jacket.

At the bottom of the stairs on a little table beside a curly Victorian coatrack, she saw the guest book lying open. Oliver had written: OLIVER SHATTUCK, CHARLOTTE SHATTUCK, in block capitals, and his London address. Her stomach gave an odd little twist. Brother and sister, that's what they were pretending. In the lounge, Oliver was sitting relaxed on a sofa with a can of ginger beer in one hand while he massaged Flora's neck with the other, eyes fixed on a giant television screen. His host was sprawled in an easy chair. Flora lifted her head from Oliver's knees and gave a little "worf," ears on point; otherwise Charlotte's presence went unremarked. The sound was hushed, only the hollow *tock* of racket meeting ball and ungentlemanly grunts breaking the stillness as the two players battled for a point. One of them rushed the net and the other miss-hit into it. Applause. No Bud Collins jabbering inanities, only a restrained British voice making a restrained comment on the score. The players went to towel off before changing ends, and both boys turned their heads to look at her.

"Third set," said Oliver. "McEnroe's leading on serve. This is Douglas Sinclair—Charlotte—" he almost said "Paige," then caught himself. It came out as "Pshattuck."

"You can call me Dougie," he told her, making it sound like "Doogie." "Ginger beer?"

"No thanks," said Charlotte. "I'm going out."

"What, now?" Oliver frowned at her. "It's raining."

"It's almost stopped and I feel like walking."

"Where? You'll get lost."

She ignored him, addressing Dougie. "The beach isn't far, is it?"

"Go left out the gate, turn right at the first corner, and keep walking until you get your feet wet. I'd show you myself, but—" His eyes slid back to the screen.

The players were back on the court, one of them preparing to serve, while the other danced from foot to foot. Charlotte didn't try to compete. "See you in a couple of hours."

Outside, she carefully noted the street name, Gilmour, and the number of the house, Seventy-six, so she could ask her way intelligently if she needed to, although she was determined not to need to, not after Oliver's comment. Following Dougie's directions, she found herself before long at the Esplanade, a wide strip of tarmac that separated the neatly ordered world of houses, gardens, streets, and sidewalks from the anarchic sea. Below her lay a broad, flat sweep of sand stretching in either direction. The few people on the beach only made it look bigger and more deserted. At the waves' ragged edge a couple of dogs raced, barking and wrestling, while three figures trudged behind on the hard, wet sand. A couple swung a small child between them, reminding Charlotte of Hilary. She had often wondered why children's shoulders didn't dislocate. In the distance was a jogger in a red jacket. Overhead, gulls skirled and surfed down the wind, and out on the horizon were several ominous black shapes: freighters, maybe, or factory ships.

The wind rasped across the salt water like sandpaper, coming down from the Arctic Circle, laden with a recent memory of ice, and Charlotte shivered as she stood gripping the iron railing. She needed to keep moving. As she slogged through the soft sand of the upper beach, she found herself grinning. The shiver was excitement as well as chill; excitement at the idea of being beside the North Sea in Aberdeen, Scotland. When she reached the wave-washed margin, she turned north, into the wind. It stung her face, smelling like iodine, and disinfected her lungs, scouring away the residue of exhaust fumes, cigarette smoke, previously used air. Her glasses filmed with salt and her hair felt sticky when she touched it.

As long as she kept her eyes on the shore ahead, or the twitching sea on her right, Charlotte had the illusion of walking without getting anywhere—it was very hard to judge distance without landmarks. She kept glancing left at the fringe of houses and shops to mark her progress, anxious in case she went too far. Then it occurred to her to wonder why she should worry. When she felt she'd walked long enough, she'd turn around and go back. It was that simple. She had no one to please but herself. The knowledge gave her a lovely free feeling.

A line of low, wooden groins ran out from the Esplanade across the sand, spaced like teeth in a giant comb, to keep the beach from washing away. When she reached the last of them, she went and sat on the end and fished the remainder of a roll of Polo mints out of her jacket pocket. Sucking one meditatively, she gazed out to the edge of the sea and wondered what lay beyond—some part of Scandinavia, probably. Was it Norway? Or—

"Hi. Mind if I sit with you?"

Before Charlotte could think of a polite way to say yes, the owner of the voice sat down. There were lots of other, untenanted groins available, she thought irritably, and started to say, "That's all right, I was just leaving," but only got as far as, "That's all right—"

The girl, huddled in her brown jacket, the velvet collar turned up against the wind, didn't seem to notice Charlotte staring at her. From the side, all Charlotte could see of her face was the sore-looking tip of her nose; the rest was hidden by the hair that curled frantically around her head, excited by the damp air. Chin tucked into her collar, the girl said, "I came out here to think, you know? It's usually a really good place for me, but I guess my biorhythms are off or something. I just keep going around and around and never getting anywhere. I'm not feeling sorry for myself—well, not *really* sorry. I mean, I'm not the only person it's ever happened to, right? People get dumped all the time."

"Dumped?" echoed Charlotte, unwilling but unable to

stop herself. The girl had an unmistakable American accent. Charlotte hadn't heard her speak before, but she recognized her.

"Yeah. Dumped. It's not like it's the end of the world, exactly, but it's pretty heavy when the relationship's been, you know, intense? And the way he did it—I mean, he could've waited till we were alone," she said angrily.

"It *was* you. You were in Edinburgh yesterday."

The girl turned her head to look at Charlotte, lifting her chin out of the jacket. Her eyes looked pink and swollen. "Yeah, I was. How'd you know?"

"So was I. I saw you at The Cottage last night."

"Oh, wow. This is, like, totally weird. Out of all the people in the world I could sit next to—it's the kind of thing you don't believe can happen." Her face clouded. "Then you saw the whole thing. You saw him do it, right there, in front of everybody."

Charlotte didn't know what to say, so she said nothing.

"What a bummer. The really dumb thing is I never even saw it coming." She buried her chin again. "That cow. If she's what Ewen really wants, then okay. I wish him luck. But I just bet she drops him. She'll find another guy to use and she'll be out of there, Ewen. And I'll tell you one thing. I'm not waiting around for that to happen. That's it. As far as I'm concerned, it's over. I'm gone. Jeez, I'm freezing, are you? And I've got to pee. There's a café back that way. You want a cup of coffee? Let's see—" She felt under her jacket for a pocket, and after a minute she pulled out a handful of change. "Yeah—there's enough for two. Okay?"

"I have some money myself," said Charlotte, "but I'm not—"

"Oh, come on. It's not far, I promise. I hate sitting in a place like that alone—it's so pathetic."

"Well, I guess—" She looked so hopeful, Charlotte crumbled. As long as she got back to Gilmour Street in time for supper, Oliver wouldn't worry. "My name's Charlotte."

The girl gave her a sudden smile. The effect, in the midst of all that hair, was of the sun coming out from behind clouds. "I'm Ariadne."

Eleven

Charlotte sat at a sticky little formica table, waiting for Ariadne to come back from the ladies' room, and wondered why she'd agreed to come. The café was stuffy and not terribly clean. An older man and woman sat nearby, not talking to each other, not even looking at each other. Across the room, two girls a little older than Charlotte sat deep in conversation, while a dribbly baby in a stroller kept throwing a rubber cat on the floor. One of them would reach down each time and pick it up automatically, handing it back for the baby to stuff in its mouth.

Just as it occurred to Charlotte that if she got up and left quickly she could escape without feeble excuses, Ariadne returned carrying two thick green china cups in saucers that were puddled with muddy brown liquid. "I hope you like milk, Charlotte," she said, putting a cup down in front of her. Milk wasn't the problem, it was the coffee; Charlotte had been going to have tea. "They've got some little cakes, but I didn't know what you'd want. If you're going, would you get me one of the pink ones?"

They were iced in a livid chemical hue and decorated with colored sprinkles. Against her better judgment, Charlotte bought one for Ariadne and got herself a Kit Kat bar. She found a spoon in the holder that looked fairly clean, and went back to shovel sugar into her coffee. Ariadne had shed her jacket. A grayish scarf hung from her neck, looking as if it had been knit of cobwebs, and she wore a shapeless greeny-brown pullover, stretched out at the collar, showing a green flannel shirt and the scalloped edge of a yellow T-shirt. She reminded Charlotte of the Russian doll Hilary's other grandparents had sent her for Christmas—heaven knew where they'd found it in Montana—that kept opening up to reveal ever smaller versions of itself dressed in different clothes. Except that the dolls all had round, rosy peasant cheeks. Ariadne's face, hedged by the hair, was narrow and pale and there were lilac shadows under her hazel eyes. She extracted a crumpled handkerchief from one sleeve and mopped her damp, red nose, then wrapped her long fingers around her coffee cup. "So, Charlotte. Where are you from, anyway?"

"Concord, Massachusetts," said Charlotte. "It's west of Boston."

"Oh, wow," said Ariadne. "I don't believe it! You want to hear something wild? My parents live in Wellesley. Can you believe we had to meet on a beach in Aberdeen when we grew up almost next door? I guess it was fated." She gazed at Charlotte like a long lost relative. "When I got to

Joyce's this morning and there were all these suitcases in the hall and piles of stuff everywhere, and then she told me about the plane reservations, I had this really sick feeling. I can understand why she's leaving him—it isn't that. *I* don't know why she's waited this long. She's been like totally miserable here, stuck by herself with two little kids for weeks while he's on the oil rig. And when he gets back, all he does is go out and drink beer with his mates. He never spends any time with her." Ariadne stared into the depths of her coffee mug, frowning.

Charlotte had the feeling she'd come in halfway through the movie. "Who's Joyce?"

"Hunh?" Ariadne looked up. "Oh, she's my aunt but I always sort of forget that. She's only seven years older than me. And she's a Virgo. I can talk to her. My whole family is like, totally dysfunctional. No one ever talks to anyone else, not about *real* things. You know what I mean—like life, and emotions. But Joyce is okay—maybe it's because we aren't really related, not by blood. I could never figure out why she married my uncle Jeff. He's this total chauvinist. He's always telling people what to do and how to straighten out their lives, as if his own wasn't a mess. This last time Joyce told him if he went back out on the rig without some kind of agreement, she wasn't going to stick around. She says he wasn't even listening. What a jerk."

"Where's she going?" asked Charlotte, fascinated.

"Back to her parents. They live in this place called Sewickley, Pennsylvania? I only ever met them at the wedding. They didn't seem exactly sympathetic, but with the kids, she's got to go somewhere. That's what happens when you have kids, I guess. It's not like you can just take off. What I don't see, Charlotte, is how women fall for men like that, you know? My mother—Jeff's her baby brother—she'll blame Joyce for this. She'll say it's Joyce's fault for not trying hard enough. My brothers are exactly the same. They never do anything wrong as far as she's concerned. Have you got brothers?"

"Two," admitted Charlotte. "And a sister. But they aren't—"

"Then you know what I'm saying. It's like you can't win? Whatever they do is great, and whatever you do isn't good enough. Anyway. I came up here to talk to Joyce about what happened last night, but all she can talk about is leaving Jeff and what's wrong with their relationship, and how could it all fall apart like this. I kept telling her I understood—she didn't have to go through all this whole thing with me, but then she started crying and I, like, freaked out. It'd be different if I didn't have my own problems, but I just couldn't handle it, and there's nothing I can do, anyway—"Ariadne's lip quivered.

Charlotte scrabbled desperately through her head for something safe to say that would put the conversation on solid ground. If Ariadne burst into tears, right there in that tacky little café, Charlotte thought *she* would freak out herself. She wished she could come up with the right formula for disengaging herself without sounding rude and insensitive. "Um, Ariadne, how long have you been in Scotland?" The question sounded unbelievably stilted and idiotic in her own ears, but it was the best she could do in a pinch.

Ariadne sniffed, mopped again at her nose, and pulled herself together, much to Charlotte's relief. "Since last fall. I got into this exchange program with the university here. My parents only let me come because Joyce and Jeff were already in Aberdeen, not that I've hung out with them a lot or anything. It was such a relief, you know? I'd been going to Simmons and living at home and I had to get out. I felt so stifled. All Mummy and Daddy ever think about is *things.* Getting them and having them and then junking them so they can get more expensive ones. And it was, like, I was one of their things, but they were stuck with me, so they kept trying to improve me? It was so awful. I don't see how I can ever go back to that, Charlotte. You want some more coffee? I do."

Before Charlotte could make the sudden transition from Ariadne's parents to another cup of coffee, Ariadne was halfway to the counter. "Anyhow," she said, setting down two more cups, their saucers awash, "all Mummy and I did all the time was fight. About my clothes and hair and how I don't weigh enough and I don't do anything social, and how am I ever going to amount to anything? Which means meet the right, socially acceptable guy and get married. So this came up and I applied and I got in. Big surprise. I guess Daddy was pretty fed up listening to us, so he convinced her Jeff would keep an eye on me—you know, make sure I didn't get into trouble?" She rolled her eyes. "What a joke."

Charlotte put three heaping spoonfuls of sugar into the coffee. "So how did you get mixed up with The Travellers?" she asked, curiosity overcoming common sense. "How did you meet Ewen?"

"Ewen." Ariadne's eyes turned tragic and Charlotte kicked herself mentally. "See what I mean, Charlotte? He's another one. I was so stupid. I don't believe how stupid I was. Listen to this."

The first part of her year at the university had been all right. She'd studied some—enough—and the social life was okay. Then early in January she'd gone with some friends to this concert. The first time she'd heard The Travellers she'd been totally blown away. "I mean, I've heard lots of folk groups before, but nothing like that. There's just this utterly cool thing that happens with their music, you know?"

Charlotte did. She'd felt it herself the night before. It hadn't made an instant groupie of her, but it had gotten in among her vitals in much the same way as hearing Eliot's fife and drum corps did, their music sounding shrill and brave in the dawning April light of Patriots' Day. Music like that filled her so full of emotion there was no room for rational thought. Feeling coursed through her from the soles of her feet to the hair on her head.

Anyway, after that first concert, Ariadne had gone back to hear The Travellers as often as she could, whenever they were in Aberdeen. When that was no longer enough, she began to follow them outside the city, to Stirling and Edinburgh and Perth and Durham and Glasgow. By the end of March she'd pretty much given up going to classes. School didn't seem important anymore, not after Ewen Robertson noticed her. By the end of April, she'd left Aberdeen and joined The Travellers.

Ariadne, Charlotte decided as she listened to the story, was not the sort of person you noticed immediately. But once you became aware of her, she was impossible to ignore. There was something about her smile, even though she wasn't at all beautiful. Maybe it was *because* she wasn't beautiful.

"Do you sing?" asked Charlotte.

"Me? I'm hopeless! I can't even carry a tune. But see, that's why she didn't mind, at least not at first. Before she started with The Travellers, she was with this other guy, Payton? About two months ago, in Glasgow, she dumped him. Just told him to get lost. Well, of course that's not what she told Graham, but that's what I heard and I believe it. I felt kind of sorry for Payton, even though he was basically a creep. But, anyway, she was just after Ewen, that's all. I should've seen it sooner. Jeez, I was dumb." She made a face. "I just never thought in a million years he'd do something like that. It was the music. It's like you think if someone can make music he's got to be a good person? The same as someone who writes poetry or great literature, or like a minister or a policeman. You think because they're who they are you can trust them. And then they turn out to be these ordinary creeps."

"Maybe all she wants is Ewen's music," suggested Charlotte. "They sing really well together. Maybe it's just business."

"Yeah, sure." Ariadne was scornful. "Thing is, he really took me in, you know? That's what hurts most. I was sure he was different, but he isn't. He just cares about money and being this huge success—having *things*. He even said he wasn't going to spend the rest of his life in a rusted-out van doing gigs in church halls out in the boonies. I only wish I'd dumped him first." Her voice was bitter.

"What about the others? They must have known—"

"Un-uh. She never told anyone she was talking to a record company—except Ewen must have known. How it all started is Nick and Ewen went to school together, and they started singing, just the two of them. Then they got Ewen's brother, Graham, to make a trio? So now it'll just be Nick and Graham. He didn't even tell his own brother. That's so totally shitty." There was a long silence broken only by the chink of Ariadne's spoon as she stirred and stirred her coffee.

"What will *you* do now?" asked Charlotte finally. "Will you go home?"

The coffee slopped onto the table. "I can't. I'll just have to figure something out, but that's not an option. I need some space to think, but something will work out. Anyway, what about you?"

"Me?"

"Yeah. Like, why are you here?"

"Oh. We're—I'm staying overnight in Aberdeen on the way somewhere else." A thought occurred to her. "When you were traveling around, did you ever go to a town called Cullen?" she asked hopefully.

"Cullen?" Ariadne shook her head. "Where is it?"

"It's on the coast, north of here."

"What's special about it?"

"I don't know. It's just that someone lives there. A friend," Charlotte hedged.

"Are you going by yourself?"

"Well, not exactly. No." Reminded of Oliver, Charlotte glanced at her watch. He'd think she'd walked into the North Sea and drowned. "I had no idea it was so late. I've got to go."

"So who're you with? Is it your parents?" Ariadne's interest was aroused.

"No, a friend," Charlotte replied evasively.

Ariadne fixed her with a speculative look. Charlotte could feel it bore through her forehead like a drill. Well, what was there to hide, she thought defiantly. Oliver *was* her friend. He just happened to be male, but even though they were traveling alone, that didn't necessarily mean they were doing anything wrong.

Ariadne's speculation, however, was about something else. "Look, Charlotte, if you don't want to do this it's all right with me. Really. But I was just thinking, could I, like, go along with you for a day or two? Say no if you want to—if I'd be in the way or anything."

Caught completely unprepared, Charlotte groped for an answer.

Ariadne said, "If it isn't good for you, just say. It's okay. I'll do something else. I can hang out here for a while or something."

"We aren't sightseeing," said Charlotte. "We're going to visit a friend of—a friend of my friend. He's elderly and he's been very sick."

Ariadne nodded. "Okay. I can understand that, but what about if I traveled up there with you? Once we get there, I could take off." She gave Charlotte a disarmingly naked look. "It's just I really need some company right now. I mean, I'm not suicidal or anything like that, but it's been really good talking with you. I could meet this friend of yours and then you could decide?"

Charlotte knew she ought to say no outright; it wouldn't work. But Ariadne looked so hopeful and sounded so desperate. "What about Joyce? Isn't she going to worry about you?"

"She's totally preoccupied. I'll just tell her I'm going with friends. She's closing the flat and flying to New York Wednesday, anyway."

Rashly, Charlotte made up her mind. What could it hurt if Ariadne was another passenger on the bus to Cullen? If Oliver objected, then *he* could be the one to say so. "We're staying at a bed-and-breakfast place on Gilmour Street. You can come back with me now and—"

"Oh, *thanks*, Charlotte!" Ariadne was on her feet immediately and pulling on her jacket.

The closer they got to Gilmour Street, the surer Charlotte was that she was making a mistake, and the more determined she became to make it. On the doorstep of Seventy-six Ariadne said, "If you want me to get lost, Charlotte, just say so. Okay? I mean it."

"No, it's all right." Charlotte was busy mentally shuffling the approaches she might try with Oliver. None of them seemed promising, so she rang the bell, unsure if, once you'd taken a room at a bed-and-breakfast, you had the right to just walk in as if it were your own house. Flora came barking down the hall, sounding like a giant rubber dog toy, and the door was opened by a neat-looking woman in a plaid wool skirt and green twinset. She had Dougie's red-blond curls, but they were carefully arranged.

"I'm—um—staying here," said Charlotte. "I'm Charlotte Shattuck. My brother and I came while you were out." The lie did not fall easily off her tongue.

Mrs. Sinclair looked her up and down, making some kind of private judgment. "So you'll be the other one in number three. Douglas should have given you a key." She shifted her scrutiny to Ariadne. "I've no more rooms. I'm sorry."

"Oh, I'm not staying," said Ariadne. "I'm visiting Charlotte is all."

"Visiting," repeated Mrs. Sinclair dryly. "Well, you can use the lounge for your visiting. Your brother"—she put an emphasis on the word that made Charlotte feel hot—"is upstairs, I believe."

"Charlotte?" Oliver leaned over the banister. "Do you have any idea what time it is? You've been gone *hours*."

"I was walking on the beach. I told you." She had no intention of discussing anything in the front hall with Mrs. Sinclair listening, or in the lounge where they could be overheard or interrupted. "You wait here," she said to Ariadne. "You can come to supper with us, all right? Let me go talk to Ol—— my brother, and we'll be right down." She slid past Mrs. Sinclair and ran up the stairs.

"What's going on? Who's with you? And why were you so long? I've been worrying." Oliver confronted her at the top.

"I'll bet you didn't miss me until the tennis was over."

"Of course I didn't—it wasn't late then. But the match has been over for hours," he replied crossly.

He was exaggerating, she knew. She pulled him into their room and closed the door. "It was beautiful on the beach. Miles of sand and hardly any people."

"You had time to walk halfway around Scotland."

"I'm late because I met someone and we started talking, then we went to a café to get warm and I forgot to check my watch. And what does it matter, anyway, because here I am."

"What do you mean you met someone?" said Oliver, adopting Mrs. Sinclair's tone of voice. "Someone picked you up?"

"Of course not. Not the way you make it sound. She's American, Oliver. She came back with me. Her name's Ariadne and she—"

"Ariadne? You're joking."

"Just listen a minute, will you? She was in Edinburgh yesterday. We saw her. She was at The Cottage"—guessing he was going to ask which cottage, she hurried on—"where we had supper, remember? She sat beside me while The Travellers were singing."

"She who? What are you talking about?"

She heaved an exasperated sigh. This was getting off to a very bad start. "Oh, Oliver, didn't you notice anything? She came in with Ewen—one of the singers. She has all this hair." She patted the air around her head.

"Well, why is she here? Why isn't she still with Ewen?"

"Because he's gone to London with Deirdre. She

announced it last night. Weren't you paying attention?"

"Charlotte, for heaven's sake—"

"It happened right in front of us, Oliver. Right *there*. Oh, never mind. The point is, I met Ariadne on the beach. She's having a really hard time because Ewen left her for Deirdre. She needs company, so I invited her to have supper with us. I didn't think you'd mind." She said the last defiantly.

"You didn't? We don't even know where we're going to eat," he pointed out irritably.

"We could ask Ariadne. She's been going to school in Aberdeen."

"Then she must have lots of friends she can hang out with. Why doesn't she find one of them? Oh, all right. Don't look at me like that, Charlotte. I suppose if you've asked her she'll have to come, but she has to pay her own way, and all we want tonight is a place to eat, period. No music. No atmosphere. And *no* romantic drama. Okay? Just food, and we're coming back early. Mrs. Sinclair isn't happy about us as it is. I told you we should have gone to a hotel."

Charlotte hung on to her temper. Keeping her voice level, she said, "Can you go downstairs and talk to Ariadne, please, while I comb my hair and wash? I'll come in a minute."

"Ariadne." He gave a snort, but he went.

They went to a pub four blocks away, on a main road. It had been recommended not by Ariadne but by Dougie, whom Charlotte found entertaining Ariadne in the lounge, while Oliver stood by with his hands in his pockets, looking enigmatic. She knew that look all too well. If his mother had not had his tea nearly ready, Dougie would happily have gone along with them. Charlotte rather wished he could have; he would have added some welcome leavening to what looked like a heavy evening.

Unlike The Yacht in Greenwich, The Crosskeys had nothing distinctive about it, but Dougie said it had good food at reasonable prices—"pub grub," he called it. The pub sat solid and unassuming in the middle of a busy parking lot, outlined in colored lights, its sign showing two old-fashioned crossed keys. Inside, a series of dimly lit rooms opened off one another, furnished with tables, benches, and chairs, and blurry with a fog of cigarette smoke, hot oil, and warm, hoppy beer. Even though it made her eyes smart, Charlotte liked it; being there made her feel older, adventurous. No one challenged her right to stand at the bar with Oliver and Ariadne, both of whom were legally of age.

Unfortunately she didn't have long to savor the sensation, because they were asked to pay when they ordered their food, and the contents of Ariadne's pockets turned up only thirty-seven pence. Charlotte felt Oliver stiffen and willed him not to say anything. Hastily she pulled out one of her remaining twenty-pound notes and thrust it at the barman. "For all three," said Oliver smoothly. "Gosh, thanks, Charlotte," said Ariadne. "I left my bag at Joyce's. I just grabbed a handful of change and took off, but I'll pay you back tomorrow." Charlotte winced inwardly, hoping Oliver wouldn't attach any special significance to that promise. Oliver said nothing until they had settled themselves at a corner table with their drinks, and Ariadne had excused herself to go to the ladies' room.

"You should have guessed she wouldn't have any money," he said as soon as she was out of earshot. "All she wanted was a free meal, Charlotte. What do you know about her, anyway? How do you know there *is* a Joyce?"

"Of course there is," returned Charlotte defensively. "Ariadne's uncle works on an oil rig in the North Sea. Joyce is his wife and they've got two kids. Ariadne said—"

"You don't honestly believe her name's Ariadne, do you?"

"That's what she told me."

"Oh, Charlotte. What's her last name, then?"

Charlotte gazed unhappily into her glass. "She didn't say."

"I'll bet she didn't. She saw you coming."

"That's not fair. You've only just met her, Oliver, and you won't even talk to her. You may not have noticed what happened last night, but I did. It was really rotten, and she was very upset. He hadn't told her he was leaving. She didn't know."

"So?"

"So it wouldn't hurt to be nice to her, just for a little while."

"Right," said Oliver. "Buy her supper to cheer her up."

"She said she'd pay me back tomorrow and I know she will."

"How can she? We'll be on our way to Cullen."

"I think," said Charlotte, standing up, "I'll go to the ladies' room myself."

She hoped there was only one, and that she'd find Ariadne still there, although she hadn't any idea what to say to her. She'd been foolish to think this would work. Not for the first time she wished Oliver was looser and more accommodating, but she supposed that had to do with the way he'd been forced to grow up, being passed around from school to school like a package nobody wanted. He and Ariadne seemed to be at opposite ends of the scale.

"Have you asked him?" said Ariadne. She was drying her face with paper towels in the dingy little washroom. Someone had written on the mirror over the sink in magenta lipstick: "Tell Jack I was here."

"Asked him?"

"You know. About me coming with you. I thought it might be better if I left you alone."

"No, actually, I haven't. I'm afraid he isn't in a very good mood," admitted Charlotte.

"Yeah, I kind of guessed. It's his friend, isn't it? The one who's sick?"

Charlotte nodded glumly. It was much more complicated, but if Ariadne was willing to accept that as an excuse, she was grateful. How on earth had she gotten herself into this? Oliver was probably right: Ariadne had marked her as a sucker. She felt annoyed with herself and angry with Ariadne. It was on the tip of her tongue to say, "Look, Ariadne, I'm afraid you just can't come with us," when Ariadne beat her to the punch. Turning to Charlotte, her expression earnest, she said, "See,

Charlotte, I don't know what else to do. I'll be all right, I know I will, once I've got things figured out. But when I'm by myself, like at the beach this afternoon, I can't seem to think straight. There's this panic that takes over. It helped so much just to talk to you."

Charlotte had a sudden premonition. She wasn't sure exactly of what, but she knew she was going to be sorry if she didn't turn and flee—and there she stood, rooted to the spot.

"I guess you know already, don't you," said Ariadne, working her fingers through her hair.

Charlotte swallowed hard. She wanted to say, "No, don't tell me."

"I don't know how it happened. I thought I was being careful and everything—really I did. Anyway, I'm pregnant."

Before Charlotte could gather her wits, there was a sudden *whoosh* behind the closed door of one of the cubicles, and the latch rattled. Whoever was in there had heard everything. Charlotte couldn't bear the thought of meeting her face-to-face. She grabbed Ariadne by the arm and pulled her to the door. They barely avoided colliding with two gray-haired women in pantsuits. One was saying, "Aye, well, Isobel. It wouldna be so bad if he didna snore so loud. But you can hear him through the wall. He rattles the teacups."

"Excuse us," said Ariadne as Charlotte jostled her past them. Charlotte felt the pecking of a headache behind her eyes. Luckily their food was on the table when they got back: heaped plates. In her experience, food almost always made her feel better. Oliver, being ostentatiously polite, stood while she and Ariadne sat. "I was afraid it would get cold," he said. Ariadne tucked into her ham salad with good appetite, as if she had not a care in the world, while Charlotte found to her dismay that her stomach had knotted itself unreceptively; her steak was resilient, her peas overcooked, and her French fries soggy.

While they ate, Oliver asked Ariadne what she was doing in Scotland. When she told him she'd spent the year at the University of Aberdeen, he asked her careful, noncommittal questions about it. He'd clearly made up his mind to be pleasant, though not really cordial. That was a skill he'd polished since Charlotte had first gotten to know him four years earlier. She guessed he used it with his mother, and that gave her a hollow, sad feeling. It was the way adults sometimes kissed each other without actually making contact. At least Ariadne didn't know him well enough to know that was what he was doing.

"Aren't you going to finish your chips?" asked Ariadne. Charlotte blinked her back into focus. Both Ariadne and Oliver had cleaned their plates while she had only picked at her meal. "No," she said. "I'm not very hungry."

"Do you mind? I'm starving. I think it's the walking."

Charlotte shook her head. Oliver got himself another half pint of beer, while Ariadne ate Charlotte's french fries, sprinkling them liberally with vinegar from a smudgy cruet she borrowed from the next table. She was eating for two, thought Charlotte in dismay, although Jean said her new obstetrician had sternly warned her against falling into that trap; she'd have a terrible time taking the weight off later. It isn't how much you eat, it's what, he'd said. She bet french fries weren't on the approved list . . . but maybe Ariadne was the type who could eat anything without gaining pounds and pounds. Charlotte found it hard not to stare at her. Her mind boiled with questions. She was afraid to open her mouth in case they spewed out. Is it Ewen's? Does he know? Are you going to tell him? Are you *sure?* What will your parents say? Did you tell Joyce? What about Nick and Graham? When is it due?

"Well," said Oliver, draining his glass. "I'm afraid we have to go. We're making an early start in the morning. Charlotte?"

"Charlotte says you're going to Cullen," said Ariadne brightly.

"That's right." Oliver glanced from her to Charlotte.

"You know, I've never been there. Isn't it, like, on the way to Inverness? I was thinking of going to Inverness."

At that moment Charlotte was very glad she hadn't eaten any more of her supper. She took a deep breath and fixed her gaze on Oliver's empty glass. "Ariadne wondered if she could travel up with us as far as Cullen, Oliver. On the bus. For company. I said I thought it would be all right. I mean, why not?"

"Yes, why not," said Oliver, ominously calm. "For company."

"Well, neat!" said Ariadne. "I mean, if you really don't mind? I hate traveling alone—it's so, like, antisocial. I can meet you at the station. What time?"

Twelve

When Ariadne left them, wafting away into the dusk, there was, much to Charlotte's surprise and relief, no big explosion from Oliver. He said good night to Ariadne and then was silent the rest of the way back to Gilmour Street. The raw, chilly air felt soothing to Charlotte, and the knots in her stomach loosened. But her relief was short-lived, as it became clear that Oliver was not simply being silent, he was not speaking to her.

A good, rousing argument would have given them a chance to shout at each other and clear the air; instead, the silence thickened poisonously. Oliver had a door key so they didn't have to disturb the Sinclairs. There was a light on in the lounge, and through the half-open door Charlotte could see the flicker of the television. Oliver shut the front door and they went upstairs without even rousing Flora. Charlotte flipped the switch by the door and a thin, depressing light trickled out of the single bulb hanging on a cord from the middle of the ceiling. It had a rose satin shade on it, like a bell with fringe. Charlotte wanted to cry. Oliver brushed past her and went to close the drapes. "Do you want to use the loo first, or shall I?" he inquired formally.

"I don't care."

Once he'd gone, it occurred to her that she ought to seize the chance to put on her nightgown and robe. She did it in such haste that she had to take them off again and turn her nightgown right side out when it was her turn in the toilet. She got back to their room to find Oliver in bed, composed for sleep, his towel neatly hung over the rack by the washbasin.

"Oliver," she said, "we ought to talk about this."

"There's nothing to talk about. Turn the light out, will you?"

"But don't you think—"

"I think it's been a long day, Charlotte. I'm really tired."

He'd shut her out, and she wasn't going to waste energy banging her head on a closed door. She wasn't going to beg. She lay rigid in the darkness for what seemed like a very long time, but at some point sleep got her because she was jarred awake suddenly by a loud thump. Daylight outlined the curtains although the room was still dark, and Oliver was up and moving purposefully around. She rolled over and sat on the edge of her bed, rubbing her face with both hands.

"Oh, sorry," said Oliver, sounding not in the least sorry. "Did I wake you?"

"What time is it?"

"Just after eight." He jerked the drapes open and bright sunshine flooded the room. The sky was deep blue and cloudless. The weather outside was better than the weather inside, Charlotte thought sourly. Oliver was already dressed. Charlotte stood up, self-consciously pulling down her robe. It had seemed a good idea to keep it on in bed, in case she had to go to the bathroom in the night, she told herself, knowing that wasn't the real reason.

"I'm going down to breakfast," Oliver announced, and left before she could object. As he closed the door, she hurled her pillow at it—a childish gesture, but it made her feel better. He hadn't changed. He *looked* different, but inside he was the same boy who had roused her to fury in the seventh grade. During the year and a half they'd been apart, she had allowed herself to forget how thoroughly he could irritate her. She had reshaped the person writing letters to her, smoothing the jagged edges, rounding the sharp corners, softening the focus. How could she have been so naive? If only Deb were here to talk to; Deb would be brisk, sympathetic, and practical. At that moment Charlotte did not need to be told she should never have gotten herself into this mess, she needed some sound advice on how to handle it.

She splashed cold water on her face and regarded herself in the mirror. She looked better than she had expected, considering the last two nights. As she dressed, she watched Flora in the back garden investigating the flower beds. Perhaps Ariadne had gotten back last night to find Joyce calm and receptive. Perhaps she'd been able to talk to her after all, and Joyce had agreed to help her. Perhaps there'd be no Ariadne waiting at the bus station, and she and Oliver could go to Cullen by themselves as they'd planned. They could pretend Ariadne hadn't even happened.

By the time she went downstairs, she was feeling quite cheerful. Oliver had found a place for himself at the large dining room table, and was eating a bowl of cornflakes as if he were the only person present. There was an empty chair next to him, but the other four seats were taken by a couple about Max and Jean's age and two identical little boys. A man in a brown suit had appropriated the small table by the window and was absorbed in a newspaper.

Mrs. Sinclair bustled into the room with a tray and distributed racks of warped toast and stainless steel pots of tea and coffee. "Good morning. Grapefruit segments or cornflakes?" she asked Charlotte.

Charlotte's appetite had returned overnight and her stomach reminded her about the supper it had refused. The grapefruit segments were canned but edible, and Mrs. Sinclair didn't stint on her cooked breakfasts: sausages, fried eggs, mushrooms, and tomatoes. When she'd taken the edge off her hunger, Charlotte glanced across the table. The woman, who'd been supervising the pouring of milk on Rice Krispies, caught her eye and smiled inquiringly. Charlotte smiled back and asked how old the twins were and how she could tell them apart, and by the time the last chewy triangles of toast had been reduced to a few crumbs, they were chatting away like old friends. Oliver remained obstinately silent, but the husband joined the conversation. He worked for the Royal Bank of Scotland, which was sending him to Aberdeen, so they'd come up to look around, find a place to live, and see some of the sights as well. After breakfast they were going to Craigievar Castle—had Charlotte been? No, she said, thinking wistfully how nice it would be if she and Oliver were looking forward to as pleasant and uncomplicated a morning.

Back upstairs, in their room, Charlotte said, "I suppose there'll be a bank near the station? I don't have much money left."

Mrs. Sinclair had intercepted them on the way out of the dining room, asking rather pointedly about their plans for the day—it *was* only the one night they'd wanted the room, wasn't it? Yes, they could pay her now, thank you very much.

"You can blame Ariadne for that," said Oliver. "We don't have time to hunt for one now, but there'll be banks in Cullen. It's not the back of beyond, you know."

"No, I don't," replied Charlotte, adding mentally, "and neither do you."

Ariadne was already at the bus station when they got there.

"Cripes," said Oliver. Clearly, he, too, had been hoping she wouldn't turn up. But she had, and Charlotte was determined to make the best of it.

"Just don't be rude."

He shot her an evil look and said, "I'm not buying her ticket."

"Isn't it a beautiful day?" exclaimed Ariadne. "It must be a sign. You know, like an omen? I've bought my ticket."

"Is that all you have?" Charlotte eyed the scuffed leather shoulder bag. Ariadne was wearing the same clothes as the day before as far as Charlotte could tell; at least the outer layers were the same. "What about the things you left in the van?" On the way to Gilmour Street, Ariadne had told Charlotte about running away from The Cottage and hitchhiking to Aberdeen. She'd gotten a ride in an empty fish truck to Perth, where she'd had to get out because the smell was making her sick. She'd come the rest of the way with a pipefitter. But she'd left all her possessions in The Travellers' van in Edinburgh; she couldn't bear to see Deirdre and Ewen again.

"They'll be safe with Nick and Graham. I'll get them back sometime. Anyway, I've got everything I need. It's good to travel light, you know? It's freeing. Stuff just drags you down—you lose it or it breaks. I think it's better to get what you need when you need it."

"I'll get our tickets," said Oliver.

"But won't they worry about you?" persisted Charlotte. "How will they know you're all right?"

"Why wouldn't I be all right?" Ariadne sounded surprised.

"You left without telling them, and after what happened—"

"Mmm, but they'll guess I've come to see Joyce, and

she'll give them my note. I told Joyce I met some friends last night—that's you—and that I was taking off for a couple of days. She was really relieved. Not that she said so, but I could, like, tell. See—it's all working out, Charlotte, like I said it would. You don't have to worry. Oh, before I forget"—she rooted around in her bag—"I need to give you the money for last night."

"Did you talk to Joyce when you got back?" Charlotte already knew the answer. Ariadne wouldn't be here if she had.

"You mean about the baby." Ariadne handed her a very crumpled bank note and some coins. "Well, I was going to. Really, I was. I thought about it all the way, after I left you. But Darren's got this ear infection? He gets them all the time. Joyce says it's the climate. Anyway, he was crying and she couldn't get him to sleep and she was feeling really ratty. So I just couldn't, you know? What about your brother? Did you tell him? It's okay if you did—I don't mind."

Charlotte shook her head. "He's feeling pretty ratty, too," she confessed. She hesitated on the verge of further confession, then said, "Actually, I should tell you, he's not my brother."

Ariadne gave her a conspiratorial grin. "Yeah, I guessed."

"You did?" Dismayed, Charlotte realized her suspicions about Mrs. Sinclair were well founded. She wondered if they would have been given a room if Mrs. Sinclair had answered the door instead of Dougie.

"Well, sure, it's pretty obvious. But who cares—it's your

life, right?" Somehow, coming from Ariadne, Charlotte didn't find this very comforting. Just then Oliver returned to tell them the bus was waiting. They found two seats across the aisle from each other. Oliver wedged his and Charlotte's packs onto the luggage rack, then slid in next to the window, and Charlotte sat beside him. The bus didn't fill, so Ariadne had a whole seat to herself.

As the bus thrust its blunt snout into the Monday morning traffic, she wriggled down, making a kind of nest out of her jacket, and said, "I am so glad I met you yesterday, Charlotte. If you hadn't been sitting there I'm not sure what I'd've done, you know?"

"You'd have found some other sucker," muttered Oliver, and Charlotte gave him a jab with her elbow.

Ariadne did not seem to have heard him over the rumble of the engine. "Where were you? I mean, before you came here?"

"London," said Charlotte, turning away from Oliver. "I only got there—" she frowned in amazement. Already her arrival at Heathrow seemed shrouded in the mists of ancient history. "It was last Wednesday. Only five days ago."

"I didn't like London. I kept thinking about terrorists and bombs the whole time I was there. You know, all that stuff about leaving packages unattended in the subway that they warn you about? I mean, how could you even tell who was standing beside you? But Scotland's so different—I really love it. It's like I've lived here in another life. I feel at home. I didn't use to think about reincarnation, but I have this weird feeling about

Scotland. It's so *familiar.* I could stay here forever."

"Your visa would run out," put in Oliver, heartlessly practical.

Ariadne's eyes darkened. "That's just so totally unfair. I don't see why I shouldn't be able to stay as long as I want. It's not like I'm hurting anyone."

"The government's afraid you'll take a job away from someone."

"Yeah, but I wouldn't. I mean, it's not like I'm qualified to do anything. I could wash dishes or something like that—"

"Then they're afraid you'll go on welfare."

"My parents would absolutely freak out if I ever did that! I mean totally freak. I'd never hear the end of it." Suddenly she yawned, covering her mouth like a guilty child, then yawned again. "I must not have slept at all last night. You wouldn't believe how much noise a little kid like that can make. He's only two and a half."

Charlotte nodded. "I know." Hilary didn't cry very often, but she'd recently entered a new developmental phase, which they all hoped she'd pass through quickly: for no particular reason and without warning, she would emit a long, piercing shriek, then grin devilishly, delighted by the volume of sound she could make, and the instant attention she got by doing it.

Ariadne wriggled down still further, reminding Charlotte of a picture she'd seen somewhere of a hedgehog, and went immediately to sleep.

"Well," said Oliver. "I hope you're happy. We'll never get rid of her. She's like Velcro."

Charlotte sighed. "You could have said no last night," she reminded him.

"How? You'd already said yes."

"If you refused, I'd have backed you up."

"Oh, Charlotte." He turned to look out the window.

"Are you angry?"

He didn't answer for a minute. Then he said, "Well, I was."

"I know you were," she replied dryly. "You made that very clear. But are you *now?* I just want to know where we stand."

"What good would it do?"

She almost said, "I wish you'd thought of that yesterday," but instead, she said, "I told her why we're going. I mean about Captain MacPherson being sick."

"I suppose you told her I'm not your brother, too."

"I tried, but she'd already guessed. And I don't think we fooled Mrs. Sinclair, either."

Oliver snorted. "I never thought we would. There goes your reputation, Charlotte. You'll never dare show your face in Aberdeen again." There was a silence between them for several minutes, then he said in an oddly stiff voice, "Your mother won't forgive me, will she?"

It was useless for Charlotte to point out that her virtue was still intact; that he hadn't made any improper advances since she'd arrived, nor had she. They seemed to be inhibited by opportunity. But it would be useless to point it out to her mother as well. At least initially. Maybe after things cooled down a bit. "Yours isn't going to like this, either," she said.

"I don't care about Paula—it doesn't matter what she thinks. I'm sorry about your parents."

Charlotte reflected wryly that it was a little late to feel twinges of remorse. As Jean was always saying to Hilary, "You should have thought of that before we left the house." She said, "They'll be furious with us, Oliver, but they'll get over it. They always do."

"You've never done anything like this. How do you know?"

"My brothers have. And Deb. Once when she was in high school she borrowed Dad's car and drove to New York City for an opening at the Museum of Modern Art without telling anyone. She went with a boy and they didn't have any money to stay overnight, so they started home and pulled off the road somewhere in Connecticut and slept in the car. My parents thought she was visiting a friend on the Cape. She'd have gotten away with it except that one of Dad's colleagues from Harvard saw them at the museum. I was only about four so I don't actually remember the fuss, but—"

"This is different." Oliver cut her off.

"I told you in Edinburgh, it's too late to go back," she reminded him.

"Andy would never have done this to you."

She was too surprised to think of anything to say. Andy, until that instant, couldn't have been further from her thoughts. Oliver didn't seem to expect a response; she felt him retreat into himself, leaving Andy in the air between them.

She thought suddenly of the last day of April vacation

when she and Kath had been delegated to clean out the farm stand. They'd put it off as long as they could. During the winter it became a refuge for plant flats, flowerpots, bushel baskets, odd crates, buckets, rakes and shovels, bags of lime—anything that needed a roof over its head. When they opened the door in the spring, thinking about using it again, it always looked hopeless.

"Yuck," said Charlotte. "Cobwebs *everywhere.* Give me the long-handled broom, will you? Who knows how many spiders are under there." When Kath made no move, Charlotte threw her a questioning look.

"I need to talk to you about something." Kath stopped, heaved a gusty sigh, started to go on, stumbled over the words, and stopped again.

"What's the matter?" Charlotte frowned.

"It's just not easy, okay?" She sounded defensive.

"It's not Paul, is it? You haven't had a fight?"

"No, of course not."

Back in the early days, after Oliver had left Concord to go to Washington and then to London with his mother and stepfather, Charlotte had doubted that she and Kath would ever really be friends again. It was the middle of their sophomore year in high school; the four of them, Kath and Andy Schuyler, Charlotte Paige, and Oliver Shattuck, had been together since seventh grade, but that fall Charlotte began to sense a change in their relationship. Instead of being four friends, they were becoming two boys and two girls. The obvious pairing was Charlotte with Andy, and Kath with Oliver, but real life seldom followed the obvious, and while Oliver accepted

Kath as one of the group, he was not in the least romantically attracted to her. Kath, on the other hand, had developed a painful crush on Oliver. If he noticed, he gave no sign, and she was much too self-conscious and tongue-tied to approach him. She burned with hopeless longing and had finally been driven to expose her feelings to Charlotte when it became clear that Oliver was leaving Concord. With his uncle Sam dead, his one remaining connection was to the Paiges; Kath was losing him, and was unlikely to forgive Charlotte, who wasn't. All that spring they had been distant, barely speaking, although there was no obvious rift. Charlotte and Andy were still friends; she still went out to the farm regularly and spent time with the twins' mother, Pat; she saw their uncle Skip frequently. By then he was always with Deb. Charlotte had begun to think congenially of him as a brother-in-law, in fact. Being related to the Schuylers by marriage would be all right—not the disaster she once might have envisioned.

But there was Kath. Charlotte couldn't see a way to solve their awkwardness and it bothered her. Nor did she feel comfortable discussing it with Deb, to whom she usually took such problems, because that would mean putting out in the open, in real words, her own feelings, and she was trying very hard not to formally acknowledge them. Oh, she knew that Oliver liked her—no, it was more than that. He loved her. But, she hastily amplified, there were lots of kinds of love. He needed her, he relied on her, because she was rooted and stable and he was not. And she loved him, too, as a friend. She was secure in their relationship and sorry for Kath. And she felt regret, because different as they were, she'd gotten to like Kath.

But then Paul Watts lifted his head out from under the hood of his beloved green Ford Mustang and saw—actually *saw*—Kath Schuyler coming out of his father's barn, smelling of horse and covered with horsehair and straw dust, and in an instant everything changed. They'd passed each other in the yard hundreds of times without paying any attention, but that hot July day—*whammo!* Before she quite knew what had happened, Paul slammed down the hood of his car and whisked her away to Bates Farm in Carlisle, where they shared a Doubledae: two flavors of ice cream, two toppings, marshmallow and nuts. What cemented the relationship was the fact that they didn't argue about flavors or toppings and Paul paid extra for two cherries. It was meant to be.

Charlotte was astounded. She'd never seen such a thing happen before in real life, had believed it to be the stuff of romantic film and fiction. Even Deb was surprised. Of course, once it happened, everyone saw how perfectly suited they were. Kath stopped looking like a clenched fist; she let her unrequited passion for Oliver run through her open fingers and became positively sunny.

Said Pat to Charlotte one rainy day in August, "Naturally I've always *loved* her, Charlotte, but it's such a relief to be able to *like* her again!" And Charlotte understood exactly what Pat meant. Deb had gone through a similar spiky phase three years earlier—although Charlotte wasn't so sure she'd continued loving her older sister at the time, but maybe it was just mothers who had to love you no matter what. It occurred to her fleetingly to wonder if her own mother had ever felt the same way about her—or was that period in their relationship still to come?

In any event, what it meant was that Kath could once again afford to be friends with Charlotte. They were better friends than before, although they really hadn't much in common. Charlotte had neither interest in, nor skill with, either horses or internal combustion engines, and Kath had little time for anything else. There was school, and there was the farm. And there was Andy.

And that's what Kath wanted to talk to Charlotte about that April day: Andy. And it was a difficult conversation. At first, when Kath said, "You know he likes you very much," Charlotte had tried to steer away from the rapids by saying it was only because she'd learned so quickly the difference between pea seedlings and weeds and could pick strawberries as fast as Pat.

But Kath was not to be rerouted. "That's not what I mean. Of course he's glad to have you working here, but even if you didn't—if you told him tomorrow you were quitting—that wouldn't change. He'd still like you."

"And I'd still like him. But I'm not going to quit, Kath, I'm only going away for two weeks at the end of June. I know it's a bad time, but the whole summer's busy and it gets worse later in July and August."

"Look, Charlotte, I think it's really neat that you're going to London to see Oliver. Honestly." She met Charlotte's eyes steadily. "I'd like to see him again, too, but as a friend. There wouldn't have been anything else, ever. I thought for a while—well, you know, don't you? It never would have worked, though. I'm really happy where I am. Besides, Oliver never felt anything special for me, did he?"

"He always asks about you when he writes," said Charlotte.

Kath grinned. "Yeah. And about Andy and Dan and Ma and Pa and the twins and Skip and Amos and—"

Reluctantly Charlotte grinned back.

"It's all right, Charlie. I don't mind. It's Andy. Being twins isn't like being two people—it's like being a person and a half. Part of us is separate, but a lot of us isn't. Does that sound stupid?"

"No."

"Well, I don't usually talk to anyone else about Andy, and I know he doesn't talk about me. It doesn't feel right—it's like an invasion of privacy. But I need to be sure you know he's serious about you. Even if it doesn't make any difference, you've got to know it."

"Oh, Kath—"

She gave her head a quick shake. "I don't want you to tell me anything, Charlie. It's just—well, Andy could get hurt, you know? And maybe he'll just have to. That's what was so hard for me before—thinking about you and Oliver and that I couldn't compete. I didn't have what you've got. But I guess I've got something else instead, so it worked out. With Andy, I'm not so sure."

Charlotte felt as if she were being backed into a dark, spidery corner. She thought for a moment about getting angry with Kath, asking what business it was of hers, anyway, how Charlotte felt about either Oliver or Andy?

What right did Kath have to force her to choose between them? Except that Kath wasn't doing that. She wasn't asking for an answer or looking for excuses or promises. She was only trying to help Andy because he was her brother and she cared; she wasn't challenging Charlotte, only trying to make her see how things were with her twin.

Charlotte looked at Kath and found her watching with an anxious expression. "I wish they weren't so complicated—feelings, I mean. Do you remember—almost exactly four years ago? How unfriendly we all were? I didn't want anything to do with any of you, including Oliver, and he didn't want anything to do with the three of us."

"Yeah," said Kath. "I've thought about that quite a bit. I remember Andy dragging me to your house that Sunday—after Dan disappeared. He was so sure you could help find him. I thought he was off his rocker."

In the semidarkness they smiled at each other. "If it hadn't been for that weekend, and Commodore Shattuck, we'd probably never have spoken."

"There was always Eliot and Skip," Charlotte pointed out.

"You didn't like Skip."

"How do you know?" asked Charlotte, embarrassed. She hadn't. She'd been extremely jealous of Eliot's friendship with him.

"He mentioned it. Oh, he didn't say, 'That Charlotte Paige hates me,' if that's what you're thinking. He was asking Ma what to do about it."

"What did she say?" Charlotte was curious.

"She told him not to try. She said it was because of Eliot and he should just leave you alone because he'd only make it worse. And then he married your sister."

"Yup."

They were silent a minute or two, contemplating the strange course of human relationships. Then Charlotte said, "Listen, Kath. I don't know what's going to happen to us. I really don't. I'm very fond of Andy, truly I am. And I'm fond of Oliver. They're very different."

Kath nodded. "It's so much easier the way it happened with me and Paul."

Inexperienced as she was, Charlotte somehow doubted that it happened that way very often. She couldn't help envying the unambiguous rightness, the simple, uncomplicated mutual recognition that had fizzed between Kath and Paul. Her own situation seemed so muddy by comparison. She wished she knew how it would work itself out. They fell to cleaning at that point, both relieved that the conversation was over and they could be easy with each other again. Before they parted, grubby and tired, Kath said, "Don't tell Andy what I said, will you?" and Charlotte said, "Of course not."

Self-consciously, she stared out the bus window, past Oliver. He seemed to be asleep, but she was sure he wasn't. He was deep in his own thoughts, and at that moment she didn't want to know what they were, any more than she wanted to tell him hers. Instead she studied the landscape: billowy gold and green fields, square black cattle, small scattered buildings hunkered down under the enormous stretch of sky. In the middle distance, a bright red tractor crawled across one of the brilliant fields, raising a cloud of gulls that glittered in the sunshine like tiny flakes of mica.

At Macduff they returned to the sea. When they got out to change buses, Charlotte could taste the salt of it. Ariadne uncurled, yawning, and went on a fruitless search for a rest room. "The driver says it's only half an hour," she reported back. "I hope I can hang on." As soon as the coach started to move, she went back to sleep. They stopped three more times, at villages that clung to the coast like limpets, where people got on and off with no particular haste, and greeted one another with a nod or a few words. If Cullen was no bigger, Charlotte reflected, Captain MacPherson shouldn't be hard to find, even though Oliver had never gotten around to telephoning him. But in a place so small, she and Oliver would never go unremarked. After Mrs. Sinclair's disapproval, Charlotte had been making up her mind to give in to Oliver and check into a hotel. That was assuming there'd *be* a hotel. She was enormously glad they hadn't arrived late and in the rain the day before.

Thirteen

A little after twelve the bus pulled into the main square of Cullen and shuddered to a stop beside the brownstone market cross. Parked cars lined the streets, and overhead strings of red, white, and blue vinyl pennants fluttered cheerfully between the rows of earth-colored buildings. As she stepped off the coach, Charlotte experienced a sudden emptiness in the pit of her stomach that had nothing to do with anticipation of lunch. They were no longer traveling to Cullen; they had arrived.

Ariadne tripped going down the steps, catching the hem of her skirt with a boot heel. "Oh, help!" she said, falling against the man in front of her. "I'm really sorry."

"Here, lass!" he exclaimed gruffly as he caught her. She favored him with the smile at close range, and Charlotte saw his sandy eyebrows shoot up under the peak of his cloth cap. She could almost hear his weathered cheeks crack as he smiled back.

Anxiously, Ariadne scanned the square. "Charlotte, do you see—oh, there it is. I'm about to burst! I'll be right back."

Oliver said, "She must have kidney problems."

But Charlotte knew better; her sister-in-law, pregnant with Hilary's brother, was always on the lookout for the nearest ladies' room.

"Now's our chance, Charlotte. There's a sign for tourist information." Oliver pointed up the street.

"We can't go off without telling her," Charlotte protested.

"Why not? She didn't ask us to wait. Anyway, *you* said she only wanted someone to travel with."

"But it'll look as if we're trying to lose her."

"Aren't we? Look Charlotte, she attached herself to you. You're too softhearted to tell her she's not wanted, but she isn't. *I* don't want her—do you? She's not part of our plans. If we disappear she'll latch on to someone else. So let her."

Charlotte chewed her lower lip. "Why don't you go and find out where Captain MacPherson lives and I'll wait here with your pack. You don't need me. Then I can explain to Ariadne and at least say good-bye. I'll feel better."

He gave her a calculating look. "I do not want to be stuck with her, Charlotte. Okay? We've got enough to deal with. You have to be firm."

"I know. Go on, Oliver, hurry up or she'll be back while we're discussing her."

"Just remember—"

"Yes, I hear you." She sat down to wait on a bench beside the cross. Around her the business of the town went on in blissful ignorance of the little drama she was involved in. A man in shirtsleeves swept the pavement in front of the chemist's; a woman came out of the greengrocer's with three large cabbages in a string bag. A grizzled dog trotted stiff-legged up the street, pausing to read the messages left by his colleagues on doorsteps and at the curb before leaving his own. Behind him, at the foot of a steep hill, Charlotte glimpsed the sea and a distant bleached green and brown headland. Cullen seemed peaceful and ordinary in the afternoon sun.

"Where's Oliver?" asked Ariadne, sitting down beside her.

"Gone to ask directions." Charlotte had allowed herself to drift, avoiding thought.

"Oh." They sat in silence for a while, then Ariadne said, "I was afraid—well, I wondered if you'd've gone."

An elderly tweedy couple walked by arguing in a desultory, habitual way about whether to stay the night or push on to Elgin.

"If I just knew what I should do, Charlotte. You know? Yesterday I thought, 'If I get away—go someplace I've never been—I'll see things differently.' Without all that emotional garbage messing up my head. But it's not going to work. I can tell, there's no way I can leave all that stuff behind. So what do you think?"

"Think?" said Charlotte faintly. "About what?"

"What I should do." She faced Charlotte, her expression intense. Oliver had been right. Charlotte should have gone with him. He'd be back any minute, and here was Ariadne attaching herself more firmly than ever. "See, I'm not sure I can do this. One minute I think, well, but women do it all the time, right? It's no big deal. It's part of life, right? And the next minute it just blows my mind. Say you were me. What would you do?"

"You can't ask me that," Charlotte almost wailed. "*I* don't know, Ariadne. I can't imagine it—being pregnant."

"Yeah, well, try," Ariadne urged. "If it were you, right here, right now—"

"I'd go home."

Ariadne's face closed up. "I can't."

"If it were me, that's what I'd do. I couldn't handle it alone." A thought struck her. "Is it the money?"

Ariadne shook her head. "I could get the money, all right. That's not a problem. It's my parents. They'd freak out, wouldn't yours?"

"Well, of course they'd be upset, but—"

Ariadne sniffed and pushed her face into her jacket collar so it muffled her to the nose. "You know how people say you've got nothing to be ashamed of, it could happen to anyone? Yeah, right. What they really mean is they don't understand how you could have been so totally dumb. That's my parents. They'd never get over it. And they'd never let me forget how I messed up. How I can't do anything right—I never have. That's the way I grew up, Charlotte. I've always been this major disappointment to them no matter how hard I try. I can't go back to that. If I have this baby, it's not going to grow up that way, either."

Charlotte heard the "if." "You aren't really thinking about not having it."

Ariadne hunched her shoulders. "The easiest thing would be to get rid of it—there's still time. I'm only two-and-a-half months. But I'm not sure I can do that."

Charlotte shivered. "What about the father?" Against her better judgment she was pushing further into the trackless swamp instead of backing sensibly out of it.

"You mean Ewen." Ariadne retreated deeper into the collar, reminding Charlotte of a painted turtle pulling its head into its shell. "He doesn't know and I'm not telling him, either. That's not an option. I don't ever want to see Ewen again."

"What *are* your options?" demanded Charlotte, aware time was running short.

"See," said Ariadne, lifting her chin slightly, "see, I was going to stay with Joyce for a while, just till I figured things out. She's at least *done* it. And I was really sure she'd understand about Ewen. They'd only been married about three months when Darren was born—I'm pretty sure that's why they got married at all."

Charlotte thought about Max and Jean waiting until they found the right apartment and Jean could take a leave from her job in the Cambridge Public Library. She thought about Deb and Skip, and wondered—but they hadn't had to get married. So many things were unclear; the older she got, it seemed the less she understood. Or maybe it was simply that she was increasingly aware of how much more there was to understand. Although it hadn't felt so at the time, now when she thought back on life when she was ten or eleven it seemed so much simpler and safer.

"And, anyway," Ariadne went on, "listening to Darren screaming all night, I got really spooked, you know? I kept thinking he's her kid—she's stuck with him. She can't even leave him for a few hours, not unless she gets someone to take care of him. Jeez, Charlotte. What if my kid gets ear infections all the time, too? That's when I thought about, well—you know."

Oh, help, thought Charlotte. "What other choices do you have? You've got to go *somewhere*."

"Yeah, I know. But—"

"Come on, Charlotte. I found out where Captain MacPherson lives." There was Oliver glaring down at her. He ignored Ariadne pointedly.

Charlotte felt squeezed. Not only had she not gotten rid of Ariadne, she realized she wasn't going to, at least not immediately. Which meant she was somehow going to have to counter Oliver's hostility. "First we need lunch," she said, improvising rapidly. "And then we need to find a place to stay. *Then* we'll go see Captain MacPherson. There's no point turning up on his doorstep starving and homeless, Oliver." She thought, but did not add, that if the news was bad they should do what they could to fortify themselves beforehand. "There's a café over there." She stood up. Ariadne stood up, too. Oliver gave Charlotte a meaningful look, and she braced herself. "We'll get two rooms—Ariadne and I can share."

There was a brittle silence. She could hear Oliver's fuse start to fizz; before the explosion, Ariadne said, "No, really. That's all right. I promised not to bother you guys once we got here. I'll find something myself."

"You won't bother us." Charlotte was surprised at how resolute she felt. "It's silly to pay for three rooms, and we all need lunch." She dared Oliver to object. His eyes were sharp as splinters of glass, but he said nothing. That, she knew, was not necessarily a good sign.

"Well, if you're sure you don't mind—" said Ariadne hopefully.

That Oliver minded was obvious to Charlotte, but she simply couldn't cut Ariadne adrift no matter how much he wanted her to. Even though she had no solution for her, she was at least someone for Ariadne to talk to. It was also true that the three of them would attract less suspicion than two.

After lunch, they tried the hotel just up from the square only to find it fully booked save for one double room, which was free only because of a cancellation that morning. The plump, dark-haired woman at the reception desk pointed out apologetically that it was July, high tourist season, and Cullen was busy with visitors.

"Maybe," said Ariadne, "we should take it in case there's nothing else? Maybe they could put a cot in it?" Now that Charlotte had included her, she meant to stay included.

She and Oliver eyed each other, then both turned to Charlotte. "Well, I don't know—" Charlotte said helplessly.

"All right, you have this room and I'll find another." Oliver sounded cross.

"Oh, but—" Charlotte discovered too late that she really didn't want him to do that. It was her fault for not ruthlessly amputating Ariadne as he'd told her to.

"My aunt runs a bed-and-breakfast in the next street," offered the receptionist. "She might have a room for you. Would you like me to ring her and see? Or there's the Cullen Bay Hotel, though it's a wee bit out of town. I doubt you'll be finding two rooms together there, either."

"What do you think?" asked Charlotte. Ariadne raised her eyebrows.

"Oh, for pete's sake!" exclaimed Oliver. "I can't stand dithering. I *hate* it! Where's this bed-and-breakfast? Would you call?"

When she hung up, the receptionist said, "Auntie Joan can fit you in. It isn't elegant, but you'll be comfortable and she does a lovely breakfast."

Five minutes later, with a sinking heart, Charlotte watched Oliver set off for Mrs. Findlay's house, Nineteen Reidhaven Place.

"Well," said Ariadne as she and Charlotte took possession of the double room, "that worked out all right, didn't it? I don't mind sharing—unless you're a kicker?"

It wasn't just the room they were sharing, it was the bed. Although it was extra large, Charlotte wondered for a precarious moment if this might be the final straw. She wavered dangerously, then took a long, deliberate breath and decided she had better not let it be. The hardest part still lay ahead; she couldn't afford to go to pieces now.

The room was sunny and pleasant, on the back of the hotel, overlooking a terrace bright with flowers overflowing their big wooden tubs, and chairs set around little tables shaded by red-and-white umbrellas. Several people were sitting relaxed and peaceful in the sheltered warmth. Looking down at them, Charlotte was assailed by envy.

The bathroom delighted Ariadne; she dropped her bag on the bed and disappeared into it. Charlotte folded onto the chair, flat and weary. She supposed Oliver would come back once he'd seen Mrs. Findlay, but he'd gone off in such a rush they hadn't arranged anything. Eventually Ariadne reemerged, her hair damp and excited, her cheeks tinged faint pink. "You know, Charlotte, I'd forgotten what it's like to have a private bathroom? And it's so clean. I was thinking I might, like, take a bath while you and Oliver go off and see this friend? There's all this hot water and they even give you little bottles of shampoo. I can just soak and no one'll mind."

"Why not?" said Charlotte, wishing she could do the same.

Ariadne sat on the edge of the bed facing her. Confidentially, she said, "I was so relieved when you said we'd share. I hope you really don't mind. I'd never stay in a place like this on my own. It must cost a mint."

"Look, Ariadne," said Charlotte, faintly alarmed, "you've got to decide what you're going to do. I mean, after we leave. Oliver and I aren't staying here very long, just to visit his friend, and then we're going back to London. You know you can't just drift around."

"Yeah," agreed Ariadne, combing her hair with her fingers. "You know, Charlotte, it's a really good thing that I met you in Aberdeen—you're practical. And it's such a relief to talk. You probably think I'm not very responsible, but I can be. It's this whole thing, you know? I only found out about the baby for sure a couple of weeks ago. I kind of wondered, but I didn't want to find out and then I had to. Anyway, I was going to tell Ewen after Edinburgh—I had it all planned. The next gig wasn't until Wednesday in Pitlochry, so I figured we could go someplace special for a few days, just him and me? And I'd tell him he was going to be a daddy. And we'd live happily ever after." She gave a bitter little laugh. "What a jerk! I can't believe I ever thought it would work out, you know? Well, so it didn't. And now I'm really glad I didn't tell him."

Deeper and deeper, thought Charlotte, feeling the quicksand sucking at her knees. Ariadne looked determined and very fragile. "So how much money do you actually have?" Charlotte asked, afraid of the answer.

"Money? You mean with me? Well, not a lot—it's in the bank in Aberdeen and I left my checkbook in the van. But I don't need much. I was going to ask Joyce for some, but I kind of forgot."

Charlotte opened her mouth to ask how Ariadne could kind of forget something like that, then snapped it shut again. Instead she rummaged in her L.L. Bean haversack. "I haven't got a lot of cash—"

"Yeah, but you've got Oliver," said Ariadne.

And Oliver had Eric's credit card, but Charlotte certainly wasn't going to mention that. "If I pay for the room, do you have enough for food?"

"Oh, sure. I don't eat a lot." She made a face. "At least I didn't used to. But I'm okay, really."

There were banks in Cullen, and Charlotte still had quite a few travelers' checks. She took out a twenty-pound note. "Here—you'd better take this. Only you've got to promise you won't say anything to Oliver about it."

Ariadne sat still, her hands in her lap. "You think that's why I came with you, don't you? Just so I could sponge off you."

Charlotte shook her head. "No," she said. Oliver might think that, but she was determined not to. "Go on, take it. I'll feel better."

Ariadne searched her face, then reluctantly took the note. "Okay, but I'll only use it if I really have to, Charlotte. And I'll pay you back, I mean it. This is only a loan."

There was a knock on the door and Charlotte jumped guiltily. "Promise," she hissed.

"Oh, yeah," Ariadne said, giving her a sudden smile. "I promise." She went and opened the door. "Hey, Oliver. We were just talking about you," she said innocently.

He shot Charlotte a suspicious look. Hastily she asked, "Did you find Mrs. Findlay's house all right?"

"Yes, of course. Are you ready?" His face was impassive, but there was an expression in his eyes that betrayed him. Seeing it, Charlotte remembered the bitter January afternoon he'd told her his uncle Sam was dead. Commodore Shattuck had died peacefully in his sleep; there'd been nothing Oliver could do. He was gone before Oliver even knew it, and Oliver had waited almost a whole day before telling anyone, hoping he could think of a way to protect himself from adult intervention. When he realized he couldn't, he turned to Charlotte knowing she'd have to tell her parents, and that her parents would inevitably tell his mother.

From his behavior, it would appear to most people that he'd felt no real affection for Commodore Shattuck, who, for almost three years, had given him a home, not merely a roof over his head. Oliver seemed more upset at losing the roof than at losing his great-uncle. That's what had bothered Charlotte's parents, her mother especially. Initially, Charlotte almost had been willing to believe it herself.

But that was Oliver. Like the Schuylers' pond in winter, his surface was cold and smooth, but under the ice bubbled invisible springs. Whatever he'd felt when he discovered his uncle Sam's body, he'd frozen it over so no one else could see.

"Charlotte, are you ready?" he repeated impatiently.

She'd meant to comb her hair and wash her face, maybe put on her last clean jersey, but she realized there wasn't time. Oliver had to go now. She stood up and straightened her layers as best she could, and gave her hair a pat.

"Well, bye," said Ariadne. "I hope everything's—you know—okay?"

It was clear Oliver knew where he was going. Unerringly he got them to Deskford Street and turned right. It ran gently downhill for a block, then pitched steeply toward the sea. The hazy afternoon sun gave the view a flat, milky quality, as if the bay and the distant headland were painted on a backdrop. Low stone houses hugged the street. Where the curtains weren't pulled, it was possible to look right in the front windows to the shadowy rooms beyond. Staring into one curiously, Charlotte was startled to see the glitter of eyes in a wrinkled face peering back at her. Quickly she looked away; she felt as if she'd been caught eavesdropping.

"What's the matter?" asked Oliver sharply.

"Nothing." She recovered her balance and walked on, but Oliver stopped. "Are we there?" She glanced around apprehensively. She wished they could just keep walking and never arrive. "Which house is it?"

"It's called Bayview Cottage," he said tightly.

"Oliver—" She went back to him and impulsively took his hand. For a moment he didn't respond, then his fingers closed hard around hers and he gave her a funny little smile that made her breath catch. "It'll be all right," she told him, although they both knew it might very well not be.

Bayview Cottage was the next to last on the left: whitewashed, with a low slate roof, two dormers, and a row of chimney pots at each end. There was a varnished ship's weatherboard beside the door with the name painted on it in good, well-proportioned plain capitals—none of the fake Gothicky letters Charlotte had noticed on other house signs. Right against the pavement was a scrubbed granite doorstep, and in the center of the black door was a polished brass knocker above the letter slot. White net curtains obscured the two downstairs windows. Suddenly they had run out of room to maneuver. Oliver stood motionless. Charlotte let go of his hand and banged the knocker. There was a long silence.

"He's not there," said Oliver tonelessly. "He's gone, Charlotte."

She thought if she could just will it strongly enough, Captain MacPherson would surely appear in the doorway and invite them in. She knocked again, harder. "If no one answers, we'll ask one of the neighbors." Even if the news was bad, they had to find out. They couldn't leave without knowing—that would be worse.

The door opened six inches and a cautious voice said, "Yes? Who is it?"

Charlotte adjusted her gaze downward slightly to meet the eyes of a small woman with fluffy white hair and a soft anxious face. It was the obvious question, but for a moment, Charlotte couldn't think of the answer, then she remembered. "Are you Mrs. McCaig?"

"And if I am? I don't know you, do I?"

"No," said Charlotte. "No, you don't." Behind her, Oliver was stone silent, no help at all. "My name is Charlotte Paige, and this is my friend, Oliver. Oliver Shattuck." She paused, looking for a glimmer of recognition, but there was none. "He's come from London to see Captain MacPherson," she pushed on valiantly.

At that moment Oliver shook himself loose and took over. "I wrote to Captain MacPherson last month. You answered the letter for him."

"Oh, aye. I do remember that. You asked about visiting James. But I told you not to come, I know I did. I told you he'd been very ill."

"Yes," said Oliver. "I had to come. Please can I see him?"

"Och, I'm afraid not. I'm sorry—"

Charlotte felt a finger of dread uncurl under her breastbone.

Fourteen

"Una? What's going on down there? Who's at the door?"

"Och, and I was just about tell you, he's having his nap and mustna be disturbed," said Mrs. McCaig. "Dr. MacLaren's orders."

"Do you mean Captain MacPherson?" Charlotte's heart leaped.

"Aye. Who else would I mean?" Mrs. McCaig sounded genuinely puzzled.

"But if he's awake," said Charlotte, not quite daring to believe, "then can't we see him?"

"He's been so ill—he's not himself yet. I don't think it would be—"

"Una? What are you whispering about down there? Who is it?"

"Captain MacPherson?" Carefully but firmly, Oliver pushed the door all the way open and stepped past Charlotte into the dark, cramped front hall. He towered over Mrs. McCaig, who retreated several paces. "Captain MacPherson, I expect you don't remember me." At the foot of the staircase he stopped, looking up. Above him stood a figure gripping the banister. Charlotte, who'd followed Oliver, blinked rapidly, trying to adjust her eyes from the brightness outside.

"What you mean," said the Captain, leaning forward, "is that I should remember you. Well, give me a minute or two, laddie. My brain's still functioning even though the rest of me's not what it was. Don't tell me."

"I wrote you from London. About my Uncle Sam."

"Ah." It was little more than a breath. "You're Samuel's lad. Oliver."

In the silence, Charlotte felt tears sting the insides of her eyelids.

The Captain cleared his throat and said gruffly, "I'd hoped you'd get up to see me before I snuffed it. You almost missed me, laddie, do you know that?"

"Och, James, you mustn't talk that way," implored Mrs. McCaig.

"It's the truth, Una, and there's no point denying it. I've been down in Aberdeen, you know, at the clinic. I've been poked and prodded and x-rayed and stuck full of tubes, until I'd a gizzard full of it. I told them they couldn't keep me—I was off home and there was nothing they could do to stop me. They said"—he began to descend the stairs, still clutching the banister—"they said they'd no be responsible if I left." He snorted. "As if I asked them to be! So now I'm home and I'm better for it, I can tell you." Reaching the bottom, he paused and took a couple of quick, shallow breaths. Charlotte remembered Captain MacPherson as a small, leathery man with a brush of stiff gray hair. He was still small, but the hair was gone, replaced by a thin, white fuzz, like peach down, and his face glimmered palely in the dim light. "I miss your uncle, Oliver. He was a good man. The world's not the same without him. You said he'd had an easy passage, though. In the end, I guess that's the best we can ask."

"He died in his sleep," said Oliver, his voice not quite steady.

Charlotte's throat was tight. Mrs. McCaig had wrapped her hands in her apron. Letting go of the banister, the Captain transferred his grip to Oliver's arm. "I'm not as steady on my pins as I was. Damn nuisance. That's it, lad. Aye, well. I think tea's in order, Una, don't you? It isn't often we have guests all the way from the States."

"Och, but James—" Mrs. McCaig squeezed and squeezed her apron as if she were wringing water out of it.

"And some of your excellent Dundee cake. It should be whiskey, of course. We should drink a toast to Sammy: a fair wind home."

"You know what Dr. MacLaren said about spirits, James."

"Aye, Una, I do. You needna tell me again. But this is an occasion!"

"You go along into the lounge and I'll bring your tea," she said.

"Right, laddie. We've got a lot to talk about." Oliver and the Captain disappeared through the door on the right, and Mrs. McCaig scuttled down the hall toward the back of the house. Charlotte was left wondering if she'd suddenly become invisible. Sternly she told herself she should not feel hurt, rather she should be glad for Oliver's sake: he had not come too late. And she *was* glad, but she couldn't help wishing he hadn't forgotten her so completely. Deciding to make herself useful, she went after Mrs. McCaig.

"I'm sure I don't know," Mrs. McCaig was saying distractedly. "We've nothing in the house for company. If only I'd known they were coming I'd've baked scones this morning, but I'd no warning. Tea, he says calm as you please, and I don't know what to give them." She was darting around the little kitchen, filling the kettle, opening drawers and cupboards. "Och, he's such a stubborn man! He's only just out of hospital—he forgets how ill he's been—"

Charlotte watched from the doorway. She seemed to be talking to the room, addressing the elderly stove, the wooden drain-board, the woolly socks and lisle stockings on the drying rack by the sink; or perhaps she was talking to the creamy yellow canary hopping about its cage in the window. Afternoon sun warmed the room, brightening the tired paint and shabby linoleum. "Can I help?" offered Charlotte, as much to let Mrs. McCaig know she was there as anything else.

"Oh, my!" Her hand flew up to her throat. "You did give me a turn!"

"I wondered if there was something I could do." Charlotte was apologetic.

"Oh, I don't think so. You dinna ken where anything is

kept. Tea, he said. But he doesna ken that you drink tea. I thought Americans drank coffee or Coca-Cola. There's a jar of Nescafé in the cupboard, but I've no idea how old it is—"

"Tea is fine," Charlotte assured her.

"And there's the Dundee cake, but you'll have to make do with plain bread and jam. Och, if only I'd *known*—"

"It doesn't matter, really it doesn't. We don't need anything—we've only just had lunch."

"Aye, well, that's what there is. If James invites strangers to tea when they turn up on the doorstep, he canna blame me." As she spoke, she took a large loaf out of the bread-box and, clasping it tight against her chest, began to shave thin, even slices off it with a murderous-looking knife. She stood the remainder on its cut end and gave Charlotte a worried look. In the daylight, Charlotte saw that she had the most beautiful blue-violet eyes, fringed with thick dark lashes. Otherwise she was an ordinary, timid little woman, the kind you'd pass in the street without noticing. "Well, if you're wanting to make yourself useful, I suppose you could butter the bread."

Steam was spouting from the kettle. Mrs. McCaig poured a little hot water into a fat brown teapot and sloshed it around, while Charlotte, glad for something to do, set to work on the heap of slices with a butter knife. The blue tin tea caddy Mrs. McCaig took down was decorated with pictures of Prince Charles and Lady Diana. It occurred to Charlotte that Jean would love one like it: a memento of the royal wedding, just shy of garish. She was about to ask where she could buy one, when Mrs. McCaig exclaimed, "Och, no! Not like that. You must spread the butter right the way to the edge and not so thick. He's very particular, is James."

Then why doesn't he butter his own bread, thought Charlotte mutinously. How could there be a wrong way to do it? But she kept her mouth shut and surrendered the knife to Mrs. McCaig, who repaired the damage and cut the slices in half, then arranged them like overlapping shingles on a plate painted with blowsy pink roses. "There, that's better. Of course you weren't to know," she added generously. "There's the cake and the bread and strawberry jam—I've opened a fresh pot. And there's a wee bit of parkin left from Thursday last. I'm almost ashamed to put it out, it's that old. The shortbread's from the bakery, but it's quite nice." She put each plate on one of the shelves of a tall, cylindrical table with feet and a handle.

"It looks wonderful," Charlotte told her honestly. "Almost good enough to eat."

Mrs. McCaig gave her a stricken look. "Almost?"

She was not used to the kind of conversational nonsense Charlotte had grown up with. "No, no—it looks wonderful. Really." Then to change the subject, "What *is* that?"

"Which? The cake stand, do you mean. Have you no seen one before?"

Charlotte shook her head. "I've read about cake stands in Dorothy Sayers novels, but I could only guess—"

"Och, but how would you serve tea without one? I sold mine when I moved in with Belle and Andrew. I had to sell most of my things—I've only a wee room. But there, I shouldna complain. They've been very good to me. This one was Mairi's. 'Twas a wedding present from

James's aunt in Ballater—that would have been his mother's sister Agnes. Or was it Margaret? No, it was Agnes, I'm sure."

Forgetting the cake stand, Charlotte said, "Do you mean Captain MacPherson was married?" She had assumed that James MacPherson, like Samuel Shattuck, was a lifelong bachelor. She had no reason to make that assumption, but it was a surprise to find otherwise. Although she ought to have guessed from Mrs. McCaig's name—

"Aye, he married our youngest sister—that was August of nineteen thirty-two. Mairi was the first to wed—Belle was a wee bit put out, I remember. She thought as oldest she should have been first, you ken, but she didn't marry Andrew Dalrymple until almost a year later."

"What happened? Mairi isn't—I mean—"

"Och, Mairi passed on these long years since. Carried off by the influenza, she and the bairn both. They'd only been wed two years. It was gey sad."

"I didn't know. I'm sorry."

"She was a lovely girl, Mairi, but never strong. It broke his heart when she left him, and he's been alone ever since."

The sadness in her eyes touched Charlotte. She said gently, "How fortunate that you could come and help."

"What else would I do? James wasna fit to manage on his own, not just out of hospital."

"Oliver wasn't sure exactly what was wrong," said Charlotte, hoping Mrs. McCaig wouldn't think the implied question impertinent.

"Aye, well, it was gey serious. Dr. MacLaren sent

James to Aberdeen to a specialist. He was there more than a month having treatments and there was talk of an operation. But he's done so well he's no need of it. He's on the mend now. I told him I'd stay on until he's back on his feet again, no matter what Belle says"

"Why should Belle mind?"

"She puts great store by appearances, does Belle. There's the family name to think of. She says it's not proper for James and me to live under the same roof, but I told her, James is family, too, even though Mairi's been gone such a long time. I told her it would look worse if we didna help. What would people say then? In the end she saw my mind was made up and she had to let me come. But she warned me she'd no be responsible for Bruce while I was away. Andrew'd promised her a holiday in the Isle of Wight. They'd a fortnight booked for June and she couldna disappoint him. Well, at first I didna ken what I'd do, but then it came to me."

"What?" asked Charlotte, intrigued. Who was Bruce?

"I brought him with me, that's what I did. All the way by coach from Perth. Bruce traveled right on the seat beside me as if he'd done it all his life." She smiled triumphantly. "And he's settled in ever so well, haven't you, my pet? I think he was pining. Belle wouldna have him in her kitchen, she said it was unhygenic, so he was shut away in my room. But he's a different bird since we came. He sings all day now." She gazed lovingly at the canary as it hopped from perch to perch, cocking its head and talking to itself. It suddenly paused, puffed out its chest, and sang a whole clear aria. Mrs. McCaig looked as proud as if she'd done it herself. "What did I tell you?"

"Very nice." Charlotte tried to sound enthusiastic. She wasn't awfully fond of pets. Long ago she'd inherited a pair of useless rabbits from her brother Max, and she'd tolerated Eliot's collection of cats because they were Eliot's. Amos she'd actually become quite attached to; he was a living, breathing, ingratiating connection with Oliver. A reminder of the side of Oliver he usually kept buried. He loved the dog, she knew. The look on his face as he'd studied the photograph she'd given him was the same as that on Mrs. McCaig's as she watched her canary.

"My daughter Sheila gave me him when she went away to Capetown with Kevin. For company, she said. She knew I'd be lonely with her so far away, and he's been such a comfort—och, goodness! That's never the time! Here's me havering and the tea'll be stone cold." In spite of her wispiness, she picked up the laden tray as if she were used to lifting heavy loads. "James must wonder what's become of us by now." Charlotte carried the cake stand behind her, feeling like one of the Three Kings.

When they reached the lounge, it was immediately clear that neither James nor Oliver had wondered about them at all. They sat on either side of the single front window, silhouetted against the white net curtain, so deep in conversation they didn't even turn their heads when the door opened. After the warmth and sun of the kitchen, the room was cavelike.

"Och, James, whatever did you think? I'm sorry we've been so long. We fell to talking and I'd no idea it was so late." Mrs. McCaig set the tray on the table in front of the sofa and perched behind it, arranging cups and saucers and spoons at great speed.

"Ah, there you are, Una," said the Captain belatedly. "What's that?"

They haven't missed us at all, thought Charlotte. They'd forgotten we exist. She reminded herself again that this was the point of their trip.

"I'll pour out and you can hand round the cups. There's milk and sugar. What does your friend Albert take?"

"Oliver, what do you want in your tea?" Charlotte asked, itching to tell him he could come and get it himself.

"Tea? Oh, sugar. Thanks. I didn't know Uncle Sam had been to Scotland after the war. He never told me."

"Och, laddie, I don't suppose he told you everything. He never would have had the time. That was back before you were a gleam in the eye. He came in the autumn of fifty-nine. We went back to the Orkneys by ferry—went back to see Scapa Flow. That was twenty years after the *Royal Oak* went to the bottom. We'd meant to go on to the Faeroes, but the weather was playing up. Nothing to what we had in nineteen forty, forty-one, you ken, but back then there was no choice did we go or not. Aye, and we both knew how dirty the North Atlantic can be in October. 'Next time,' he said. 'Next time.'" He was silent for a moment, then he cleared his throat and said, "I've a box full of photos somewhere. We went south to Fort Augustus. Sammy was keen to see the Caledonian Canal. You ken he'd worked on the Saint Lawrence Seaway?"

Oliver nodded. "He told me quite a lot about that. Do

you think I could see the photographs?"

"Of course you can. I'll have to dig a wee bit to find them." The Captain started to struggle to his feet.

"Och, James, your tea!" protested Mrs. McCaig.

"Here." Charlotte thrust Oliver's cup and saucer at him and went back to sit on the sofa.

The Captain subsided. "Aye, I guess they can wait a wee bit longer. Could be you've seen the box they're in, Una."

"What box is that, James?"

"The cardboard box with the photographs in it. Are you deaf, woman? I've just been talking about it."

"I've seen lots of boxes since I arrived. How should I know which one you mean? I've not been prying, if that's what you're saying."

"No, no, of course not. I never thought that," he said soothingly. "I just thought you might have come across it in your cleaning." He took a swallow of tea and spluttered. "You've put sugar in it again."

"Dr. MacLaren says it's good for energy, James. It's only a teaspoon. If you don't want it, I'll drink it myself."

"You'd better give me a slice of that cake to take the curse off it, then," he grumbled.

Charlotte, thinking that if she were dressed in a frilly apron and cap at least she'd be getting paid, took him a plate on which Mrs. McCaig heaped three slices of bread spread with strawberry jam, two pieces of shortbread, and a piece of dark, raisin-speckled cake. "For pity's sake, woman—I canna eat all that!"

"It'll build you up, James. You need your strength. Albert, what can I give you?"

"Nothing, thanks," said Oliver.

Seeing her face fall, Charlotte said quickly, "I've never had Dundee cake. What's in it?"

The Captain set his full plate on the table and leaned toward Oliver. They looked like conspirators, locked in a private conversation. Charlotte resigned herself to listening to Mrs. McCaig's recipe for Dundee cake, making appropriate noises from time to time. After a while she became aware that Mrs. McCaig had run out of words, but she hadn't the energy to search for another subject, so they sat on the sofa in silence. Several times the Captain threw himself back in his chair with a seal-like bark of laughter; once Oliver joined in, and Charlotte felt an actual pang of jealousy.

Mrs. McCaig finished her tea and set her cup on the tray. From a workbasket on the floor she took out a thick gray sock and began to darn it with black thread. Charlotte didn't understand how she could see what she was doing in the semidarkness; her fingers moved like spiders, weaving thread in and out of the worn heel. She seemed absorbed and content. Clearly she didn't expect to be included in the conversation across the room, so wasn't bothered that she wasn't. Charlotte wondered if sock-darning was therapeutic. She couldn't remember ever seeing anyone do it before. When socks in her family wore out, they were discarded.

At last Mrs. McCaig paused, examined her work critically, and decided it was done. She bit off the thread and carefully rolled the sock with its mate, turning the top inside out. Nervously, she smoothed her skirt over her knees as if wiping her hands and gave a tiny cough. After a minute she coughed again, a little louder, and Charlotte realized it was a signal. She stood up. Her legs were stiff, from sitting on the bus all morning, and from being tense ever since. "Oliver, I think we ought to go. We've been here almost two hours."

Oliver gave her a blank look. He was probably trying to remember who she was.

"Och, you canna go now. We've barely started," protested the Captain, but his voice sounded thin.

Oliver rose. "We interrupted your nap. I'm sorry."

"I can sleep any time. Don't mind Una, she's always fussing."

"May I come back tomorrow, sir? There's so much I want to ask you and perhaps I can find the photographs. Would you mind?"

"Mind, laddie? Of course not! You're welcome to come as often as you like and stay as long as you want."

"Come on, Oliver," said Charlotte, suddenly eager to be outside in the windy, salt-smelling sunshine. From three thousand miles away, her mother gave her a gentle nudge. Reluctantly she turned to Mrs. McCaig. "Can I help you clean up?"

"Och, no. I can manage, thank you." Mrs. McCaig seemed equally eager to have the two of them gone.

"It was a lovely tea," said Charlotte.

"Come in the morning, Oliver, and we'll make a real day of it. You can stay to lunch," said the Captain. "Half past nine, laddie."

"Half past nine," agreed Oliver.

Fifteen

This time the Captain didn't attempt to get up. Mrs. McCaig saw them to the door. "He thinks he's fitter than he is. He's a very stubborn man, James MacPherson."

"I hope we didn't tire him too much," said Charlotte. "Thank you for the tea." She gave Oliver a poke.

"Mmm? Oh yes, thanks."

He was off striding up the hill before Mrs. McCaig had the door properly shut, and Charlotte had to jog to catch up with him. At the corner he was forced to stop to let two cars pass. There was a curious, inward-turned expression on his face. Although the sky overhead was clear, for a moment the sun seemed to go behind a cloud. "You can spend the morning with Captain MacPherson and we can get a bus back to Aberdeen in the afternoon. We'll have to find out—"

Oliver blinked and the strange look was gone. "Listen, Charlotte, I'm going to ask Mrs. Findlay if I can have the room for two more nights."

"*Two?*"

He nodded. "Tomorrow and Wednesday. We haven't come all this way just to turn around and go straight back to London. That doesn't make any sense."

"Yes, but what about your mother?"

"It'll work, trust me. Paula and Eric got back to Highgate late last night and they got my note. I'll call them this evening after supper as if I'm in North Wales and tell them I'll be home Friday. There's no phone at Fred's cottage—they can't reach me in the meantime, so that's all right. And I think it would be a good idea if you called your parents, too. That'll keep them from calling Paula."

Charlotte's stomach knotted. "It's taking an awful chance, Oliver. Just because it's worked so far—"

"It'll go on working. Why shouldn't it? Only until Friday, Charlotte. Just give me two days with Captain MacPherson. There's so much I want to find out—this is my chance—but I know he isn't very strong. I don't want to exhaust him."

"I'm not very good at making things up, Oliver. What if they want to talk to Paula, what will I say?"

"It's not a problem. Your parents have an answering machine, haven't they?"

"Mom does, yes, in case clients call while she's out, but I don't—"

"It's five hours earlier in Concord, right? That means it's about eleven-thirty. There's unlikely to be anyone home. You can leave a message on the machine—tell them how busy you are and what a wonderful time you're having and you'll call them later in the week. No awkward questions, and you won't have to invent anything. You can call while I go talk to Mrs. Findlay."

He knew she was caving in, but she wasn't going to let him get away with that. "Not a chance. I want you with me in case someone's home."

For a moment she thought he was going to argue, then he shrugged. "All right. I'll be back as quickly as I can. We'll use the phone in your room and put it on the bill."

But he'd forgotten Ariadne. She was curled up on the bed under a blanket, sound asleep, and she didn't stir when Charlotte came in or used the bathroom, which she found festooned with various damp undergarments. Ariadne went in for lacy camisoles and petticoats. From the look of things, it was possible that she'd been wearing her entire wardrobe. While she waited for Oliver, Charlotte sat by the window and watched Ariadne breathe peacefully in and out, thinking that unconsciousness seemed like a very happy solution to life at that moment. In spite of the problems pressing in on her, Charlotte realized she was weary enough to go right off if she lay down. Whatever her vacation had been thus far—and it would take her some time to figure that out—it had not been restful, and she was certainly not looking forward to the next bit. Thank goodness they'd found Captain MacPherson alive and in his right mind. The alternatives didn't bear thinking about.

She tried to figure out a message for her parents that would be neither the truth nor a blatant lie, that would give them no cause for alarm while being unspecific as to detail, and sound natural and spontaneous. She was too tired to think straight. Oliver would have to advise her. If only the whole idea didn't give her a stomachache.

Oliver swore softly when she let him in and warned him to be quiet. "We'll have to use the phone in the lobby. And I'll have to use it later to call Paula. There's nowhere private at Mrs. Findlay's. I checked about your room—you can keep it, or there's a single that's cheaper. It doesn't have a private bath."

For a split second Charlotte was tempted, but she couldn't abandon Ariadne. In two more days she'd be on her own again, and maybe in the meantime Charlotte could convince her to go home to Wellesley. It was worth a try.

The telephone was in a secluded corner of the reception area. Oliver dialed the operator and arranged to put the charge on Eric's credit card, and this time Charlotte didn't object. "Okay, this is what you say. You're sorry you couldn't call when they're home, but you're going out to dinner, which is true. You just wanted to tell them everything's fine. Okay?"

"I should tell them what we did today."

"Tell them about the river. We hadn't gone when you called before. Tell them about Greenwich."

Greenwich? That seemed so long ago she'd almost forgotten it. She struggled to call it back; Oliver was speaking to the operator. The pub by the water . . . pickled onions . . . the painted ceiling in the banquet hall . . . the Meridian . . . all that was before she'd even known—

"It's ringing." He pushed the receiver into her hands. She gulped; her fingers were cold. What if her mother was spending the afternoon working at home? She might be deciding on rug samples for the branch library renovation, or calculating square footage, or—after the fifth ring there was a half ring, then a click, and in a few seconds her mother's voice was on the line: "You have reached Katherine Paige Interiors. I cannot take your call, but if you will leave your name, number, and a brief message, I will return it as promptly as possible."

"Go on," said Oliver.

Charlotte's voice sounded thin and squeaky in her own ears. She hoped her parents would think it was the transatlantic transmission. When she hung up, her hand shook slightly.

"What did I tell you?" Oliver crowed. "Mission accomplished and no awkward questions. If only I could do the same with Paula and Eric." He looked at her and frowned. "Charlotte, it's all right. You've just assured them they don't have to worry about you. That's exactly what you wanted to do."

"I know, but—"

"No but. Look." He hooked his arm under hers and guided her toward the back of the hotel, into a comfortable dark-beamed room she hadn't seen before. "You sit here and I'll get you a cider or a shandy and you'll feel better. We can decide about dinner." He settled her on a settee padded with dark red plush and went to the bar.

She hunched her shoulders to loosen the muscles and looked around. Big windows gave onto the flagstone terrace she'd seen from above. It was deserted now with the sun gone off it; the umbrellas were furled, the flowers had lost their brilliance. There was no one else in the bar, either, except the bartender, a dapper man with a neat gray beard who was working on a crossword puzzle. With his back to her, ordering drinks, Oliver looked like a tall, self-assured stranger.

"What are you thinking about?" he asked, putting two glasses on the table and sitting beside her.

"The Italian restaurant in Newburyport."

"What?" He gave her a blank look.

"When we went to Plum Island, remember? The day we skipped school after your uncle—died." She stumbled slightly over the world and went quickly on. "We had lunch at the Café Florian. I had spaghetti with clam sauce and you had fish. And coffee. That was the first time I'd seen you drink coffee."

"Charlotte, for heaven's sake—"

"You can't have forgotten? That day?"

"No, of course I haven't forgotten. I couldn't have told you what we had for lunch, or where we ate, but—why'd you think of it, anyway?"

She leaned her head against the settee-back. "I was just thinking about how you get to be adult, Oliver. The way it sneaks up on you. I've always wanted to grow up—I suppose I still do. I want to be old enough, but I'm not quite sure for what. It looks awfully complicated somehow. And I still think of myself as a kid; well, I am, really. But I must look older on the outside than I feel on the inside, otherwise I wouldn't be here. Someone would have stopped me along the way. But how did it happen? I guess I thought there'd be something official, like flying up to be a Girl Scout when you're a Brownie."

"I was never a Brownie," said Oliver.

"But you know what I mean. Don't quibble."

"Sorry."

"Look at us—right now—sitting here in a bar in Scotland by ourselves. How do we know how to do this? Stop looking at me that way—I know I'm not saying this well. I'm very tired." Charlotte took a long swallow of her drink, then frowned, tasting it. "What is this?"

"Lager and lime."

"Is it alcoholic?"

"Not very. If you don't like it, I'll get you something else."

"You're corrupting a minor."

"I thought it would help you relax. I need to talk to you." Something in his tone of voice sliced through the pleasant haze that was forming in her brain. "You know that Captain MacPherson is dying."

She stared at him. "Oh, no, Oliver. He can't be! She said—Mrs. McCaig *said* he's getting better. They thought he'd need an operation, but it turned out he didn't. They let him come home."

"They didn't let him. He told them he'd had enough and he was going home, and they couldn't stop him. He has cancer and it's killing him."

"She must not know."

"Yes, she does. At least he's told her, but he says she doesn't want to believe him. This doctor—Dr.

MacLaren—sounds all right. He knows and he's agreed to help, to make it as painless as he possibly can."

"An easy passage," said Charlotte softly.

"That's why I have to stay. You understand? I won't ever see him again." He was very calm, not frightened or upset by what he was telling her. She had to believe him. He gave her a long, level look and went on. "He talked about it while you were getting tea. Anything they could do for him in Aberdeen would only be temporary and the chemotherapy made him feel rotten. He decided he'd rather die his own way in Cullen."

"But Oliver, don't you mind?"

"Of course I mind. But don't you see? I was right to come, Charlotte. I got here in time. I can talk to him about Uncle Sam and he understands, and I can say good-bye. I never said good-bye to Uncle Sam, because I didn't know. This is like a second chance. I suppose you think it sounds crazy."

He was waiting for her to say it didn't. She reached over and put her hand on top of his; he turned it over and curled the fingers through hers. After a moment he said, "I don't think I could have come if you hadn't agreed to come with me. I ought to have been able to, but—everything would have been so different. Whatever happens after this . . ." He let the sentence go and sat looking at their hands. Neither of them moved, then finally he gave her fingers a squeeze, released them, and picked up his glass. When he put it down again, he said, "He's leaving her the house."

"Mrs. McCaig?"

Oliver nodded. "He hasn't told her that yet. He can't stand her sister, Belle. He says she's just like their mother, a narrow-minded bully. His wife was different, though, and she got away, but Una's never had a chance. I guess her husband was no prize, either, and when he died there wasn't any money. So Captain MacPherson's leaving her everything."

That meant Bruce could stay in the kitchen window at Bayview Cottage, singing his little heart out. Charlotte found that comforting.

Oliver drained his glass and went to get another. He returned with two bags of salt-and-vinegar potato chips. "I think we ought to celebrate tonight—have a really good dinner. Mrs. Findlay told me about a restaurant near the harbor—I can make a reservation."

Under the circumstances, celebrating sounded odd, but Charlotte understood. She propped her chin on her hand and looked at Oliver assessingly. "Same problem as Edinburgh, of course. No clothes."

"Doesn't matter. People wear anything in a holiday resort," he countered. "Not that you have to worry, anyway, Charlotte. You could wear ratty blue jeans and still look terrific."

"Oliver Shattuck, what a line."

"Wrong. I don't do lines. I mean it."

She met his eyes and felt the fizz of electricity from the soles of her feet all the way to the end of her French braid. She thought it was a very good thing they weren't sharing a room this time. Then she smiled at the thought of Ariadne as a chaperone.

"You do look terrific," he said, settling his arm comfortably across her shoulders. She fit very naturally against him. Other people began to trickle into the bar, order drinks, fill the benches and chairs, furnishing the space with the pleasant hum of sociability: quiet talk and laughter. Charlotte would have been quite happy sitting there all evening, part of a couple, not thinking about any of the things that had to be thought about, just being aware of Oliver. She felt drifty and content.

After a bit, he said, "Have you gone to sleep?"

She shook her head slightly.

"Then we'd better move."

"Why?"

"Because I have to call Paula after dinner and I can't wait too long. I'll call the restaurant and you go wake Ariadne."

She sat up, shifting away from him. "Ariadne? Why?"

"So she can come with us. It's all right, Charlotte. I don't mind."

But I do, thought Charlotte. Oliver was being magnanimous at just the wrong moment, but she couldn't bring herself to tell him. Her lovely shimmery mood burst like a soap bubble.

Maybe Ariadne would be sleeping so soundly, it would be a pity to wake her. Or better yet, Charlotte would find she'd gotten up and gone out by herself while they were in the bar.

But she found Ariadne sitting on the bed, propped against a mound of pillows, leafing through a full-color tourist magazine thoughtfully provided by the hotel, full of photographs of picturesque fishing villages, turreted Disneylike castles, and hillsides magenta with heather. She greeted Charlotte with happy anticipation. "Jeez, I'm *starving!* I had this incredible dream about pepperoni pizza, it woke me up. Wouldn't you think there'd be a pizza place somewhere in this town? Maybe they'd know at the desk."

"Pizza is empty calories," said Charlotte severely, quoting Deb. "You shouldn't eat junk food." Ariadne looked abashed. "But what about the tomato? I mean, that's a vegetable. And cheese? That's got, like, calcium." Charlotte shook her head and Ariadne sighed. "Yeah, I guess I'm going to have to really think about what I eat from now on, hunh?"

"Anyway," said Charlotte, "If you want pizza you'll have to find it yourself. Oliver and I are going to a restaurant for dinner." It was neither gracious, nor an invitation. Feeling ashamed, Charlotte turned her back on Ariadne to hunt for something in her knapsack.

There was what her brother Eliot would have gleefully called a pregnant pause. Then Ariadne said, "I guess it was pretty bad? I mean, Oliver's friend?"

To her chagrin, Charlotte actually had forgotten Captain MacPherson for the moment; her brain was overloaded. She didn't know how to answer Ariadne.

"It's okay. You go on. I expect you want to be alone with him. If there's anything I can do, Charlotte—besides stay out of the way I mean—"

Oh, shit! thought Charlotte, surprised at herself. "Oliver's making a reservation for us, for all three of us.

We—we—want you to come with us."

"Are you sure? I mean, I know I'm not exactly his favorite person—"

"Yes, we're sure," said Charlotte resignedly. She dreaded the evening ahead, fumbling for subjects on which to make polite, vague conversation, talking about things that didn't matter to avoid silence. But she knew she wouldn't enjoy herself now if they left Ariadne out. Oliver was just going to have to make a real effort this time.

Sixteen

They were early for dinner; there were only a few other people in the dining room, but Oliver's reservation had procured a table in one of the front windows. From it, they had a wide view of the bay, and of the harbor just below, clasped protectively by its seawalls. People were walking on the broad flat walls in the softening light of early evening, and a few little boats sat placidly inside like well-fed ducks on a millpond.

"Oh, wow," said Ariadne, surveying the room appreciatively. "This is really nice." It was, too. The tables were covered with pale rose cloths, the napkins folded like fans, the silver carefully arranged, and each place set with a goblet. The waitress who brought their menus lit a new candle in a hurricane chimney for them. Ariadne glowed. Her cheeks had color; her wild hair was mostly in the custody of a large barrette at the nape of her slim neck, but delinquent tendrils curled disobediently around her face, softening the edges, and in the warm light her eyes seemed flecked with gold. By comparison, Charlotte felt travel-weary and confused. Too much had happened.

Ariadne picked up a vase full of pink and blue sweet peas and sniffed. "Hey, they're real. Jeez, I'd forgotten what it's like to go to a place like this. All I've been to are Wimpey bars and chippies and grotty little cafés. But this is really, like, *civilized*, you know?"

Charlotte stared absently at the flowers. Her mother always said that if the flowers were real, the food was almost guaranteed to be good. She wondered what her mother was doing right at that moment. Had she been home yet? Had she gotten Charlotte's message? Perhaps she'd called Charlotte's father to tell him, or Jean or Deb—

"Charlotte? Charlotte, have you decided?" Oliver asked with just a touch of impatience. She blinked and found the waitress looking expectant, pencil poised.

"What? Oh, sorry. Not quite. You go first." She hadn't even looked at the menu.

Ariadne knew just what she wanted; she ordered poached prawns. Charlotte wasn't sure what prawns were and didn't want to ask. Oliver chose fresh Scottish salmon with hollandaise sauce and Charlotte nodded in agreement. "That's what I'll have, too, please." Easier than making everyone wait while she studied the entrées. The waitress recommended Cullen skink to start and Oliver grandly ordered it for them all.

"What is it, what she said?" asked Ariadne.

Oliver shook his head. "I thought you'd know, you've been living here."

"Yeah, and I told you what I've been eating—fish and chips and burgers. It'll be a surprise, then."

Silence descended on them. Charlotte kept her gaze averted so she wouldn't meet anyone's eyes. She felt awkward and self-conscious, and resentful because of it. If she and Oliver were alone she wouldn't mind the silence. Ariadne's presence made it uncomfortable. She wondered how it was possible to shift so quickly from one powerful emotion to another.

After what seemed like a very long time, but could only have been five minutes or so, the waitress brought wide, shallow bowls of a creamy soup with bits of smoked haddock in it, and a basket of warm, floury rolls. Over the soup, Oliver and Ariadne fell into a discussion of their experiences with the British educational system—a lot of stuff about A-levels and O-levels, student grants and bursaries, and public schools—which evidently weren't public. They argued, in a friendly way, about being forced to decide on your field of study before you even got to a university. Ariadne considered that most unfair; how would you know what your choices were? Oliver thought the system was much more efficient. You needn't waste time on things that weren't going to matter to you.

"Well, but look at me," said Ariadne. "I've only got one more year to go and I *still* don't know what I want to do. Every letter, my parents ask me what are my plans for after college? What am I going to do with my life? And the truth is"—she paused—"I'm not even sure I'm going back next year."

"To college?" said Oliver. "If it's your last year, it

would be stupid not to finish. At least you'd have a degree."

"So what? I mean, what good will it do me? And, anyway, they'll make me go home and I can't face that."

"So stay and finish at Aberdeen."

Ariadne made a wry face. "See, I don't think I can. I kind of messed up last term. My lecturers probably don't even remember me—I didn't show up very much. It was all right last fall, I went to lectures and my tutorials and I did all the work and everything, but then I got to thinking what a waste of time it was. I mean, there I was in *Scotland* and it seemed really wrong to spend every day just studying. I could do that anywhere. So I took off. Then all of a sudden the year was almost over. And now that Jeff and Joyce are splitting they wouldn't let me stay, anyway."

"I'm thinking of staying in London this fall," said Oliver.

Charlotte stopped chasing the last spoonful of soup. "You are?"

"Mmm. Eric—my mother's husband," he explained to Ariadne, "is being reassigned to Washington in another two months."

"How can you stay if they go back?" demanded Charlotte. "Where will you live?"

"Remember Timothy Harker? His parents would let me stay with them. I'd pay board, of course. His father's an Anglican minister—very respectable. Paula can't possibly object. Then I could finish at Highgate and go on to Cambridge."

"You don't—do you mean Cambridge, *England?* What about Harvard?"

"I was thinking I could do my undergraduate work at Cambridge, then go to Harvard Law. My tutor says he thinks I've got a chance at getting a place at Trinity if I work hard enough. Imagine how Paula would love that—'My son who's studying at Cambridge University.' And there'd be a whole ocean between us. I wouldn't have to go to Washington for holidays."

Or Concord. Charlotte felt as if she'd swallowed an ice cube. How long had he been thinking about this?

The waitress removed their soup plates and brought the main course. Ariadne's prawns turned out to be plump, rosy shrimp; Charlotte was fond of shrimp.

"It sounds," said Ariadne, spearing and eating one, "as if you don't get along very well with your parents, either. These are really good. Want to try one?" Charlotte shook her head.

Oliver said, "I don't know about my father. I haven't seem him since I was nine."

Ariadne nodded sympathetically. "Divorced. So, did he remarry?"

"He's got a new family in California. I've got a half-brother and a half-sister I've never seen, and probably never will. Kyle and Kristen."

"Oh, wow. It's so weird to think about that. You could walk right past them on the street and never even know. But maybe that's better, I mean, getting divorced? My parents really should have done it years ago. They don't like each other, but they don't want anyone outside the family to know, so they do things together in public for the hospital, or these benefits Mummy organizes. There they are in the paper, looking as if they're having this great time: 'Dr. and Mrs. Gerald Leavitt of Wellesley at the Gay Nineties Ball for Cancer Research.' But it's all a fake. What's the point of living like that? I mean, they aren't happy or anything." She gestured with her fork and scattered peas across the tablecloth. "So what's your mother like?"

"Paula? She's all right," said Oliver carefully. "We get along because it's simpler than not. Eric stays out of it—she's his wife, but I'm not his son, and that's fine. I guess I don't really think of Paula as my mother. She's my guardian. Legally responsible for me until I'm considered old enough to be responsible for myself."

Charlotte looked from Oliver to Ariadne, then down at her plate. There was a moist, orange-pink fillet on it, a scalloped dish of sauce, buttered parsley potatoes, and a heap of mixed peas and carrots. Everything looked good and she was hungry; she was determined not to waste it. She drew a small, invisible circle around herself, shutting out Oliver and Ariadne, who didn't need her help after all to keep a conversation going.

Charlotte knew what she wanted for desert: Jean, who shared Charlotte's weakness for sweets, had described British trifles in mouthwatering detail. Once they'd ordered, Ariadne excused herself and went off to the ladies' room, dropping her napkin and bumping into the next table on the way. Instead of making another remark about weak kidneys, Oliver sat back and regarded Charlotte. "You've been very quiet."

She spluttered into her water glass. "I didn't think you'd noticed."

"What's that supposed to mean?"

"You and Ariadne have more to talk about than you thought. Whose parents are worse—have you decided? Or do you need an impartial judge?"

"I wasn't aware that we were competing," he said coolly.

"That's what it sounded like."

"Look, Charlotte, you get along with your parents. You're lucky. Your parents are reasonable and sympathetic. When you talk, they actually listen. Even when they don't agree with you, they're willing to help—they're on your side. Andy and Kath's parents are like that, too. You have no idea how much I used to envy the three of you."

"You had Commodore Shattuck. He listened. He helped."

"Yes, I did. For three years. I didn't know him until I was almost fourteen, and now he's gone. I can't even write to him for advice."

"Do you want me to apologize, Oliver? Is that it? I'm sorry I have nice parents?"

"Don't be silly." He frowned at her for a moment, then he said more calmly, "It's like learning to ride a two-wheel bike, Charlotte. You've got training wheels, I haven't. You won't fall over before you learn to balance because they'll hold you up. I've had to learn to balance on my own from the beginning. Well, I can do it. Nobody taught me how—I've got the bruises to prove it. Mostly"—he paused, staring out the window—"mostly I'm glad you've had help. But every now and then I get angry because I haven't. Ariadne knows what I mean."

"And I don't!" cried Charlotte, stung.

"No," he replied, still not looking at her, "you don't."

She almost said, "Well why don't you two start a club, then," but caught herself. "All right, Oliver. I can understand how you felt when you were younger and she sent you away to school. But what about now? Maybe if you forgave her, Paula would turn out to be sympathetic. Her life isn't the same as it was then—it's settled, and she's got Eric, and it sounds to me as if she's really trying. My mother says—"

Oliver turned his head, his expression stony. "It's too late. I just don't care anymore. She wasn't there when I needed her, and now I don't. I'm not going to let her back in, Charlotte. I don't see why I should."

Ariadne returned and dessert arrived. The trifle was beautiful: layers of sponge cake, jam, custard, and whipped cream, decorated with candied cherries. As she ate it, Charlotte was aware that under ordinary circumstances she would have savored every morsel, but she couldn't give it the attention it deserved. Oliver and his mother kept distracting her.

How Charlotte's mother could make allowances for Paula was outside Charlotte's understanding. She decided it must be an adult thing. It hadn't occurred to her then that the allowances she made for Oliver might be considered a child thing, each side presenting a united front to the other, refusing to acknowledge the weaknesses and contradictions in its position.

But now she thought of Jean, agonizing over whether sending Hilary to day care would damage her emotionally; doubting her vocation as a mother because she couldn't help wanting to go back to work part-time and was willing to surrender her daughter to strangers to do it. Mrs. Paige and Jean had had a long talk about this one Saturday morning over cups of coffee in the Paige kitchen. Drinking cocoa, Charlotte had listened, a little surprised to find she could understand what Jean was saying, not just the words, but the feelings behind them.

And Mrs. Paige worried that she had driven Eliot to give up music. She'd told that to, of all people, Pat Schuyler: that maybe he'd gone to Montana because she'd pushed him too hard to be a concert musician. *Pat* felt guilty about Andy. She'd said so to Charlotte. Was it her fault that he wouldn't give up the farm because he knew how much it meant to her? Charlotte was sure that wasn't the main reason, but she wasn't sure that Pat entirely believed her.

Parents made mistakes. It was an eye-opening fact, at least to Charlotte. They worried about those mistakes in secret, afraid to admit to them in case their children didn't forgive them. Sometimes, whatever they did was a mistake because there wasn't a right choice. But children didn't understand that. Mrs. Paige had kept telling Charlotte this about Oliver's mother and Charlotte had resisted hearing it because that made her feel disloyal to Oliver. But what if, instead of sending him to school after school, Paula had kept him with her when she and his father had separated, while they negotiated their acrimonious divorce and she'd taken her first shaky, frightened steps alone, before she had found her confidence, her job with the NEH, and finally Eric Preston? Would that really have been better for him? Would it have been better for Charlotte if her own mother had given up the work she loved doing to be a full-time mother? There was a time when Charlotte had longed for that, but now that she was older she wasn't so sure it would have been good for either of them.

She wondered, glancing at Oliver, if Paula was aware of his feelings about her. Knowing Oliver as well as she did, Charlotte was pretty sure of the answer. Oliver was a master at letting you know things without having to tell you directly. Paula couldn't possibly live in the same apartment with him and not realize. How miserable it must be not to be forgiven and not to be able to forgive. Would Oliver have forgiven *her* if she had not agreed to come with him to Cullen? Could that have been at least part of the reason she was here—she was too much of a coward to risk their friendship? That was a depressing thought.

Oliver and Ariadne were talking about the Jacobite rebellion of 1745 when Charlotte tuned in again. Ariadne had seen a lot of Scotland since taking up with The Travellers. She'd been out to the Hebrides, to Lewis with Harris, and to Skye, where Flora MacDonald had lived, the woman who had rescued Bonnie Prince Charlie from the English. "You know, 'Speed bonnie boat'—I won't try to sing it for you," she said as Oliver paid the bill with Eric's credit card and asked Charlotte if she had any pound notes for the tip. She found two crumpled ones which he added to his.

Before they went back to the hotel, they walked down to the harbor. It was a calm evening; the wind had dropped and dusk was slipping in on the tide as the sun edged down toward the western hills. Overhead the sky was still a deep, saturated blue and the sea was glazed with a mellow golden light. A few lights began to appear in the village, like fallen stars, and beacons blinked at the outermost ends of the seawalls.

"The light is so beautiful," said Ariadne. "You forget how late it is."

"We're much farther north than Massachusetts," Oliver said.

"But it's pitch-dark almost all day in the middle of winter. That's one thing I couldn't get used to, you know? It's really depressing."

They sat on the edge of the seawall, their feet dangling, and to Charlotte's amazement, Oliver began to sing quietly. It was the "Skye Boat Song." He knew all the words; Ariadne joined him on the second chorus. Charlotte recognized the lilting, wistful tune and hummed with them softly.

"Burned are our homes,/ exile and death/ Scatter the loyal men,/ Yet ere the sword/ cool in the sheath,/ Charlie will come again," sang Oliver.

The last notes faded. After a silence, Oliver said, "You're right. You can't carry a tune, can you?"

Apologetically Ariadne shook her head. "Ewen used to say I could only stay with them if I promised not to sing.

But you've got a really good voice, Oliver. You sing better than Ewen. I'm not kidding. Maybe you should hook up with Graham and Nick—you could take Ewen's place."

"That's the only Scottish song I know," said Oliver. He smiled a little. "I wonder what Paula would do if I became an itinerant folksinger? It might almost be worth it." He glance at his watch and sighed. "And speaking of Paula, I can't put it off any longer. I'll use the phone in your room."

With more discretion than Charlotte would have given her credit for, Ariadne shut herself in the bathroom when they got back. "Do you want me to go away, too?" asked Charlotte as he settled himself by the phone. Oliver shook his head. "Just sit there and be quiet, that's all." He dialed the operator and told her he wanted to make a collect call—"Otherwise they'll wonder why I'm not feeding money in"—and waited. Charlotte found she was holding her breath, and made herself let it go. Her heart had begun to skip a little.

"Hello, Paula?" said Oliver. "Yes, it's me. I'm calling you from—"

Charlotte heard the voice at the other end, made tiny by distance like something seen through the wrong end of a telescope. The words were too small to be distinguished, but the tone—

"I left you a note. Didn't you find it? I left it—"

"Listen, Paula—"

She noticed Oliver's face had frozen. The fingers gripping the receiver had tightened so she could see the tendons in the back of his hand. Her heart began to thud.

"Yes."

"There's nothing to worry about. We're in Scotland."

"No, I am not." His voice was flat, expressionless.

Something was dreadfully wrong. What? What could it be? How did Paula know he wasn't in Wales?

"Near Aberdeen."

"How did you find out about Charlotte?"

"We're in Cullen. It's a village on the northeast coast, near Elgin."

There was silence. Oliver was silent, and the receiver was silent, but the air was charged, and he wouldn't look at her. Instead, he stared fixedly at an invisible spot on the carpet. Charlotte felt as if she were suffocating. Her heart had swollen in her chest until there was no room for her lungs.

"Airports?" said Oliver.

"But *why?* We're perfectly all right. I told you. We'll come back to London on our own; we'll fly, if that's what you want—"

"But you don't—"

"This isn't her fault."

"Yes."

He took a deep breath, then looked at Charlotte. "Here. She wants to talk to you."

"Me?" Charlotte's voice was a squeak. She cleared her throat painfully. "But Oliver—"

He held the receiver out to her. "Go on, Charlotte."

She felt sick. The plastic was warm and damp from his grip. Reluctantly she put it to her ear. She was paralyzed; she didn't know what to say.

"Now you have to speak into it, Charlotte," said Oliver savagely.

She glared at him. A healthy surge of indignation reanimated her. "Hello? Mrs. Preston?"

"Charlotte, thank heaven! Are you all right?"

"Yes. I'm fine."

"Thank heaven," said Paula again. "I'll call your parents and tell them. I'm sure they're worried sick about you, even though they tried not to show it. I simply cannot imagine what possessed him. I just can't—I told Oliver that we'll fly up to Scotland tomorrow on the first flight we can get. We should be in—in—wherever it is you are by afternoon. You just stay there in the meantime and—what, Eric? Well, how should I—? Yes, of course. Charlotte? Where are you?"

"In Cullen."

"I know that. I mean where in Cullen?"

Her mind went blank. "A hotel. Um." There was a matchbook in the ashtray. "The Seafield Arms Hotel. I don't know the address."

"Never mind that, we'll find it. I'm sure it can't be—"

Something made Charlotte add quickly, "Oliver's not staying here. He's around the corner in a bed-and-breakfast place. I'm sharing the room with a friend."

There was a moment's silence at the other end, then Paula said carefully, "A friend?"

"Yes. A girl we met in Aberdeen." She couldn't bring herself to say Ariadne. Instead, she babbled on. "She's an American, and she's been studying at the university. Actually, she's from Wellesley, and—"

"All right, Charlotte. I see. Would you put Oliver back on again, please?"

Released, she handed the phone back. She felt suddenly boneless.

"Yes," said Oliver. Then, "No . . . I don't think there are any. Not here. But—yes, I'll check, but I don't—yes, I told you. The number's 054-841326." Then he hung up, and they sat there, perfectly still. Charlotte imagined this was how it must feel to be vacuum-packed, like a pound of coffee, to have all the air sucked out of the space around you.

The bathroom door opened and Ariadne stuck here head around it. She had unfastened the barrette and her hair, given its freedom, sprang out around her face like Medusa's snakes, wild and dangerous. "Okay, you guys?" She glanced from Charlotte to Oliver and back. "What's the matter?"

"Everything," said Charlotte melodramatically. Oliver seemed not to notice Ariadne.

"Um." She frowned and went over to sit on the bed next to Charlotte. She was wearing a voluminous cotton slip and hugging the shapeless moss-colored pullover around herself. "It's not like I'm prying or anything, but—"

Oliver shook himself like a dog coming out of the water. "Well, that's that. At least I've got tomorrow." Abruptly he stood up.

"But how did she *know*, Oliver? How did your mother know?"

"Because your parents called last night, that's how."

"Last night?"

"They were having dinner in Cambridge with Max and Jean and Deb and Skip. And they thought, 'Wouldn't it be fun to call Charlotte so we can *all* talk to her.' Paula and Eric had only just gotten in when the phone rang."

"This is really confusing," said Ariadne. "I mean—"

Oliver ignored her, and Charlotte wished she'd go back into the bathroom. Oliver said, "I'm supposed to be at Captain MacPherson's house at nine-thirty."

"But if they're coming, how can you?"

"They won't get here until late afternoon, Charlotte. What's the point in wasting the day hanging around the hotel lobby? I might as well do what I came for, as much as I can. Shall I stop by for you in the morning?"

She opened her mouth to say yes, then shut it; she thought of Mrs. McCaig and the canary in its cage, and the dark little front room, and having to sit quietly for hours while Oliver and Captain MacPherson talked and talked. "I don't know."

He shrugged. "I'll stop, and if you aren't ready, I'll go without you."

Seventeen

"It must be pretty bad, huh?" said Ariadne when he'd gone.

"It's a mess," said Charlotte bitterly. "It was going to be a mess no matter what, but now it's going to be a mess tomorrow." *And it's Oliver's fault,* she added to herself. He ought to have stayed to talk this out with her instead of deserting her, but of course he'd never discuss their situation with Ariadne present. And that was Charlotte's fault, for being a soft-hearted patsy. She was frustrated, and angry at all three of them. She blinked and found Ariadne giving her a long, thoughtful look. "Hey, Charlotte. You and Oliver—you weren't running away together or anything, were you?"

"Running away?" Charlotte stared at her blankly. "What do you—you don't mean—?" Words failed her.

"Yeah, I do, but you don't seem exactly, you know, the type?"

"I'm not!" exclaimed Charlotte. "I'm not old enough. I'm nowhere *near* old enough!" That was what Mrs. Sinclair must have thought—

"You must be, like, seventeen?"

"Sixteen. But that's not what I mean. Look, Ariadne, I don't want to talk about this, all right? I just don't. I'm going to bed." She ended the conversation definitively by going into the bathroom and closing the door. She felt utterly used up. The day had been one of violent extremes and terribly complicated. Everything to do with Oliver was always complicated.

Pat Schuyler, at heart an unquenchable optimist, claimed that sometimes, if you went to sleep thinking about a problem, you'd wake up knowing how to solve it. Your brain would gnaw away at it while you were unconscious, and spit out the answer when you opened your eyes in the morning. If Pat was right, Charlotte realized as soon as she woke that this was not one of those times. She floated up out of a deep, dreamless sleep Tuesday morning to find the sky outside the window pale with early sun. In the bed beside her, Ariadne was curled under the covers; it looked as if someone had left a smallish gold-brown haystack on the pillow. Charlotte lay looking at nothing for a few minutes, wishing she could go back to sleep and postpone the day. Such a wish meant she was already too wide awake.

By the time Charlotte had washed and dressed, choosing the most respectable outfit in her limited wardrobe, Ariadne was uncurling, yawning, stretching, raking her fingers through her hair. The first thing she said was, "I hope they have good breakfasts here. I can't believe I'm so hungry! I never used to eat anything until lunchtime, you know? I mean, all you do between supper and breakfast is *sleep* for pete's sake! Maybe it has something to do with Ziggy, do you think?"

"Ziggy?"

"Yeah." Smiling, she patted her stomach. "I decided I have to call it something to kind of help me get used to thinking about it. But I don't know what it is, so I can't use a boy's name or a girl's name, and when I was in the bathtub yesterday I started talking to it. And Ziggy's what came out. You don't think I'll screw it up or anything doing that?" She disappeared into the bathroom without waiting for Charlotte's answer. When she came out again, sometime later, mostly dressed, she said, "I was kind of hoping I'd know exactly what I should do when I woke up. That's the way it happens for some people, you know? But I guess I'm not one of them."

"No," said Charlotte, plunged in gloom, "neither am I."

Ariadne came and sat down, facing Charlotte. "Okay. Be honest. Would it be easier if I just got lost? I've got all my stuff together. I could clear out right away after breakfast and leave you and Oliver alone. He didn't want me coming, anyway—I could tell that in Aberdeen. I guess he wasn't too happy with you. I thought about not turning up at the bus station, but I was really kind of desperate. I had to have somebody to talk to so I decided I'd pretend I just didn't notice. Anyway, last night? I guess you must have convinced him to invite me, and it felt so good, just being with friends."

"It was Oliver's idea." She wished Ariadne would shut up; she didn't want to feel responsibility for her.

"Yeah, but I bet it was because of you. So now you've got your own problems and it's not like you can do anything about mine. It's up to me to figure this out."

Reluctantly, Charlotte said, "But where would you go?"

Araidne shrugged. "Probably back to Aberdeen, even with Joyce gone. At least it's a place I know. And there's lots of time left—Ziggy isn't due for another six months. That's not until *December.* Who knows what'll happen by then?"

Obviously Ariadne's notion of time was different from her own. With an effort, Charlotte pulled her scrambled wits together. "I think we should talk about this over breakfast, okay?"

But they didn't work their way around to serious discussion until they'd nearly finished; Charlotte felt an immense reluctance to become enmeshed. Finally, fixing her with an earnest gaze, Ariadne leaned across the litter of smeared and crumby plates. "You know, Charlotte, maybe you ought to go with Oliver? Maybe he really wants you there, but he doesn't want to say?"

Charlotte shook her head. "He only needed me to get here, before he knew what he was going to find. He won't care whether I'm there or not today," she said matter-of-factly. "He didn't yesterday. Once they started talking I could have been back home in Concord for all the notice he took."

"Did you mind?"

"It's what he came here for, so I shouldn't." She hesitated, then said honestly, "But, yeah, I do mind. I don't like being forgotten."

"I know what you mean. I bet Ewen hasn't thought even once about me since he took off with her. I sort of hoped that by not telling him I was going—you know, after the concert? I sort of hoped I'd make him sorry. He'd look around and say, 'Hey, where's Ariadne?' I guess I knew it wouldn't work that way, though. And, anyway, I don't care. He's not worth it. I just wish he could *know* I don't care. I want him to realize I'm not heartbroken or anything."

Half-listening to her, Charlotte suddenly realized something. "I don't want you to leave."

Ariadne thrust her hair back with her long fingers. "Really? Cross your heart? Are you sure, or are you just saying that?"

"And hope to die," replied Charlotte. "I'm sure." She wasn't going with Oliver, she knew that, and she didn't see how she could survive the day alone. Besides, she had told Paula about Ariadne; if she didn't produce her, Paula would think Charlotte had invented her so that things would sound better than they actually were. What exactly Paula would make of Ariadne was another matter. "You know," she went on, compelled to be more or less straight with Ariadne, "when Oliver's mother gets here, it's likely to be pretty awful. Paula's very upset with us. I expect we'll leave first thing tomorrow, unless—if they have a car, they might want to go straight back to Aberdeen tonight."

"Well, that's okay with me," said Ariadne. "I mean, even if I haven't got all the answers, I feel much better than I did before. I've kind of got my balance again. And if you're not going with Oliver, then we have until this afternoon before the roof caves in. We might as well enjoy it, right? The sun's even shining."

Charlotte left a note for Oliver at the desk, not that he'd probably stop to ask. He'd look around, see she wasn't there, and go on by himself. But she told him, in case he bothered to inquire, that she and Ariadne were spending the day sightseeing, and they'd be back between three and four. Sightseeing sounded like such a casual, lighthearted occupation.

"I don't see how they can possibly get here before four," she said as she and Ariadne left the hotel. "They're coming from London."

"You know," said Ariadne, "I guess I'm not completely sure who *they* are. I mean, it could be the Mafia or the FBI."

"Worse. They're Oliver's mother and Eric, her husband. At least I think he's coming, too—she said 'we.'"

"Would that be good or bad, if he came? I mean, if both my parents came to get me, I'd know I was in deep trouble."

"I'm not sure. I think Eric's pretty reasonable, and he's not as involved as Paula because Oliver isn't his son, so maybe it's good. Or at least better. But I've only ever met Eric once, and it's hard to tell exactly how Oliver feels about him."

"Yeah," said Ariadne ambiguously. Before Charlotte could figure out what she meant by that, she went on, "But what I don't understand is, if you weren't running away, then how come his mother didn't know where you were?"

Charlotte stopped, studying a shop window full of beach toys: balls, spades, buckets, bright plastic boats, and cheap sandals. A green inflatable sea monster with curly painted eyelashes smiled coyly at her from under a straw hat.

"You don't have to tell me if you don't want to," said Ariadne, withdrawing behind her hair. "I mean, it's none of my business."

"It isn't that." Charlotte sighed. "I'm not sure I can sort it out."

"If you want to try, I'll listen," offered Ariadne. "I used to listen to Ewen for hours and hours. Half the time I didn't even know what he was talking about. But you know? I don't think he did, either. After he'd had two or three beers, he'd just start talking and he'd go on and on. What a lot of time I wasted on Ewen! What a jerk I've been, you know? I bet *she* doesn't listen to him. I don't think she listens to anybody. Where do you want to go?"

"I don't really care."

"Okay, what about the beach, then? That's a good place to talk—like in Aberdeen—only it's a whole lot warmer here. Start with how you got to Scotland."

They headed down the street toward the harbor, under the stone arch of the railway viaduct, and Charlotte told Ariadne about her graduation present, and why she'd gotten it a year early, but then she realized that was nowhere near the beginning of the story, and the rest wouldn't make sense unless she explained how she'd gotten to know Oliver in the first place, when he'd come as a last resort to live with his great-uncle in Concord. Even though he was nearly two years older, he'd had such a checkered history at schools that he'd been put into Charlotte's junior-high school class in the middle of the year. He had no friends; he didn't try to make any. But then, Charlotte remembered, neither had she. A late, unplanned baby, she'd been the youngest in her family by thirteen years, and her best and only close friend at that point was her twenty-five-year-old brother, Eliot. She'd had to start growing up before she realized how generous Eliot had been to share his life so thoroughly with a much younger sister.

Oliver had appeared in Concord just at the time when Eliot announced he was going to graduate school in Montana. Charlotte, bruised and angry, felt abandoned.

"Yeah," said Ariadne. "When my brother Ryan left home that was really hard. Not because we got along so well, but as long as he was around my parents kind of ignored me. As soon as he was gone, well"—she made a sour little face—"So anyway, it doesn't seem to me like Oliver would be really easy to get to know."

"He's not," agreed Charlotte. "It was accidental. A friend of Commodore Shattuck's came to Concord that year for Patriots' Day, to prove the British could have won the battle at the Old North Bridge. In the end there was a tremendous snowball fight and it was a draw. There were these two other kids as well, twins—Andy and Kath Schuyler. We all got involved and somehow we all got to be friends. Oliver's great-uncle had a lot to do with it." She lapsed into silence, remembering.

After a few minutes, Ariadne said, "He must be all right—Oliver's great-uncle?"

Charlotte nodded. "Actually it's his friend we came here to visit—Captain MacPherson. Oliver wanted to talk to him about the Commodore."

"Well, but what I don't understand is where did Oliver's mother come from? I mean, if he was living with this uncle—"

"The Commodore died."

"Oh."

"Paula decided Oliver should live with her after that. She'd married Eric Preston by then—"

"Eric Preston?" Ariadne screwed up her face quizzically. "That name sounds kind of familiar."

"He's a television reporter."

"*That* Eric Preston? Oh, wow. That's Oliver's stepfather? I never think of somebody like that being real, you know? I mean having a wife and a stepson and problems, just like ordinary people. So, what's he like? Is he nice?"

"I told you, I hardly know him. I only met him once when Oliver's great-uncle died. They came to London right after that."

"Okay, so you came to visit, right? They invited you. So why don't they know you're here?"

"Because at the last minute, Eric had to go to Germany on an assignment and Oliver's mother went with him, and Oliver was supposed to call and explain, and I was supposed to change my ticket for a later one."

"You mean he didn't tell you? So you didn't know until you got here? Oh, wow."

They had reached the bottom of the hill. The tide was out and the little harbor was nearly dry, the few boats in it stranded on the sand, tipped at awkward angles, out of their element. The sun poured warmth over Cullen out of a hazy sky, and the bay twitched lazily, like a blue-green sea horse irritated by the cruising gulls. They sat on the seawall, as they had the evening before, but nothing was the same. It was like when the Commodore died: once their parents knew, they lost control. Charlotte tried to explain to Ariadne about Captain MacPherson, and why it was so urgent for Oliver to come and talk to him. She wanted to convince them both that he'd done it for a real reason, not just to spite his mother.

"Mmm." Ariadne chewed the inside of her cheek thoughtfully. "See, Charlotte, the trouble with someone like Oliver is that he's so focused. He figures that what he's doing is the most important thing in the world, and he expects everybody else to understand. It's not like he's impulsive or anything. I mean, he thinks about what he's doing, but he doesn't worry about consequences because he's so positive he's right."

Slowly, Charlotte nodded, wondering how Ariadne could possibly know him so well.

As if reading her thoughts, Ariadne continued, "My father's like that. When they got married I'm pretty sure Mummy believed it was true, that whatever he wanted should come first because it mattered more than anything else. More than anything *she* wanted. Now she just pretends she believes it, but she doesn't. She spends her whole life acting, you know. When I was about fourteen I finally understood that. Underneath, she's just this really angry person. You know those pictures they show you in school? The ones that are supposed to scare you off smoking?"

"Smoking?" Charlotte missed the connection.

"Yeah. How your lungs would look if you smoked a pack a day—all black and yucky? Well, see, I think that's what Mummy looks like inside. I think that's what anger does to you if you don't ever let it out—if you live with it bottled up all the time. It sort of rots you."

"But I'm not angry," protested Charlotte. "I mean, I get mad sometimes—everybody does."

"Oliver's angry," said Ariadne. "He's angry with his mother, isn't he?"

Charlotte said nothing.

"So anyway, what's going to happen? I mean, when they get here?"

"I expect they'll send me home. I was supposed to stay another week, but I'm sure Paula won't want me now."

"And what about your parents? What'll they do?"

"I don't know. I'm really afraid . . ." Charlotte's voice trailed away. She was unwilling to put words to her fears.

"They might say you can't see Oliver again, after this. Right?" Ariadne had no such inhibition.

To the west the broad, toast-colored beach curved around toward the distant headland. Already the shore was dotted with figures. People bobbed in the waves and splashed in the shallows, lay stretched flat on blankets or sat with dignity in folding chairs, played ball, built forts, walked, ran, tottered. It all looked idyllic and carefree—an illustration for a holiday brochure: Come to sunny Scotland for the holiday of a lifetime. . . .

A lifetime. It would be three years before Oliver was legally independent; five years before Charlotte was twenty-one. Under ordinary circumstances, Charlotte didn't mind—she scarcely gave it a thought. Her parents' rules generally seemed fair and reasonable. Occasionally she chafed under them, but mostly she was grateful because they gave her a secure, familiar place to which she could return when the world seemed shifty and dangerous. Her parents' rules were like a bungee cord: elastic up to a point—the point beyond which it would be disastrous to fall. Then they jerked her back. Except maybe this time. This was a big thing she and Oliver had done. Would her parents really forbid her to see—possibly even to write to—Oliver? And if they did, would she obey? What would happen when he came back to the house in Concord his great-uncle had left him? Perhaps, as his guardian, Paula could make him sell it if she thought that was best. Then he would truly never forgive her, Charlotte knew. He would be like Ariadne's mother inside. . . .

"Oh, come on," said Ariadne. "Let's not just sit here—let's do something. Look at all those funny little houses over there—it's like a pretend village. Do you think they're real?"

Charlotte welcomed the distraction. They crossed the wide road behind the seawall and entered a maze of narrow streets. Ariadne's pretend village was packed densely into a rough oval, contained by the bay on one side, and, on the other, by the steep rise of land on which the rest of Cullen had been built. The low stone houses were joined together in curving rows like Siamese quadruplets or octuplets, their slate and orange tile roofs fretted with dormer windows and chimney pots. Their deeply recessed doors opened right on the street and were painted bright reds, blues, sharp white, or glossy black. Tubs of marigolds and hanging planters splashed color on the stone.

Ariadne was enchanted. "Oh, wow. This is so neat, Charlotte. Don't you just love it?"

Charlotte was used to living in a house with space around it: grass, trees, privacy. "Well, it's pretty," she said, "but it seems kind of public—"

"I bet it's a real community—where everybody knows everybody else and they all help out? I mean, you'd never be alone in a place like this."

"No, you wouldn't," agreed Charlotte dubiously.

"I need to have people around me," said Ariadne. "It's not that I have to be with them all the time or anything—I just need to know they're there. Look at this one—it's got a little garden in back. Isn't it perfect?"

"I don't think we should go down there." Charlotte hung back at the mouth of a little passageway, feeling shy. Ariadne had no such doubt.

"I'm sure nobody minds. I just want to see what it's like—I'm not hurting anything. They must have a baby."

Above the wooden fence, Charlotte saw diapers—lots of diapers—hanging limply from a clothesline.

"You know, if I had a house like this, I'd be so happy. There'd be just room for Ziggy and me, and I could have a kitten. I've always wanted a kitten. I'd have everything just how I wanted it and I'd learn to cook and there'd be lots of other kids for Ziggy to play with. They'd all want to come to our house and I'd bake cookies. There'd always be cookies, homemade ones, not the bought kind."

Pulling her back onto the street, Charlotte said, "But how would you live, Ariadne? You need money."

"I'd get a job. I'm not afraid of work, you know. There's got to be things I can do in a town like this. I'm going to have to get a job anyway, somewhere. Why not here? I could be a waitress, or I could clean rooms in a hotel. You don't need a degree for that."

Ariadne sounded so hopeful, so unrealistic, that Charlotte couldn't bear it. "You can't possibly stay here—you don't know anyone. There aren't any houses for sale and you couldn't buy one if there were."

Ariadne leaned back against a warm stone wall; red and white roses lifted their blowsy heads above it, adding spice to the salt air, and gulls mewed. "Oh, Charlotte, I know all that. Don't you ever daydream? When I was really little, I had this playhouse. It had windows and a door that opened and everything. I used to pretend I lived there with my baby. Well, now I've got the baby for real, so I'm pretending about the house, that's all."

A young woman, not much older than Ariadne, came around the corner pushing a baby carriage. Its occupant was screaming with rage, face blotched and bunched as if it had been left too long in hot water. The woman seemed oblivious; her expression said she'd heard it all before. She went right on pushing, past Ariadne and Charlotte, around the next corner. The baby's screeches mingled with the gulls' cries.

In another few months, thought Charlotte, that will be Ariadne. I would be terrified. "What happens when the baby's born? Have you thought of that? You won't be able to work because you won't be able to leave it alone."

"But see, Charlotte, I won't have to. When it's little I can take it with me in one of those cot-things. Babies just lie there—they can't walk or anything, right? Once in a while you feed them, and mostly they sleep."

"And you change them and they cry," Charlotte pointed out.

But Ariadne was confident. "Not Ziggy. Ziggy's not going to have any reason to cry. I'm just going to love this baby so much. You know, I was thinking if I worked in a hotel I bet I could have a room there. It wouldn't have to be anything fancy to start out—it could be in the attic."

"Ariadne, aren't you at all scared?"

Ariadne bent forward, pulling her hair around her face, hiding in it. "You want to know when I was really scared? When I was in Aberdeen and I met you on the beach, that's when. I mean, I kind of panicked a little when I found out about it—when I knew for sure it wasn't a mistake. But then I thought it would be okay because I was still with Ewen. I just assumed that once I told him, he'd instantly want this baby. That was really dumb. He wouldn't have. See, I have been thinking about this. I didn't try to get pregnant or anything. I know there are women who do, just to hang on to some man." She lifted her head and gave Charlotte a direct, challenging look. "That's why I didn't tell Ewen, okay? I didn't want anybody thinking I was blackmailing him into staying. So, anyway, if I didn't try to get pregnant on purpose and it just happened, then well, I figure it was meant to. Why shouldn't I have this baby?"

So many reasons crowded Charlotte's head, she didn't know where to begin.

"I know it'll work out, Charlotte, really it will. And in the meantime I've decided I can't worry. I read somewhere about your mental attitude affecting the baby before it's even born. Well, I don't want that happening to Ziggy. I've got to be really positive from now on."

They began walking again, without any real purpose. "You aren't really serious about looking for a job here, are you?" asked Charlotte.

"I don't know—I might. I mean, if I can find one, this would be a really good place for a baby—all this fresh air and the beach to play on."

"I'll bet it looks different in the winter," predicted Charlotte.

"Yeah. You're probably right. I hate being cold."

"I really don't see how you can do this by yourself," said Charlotte after a while. "Couldn't you go home—just until the baby's born?"

"No. I told you."

"They'd take care of you."

"I'll take care of myself." Ariadne didn't sound angry, just stubborn.

Charlotte thought of her sister-in-law, Jean, almost eight months pregnant with Hilary's brother-to-be. Jean was bulky, awkward, usually tired. She had lots of help and support: her husband, Max; Charlotte and

Deb; Charlotte's parents. She didn't have to work; her part-time salary certainly made life easier, but without it she and Max could manage. Since Hilary's birth, five years earlier, they had put together enough money to buy the gray frame house on Tieman Street in Cambridge, where they had lived since getting married. Now they rented the top floor to an MIT instructor, his wife, and three-year-old son, with whom they swapped advice, chicken pox, tales of disaster, child care, and equipment. Max was planning to be with Jean when the baby was born. Hilary would stay in Concord with her grandparents and Aunt Charlotte. There was a whole, close, protective web spread around Jean, to encourage and take care of her. Ariadne had no such web. Feeling desperate, Charlotte wondered how, in the little bit of time they had left, she could convince Ariadne this was not something she could do alone.

"You know, I hate to say it"—Ariadne broke in on Charlotte's thoughts—"but I'm going to have to find a john. I think I remember seeing one by the harbor."

Eighteen

By the time they found the public conveniences it was nearly midday. Ariadne suggested they walk back to the middle of town and buy supplies for a picnic. The man in the market who cut them a lump of yellow cheddar advised taking their lunch up Castle Hill, from where they'd have an excellent view, and drew a little map.

At the bench in the market square they stopped to divide their provisions. "We'll never eat it all," said Charlotte, packing oranges and Ry-Krisp into her haversack.

"I bet we will. I'm, like, starving again. I don't know what happened to breakfast. Maybe we could open the shortbread right now—so I don't faint before we get to this Castle Hill?"

Charlotte was rooting in her bag for it when Ariadne gave a sudden gulping hiccup. Charlotte felt her strong bony fingers bite painfully into her upper arm. "What? What is it?"

"Look!"

Alarmed, Charlotte glanced around. Paula and Eric—her first thought. But Ariadne had never set eyes on Paula and had only seen Eric on television, where he looked quite different than in person. She followed Ariadne's gaze and saw nothing out of the ordinary, only people on the pavement, minding their own business and paying no attention to the two of them. The bus they'd arrived on the day before stood panting asthmatically with its door open, waiting to lumber off to Elgin.

"I don't see anything."

"The van—the *van*."

There was an elderly tan VW bus parked by the curb on the other side of the square. It was the only van Charlotte could see, except for a red one with ROYAL MAIL painted on it. "So?"

"It's the van—you know, *theirs*. Oh, jeez. What should I do?"

"Ariadne, what are you talking about?" asked Charlotte crossly.

"I told you I left that note with Joyce, about coming here with friends?"

"You mean The Travellers? Are you sure?"

"I guess *I* ought to know that van. I rode in it a million times. I even slept in it. Oh, wow. I really didn't think they'd come—" Her face flamed with hope.

"They'd want to return the stuff you left behind in Edinburgh," Charlotte pointed out cautiously.

"Yeah, but they could've just given it to Joyce. I mean, they didn't have to drive all the way up here looking for me. Help me, Charlotte, what'm I going to say? He must've changed his mind after all."

Charlotte felt a chilly little draft on the back of her neck. Ariadne was electric. "But you don't know—"

"There's Nick! See?" Instinctively she mashed at her hair; it ignored her.

Nick was the dark one, the short one with the powerful shoulders and the fierce tribal beard. He stumped across the square, brows pulled low over his eyes, fists stuck deep in the pockets of his scuffed leather jacket, heading for the van. His narrow, dusty jeans revealed him to be slightly bowlegged. He looked as if he'd flatten anyone who got in his way. "Um," said Charlotte, "he seems angry about something."

"Angry?" Ariadne sounded surprised. "No, I don't think so—hey, Nick!"

He swung around, scowling. "So here you are. We came looking for you."

It sounded like a threat to Charlotte, but Ariadne said joyfully, "That's what I guessed when I saw the van."

"Why'd you do a gyte thing like that? Not a word to anyone, and all your belongings left behind." He shot a suspicious glance at Charlotte. "And who's she?"

Ariadne linked her arm through Charlotte's. "She's my friend."

"Oh, aye? So what'd you do it for then? Take off that way?"

Thrusting out her chin, Ariadne replied, "I just didn't think there was any point in hanging around, okay?"

"Well, Graham's been that bothered. He won't think

of anything else until he's seen you."

"What about Ewen?"

"Ewen's gone off to bloody London, hasn't he?"

The light went out of Ariadne's face. "Yeah. Right. So it's just you and Graham?"

"Me and Graham, that's it. Ewen cleared off with Deirdre O'Donnell. You heard him. Stupid beggar."

Ariadne let go of Charlotte and folded onto the bench. Charlotte asked sharply, "Are you all right?"

From the depths of her hair, Ariadne said faintly, "Yeah, I'm fine. I just need a minute, okay? Jeez, was that dumb, or what? I don't know why I did that. Hey, Charlotte?"

All that brave talk about Ewen and how little he mattered had been just that: talk. Charlotte's heart cramped with sympathy. "What?" She sat down beside Ariadne.

"I'm okay—really. But would you mind getting my stuff for me?"

Nick stood over them, scratching furiously at his beard, looking angry and uncomfortable.

Charlotte said, "I think maybe Ariadne needs to lie down."

"Aye, well, wait for Graham at least, will you? He won't leave until he's seen you," he said, ignoring Charlotte.

"What good will it do? I mean, there's nothing to say."

Being ignored again made Charlotte irritable. Nick hadn't even looked at her since he'd asked Ariadne who she was. "Why don't you just leave her stuff at the hotel up the street there. We'll get it later. We were just on our way—"

"Hang on, hang on—look, here he comes!" exclaimed Nick in obvious relief. "Hi, Graham!"

A large, slightly bulky figure had appeared around the gents' end of the public toilets, hitching up his pants. His face broke into a worried smile at the sight of them. "Och, Claudia! I thought we'd missed you again, lass."

"Well? So you haven't." Ariadne's face was pale but determined.

"You never said you were going—by the time we'd got out of the crush, you'd vanished. We hung around in case, then Nick said you'd be off to Aberdeen, sure."

Close by, without Ewen to dazzle her, Charlotte could see the resemblance clearly. She'd missed it earlier because although they shared the same very blue eyes and sandy hair, everything about Ewen said "Look at me!": his face, his clothes, the way he stood with his head back, straight and smooth and confident. Graham was older, baggier, more worn around the edges. The skin under his eyes was a little pouchy and his hair was slipping backward and he was slightly round-shouldered.

"You shouldn't have worried," said Ariadne. "I'm okay, really. I met some friends."

"If I had two minutes alone with Ewen I'd wring his neck for him, so I would."

"You and who else?" said Nick.

"Yeah, okay, so he might've said something first," said Ariadne, "but if it was what he wanted, why shouldn't he go? This is a big chance for him. We weren't, like, serious or anything, Graham. We had a good time while it lasted, so now it's over. It's okay. I can deal with that."

"It's my fault," said Graham glumly. "I'm the one asked her along with us in the first place. But I never thought she'd split us up, never. She was down on her luck, alone in Glasgow—"

"Ach, you always were a soft bugger," growled Nick. "Anyway, it's done. Just let go of it, will you? It isn't what's happened that's important now, it's what we're going to do about it."

"Right," said Ariadne. "What are you going to do without Ewen? I've been, like, worrying about *you*."

"We haven't figured that out yet," said Graham.

"We have," declared Nick, glaring at him.

Graham sighed and pushed at his hair. No wonder it was slipping, thought Charlotte. "It won't be the same, Nick."

"Aye, and isn't that the point, man! I've said it and I've said it, we don't need Ewen. We're better off without him, him and his Celtic twilight crap. You ken as well as I do that stuff he'd started writing was rubbish. Sons o' the heather—what a load of old—"

"But people like it, Nick. They ask for it."

"Because they don't know any better. It's up to us to educate them. I keep telling you, you daft bannock."

"I'll bet you could," said Ariadne. "I mean, just the two of you, you know?"

"There, see? It's better than painting bloody houses."

"It's not a bad job," said Graham in self-defense. "It's steady work—there are always houses need painting."

"Don't be gyte, man. You're a musician."

Graham pushed at his hair again. "I'm not as sure as you are about that, Nick."

"You're better than Ewen."

This seemed to be the middle of a long, continuous argument. Charlotte felt superfluous. "Ariadne? I think I'll go back to the hotel."

"Now?" They all stared at her. "But what about our picnic? We were going to have a picnic," Ariadne explained to Nick and Graham. "We bought all this food for lunch."

"It's a nice day for a picnic," observed Graham.

"Aye, so let's get away and leave them to it then," said Nick. "It's miles to Oban." He started purposefully toward the van.

"Oban?" said Ariadne. "Jeez, I remember when we all went there, and we stayed in that funny little cottage with the attic? Is that where you're going? It had a really good aura, you know? You could, like, feel it. There wasn't any electricity, only these oil lamps and this big old stove, and you could walk right out the back door onto these rocks and there was the sea. The air smelled so good. I really loved it there." Her eyes had gotten dreamy.

"Um," said Graham, glancing after Nick. "Why don't we all have a picnic?"

Nick turned. He and Charlotte looked at Graham in dismay. Ariadne said, "You mean the four of us? Well, why not. That's all right, isn't it, Charlotte?"

Nick said, "It's getting late."

Graham shrugged. "What does it matter? We're not

expected anywhere—we canceled the other two gigs and there's no one waiting in Oban."

"We only bought enough food for two," said Charlotte, aware that she sounded mean.

"That's easy—we can fix that. You and Claudia stay here while we get something, then we'll go off in the van. Come on, Nick."

Giving Charlotte and Ariadne a sour look, Nick followed Graham down the street.

"Why does he keep calling you Claudia?" asked Charlotte.

Ariadne leaned back against the bench and stuck her legs out, studying the scuffed toes of her boots. "I guess because that's the name on my passport."

"Your real name? Claudia?" So Oliver had been right.

"That depends on what you mean by real, though, doesn't it? I mean, it's the name my parents gave me when I was born, but how could they, like, know who I'd be?"

"Well, they had to call you something," Charlotte pointed out. "Claudia's a whole lot better than Baby X or Kiddo. In fact, it's not bad at all. There's lots worse."

"But it's not who I *am*, Charlotte. Not now. So why should I be stuck with it for the rest of my life? Maybe I won't always be Ariadne, either, you know?"

"What about Ziggy? You aren't going to name the baby Ziggy, are you?"

"No, of course not!" Ariadne smiled at her. "Don't be silly. I'll just have to wait and see it, then I'll know what name to start with. But if she—or he—wants to be something different later on, well, that'll be okay, too. See, I believe names are really important. I mean, they have a lot to do with self-image—how you feel about yourself. What about you—are you happy being Charlotte? Is that the name you'd choose right now?"

"I never really thought about it," Charlotte admitted. "I don't know. Look, Ariadne, why don't you go off on this picnic with Graham and Nick and I'll go back to the hotel. I don't mind."

Ariadne sat up. "Oh, but you can't just leave me, Charlotte. What'll I tell them?"

"They won't care. They don't know me. You're the one they came to find. Nick doesn't want to have this picnic in the first place and Graham really wants to talk to you. It would be much easier if I—"

"I don't want to talk to Graham." Ariadne stuck her chin down. "I mean, I don't mind *talking* to him—just not about Ewen. It's all over with and I don't want to think about him anymore, ever. I need you to help—you've got to come. If you're worried about getting back here in time, we'll say we can't go very far. Okay?"

"Oh, shoot." Charlotte had forgotten all about getting back in time. Now that Ariadne had mentioned it, she knew Paula and Eric wouldn't go away. If she went back to the hotel by herself, she'd only spend the afternoon imagining what would happen when they arrived, digging herself into a pit of depression.

Graham and Nick were back so soon, Charlotte suspected Graham hadn't entirely trusted them to wait. He carried a paper bag and Nick had a large brown plastic bottle of beer. Charlotte eyed it uneasily. She and Ariadne climbed into the back of the van; Nick had taken possession of the passenger seat, and Graham levered himself in behind the wheel, pulling a tangle of keys out of his back pocket. "Just mind the guitars, will you?" warned Nick.

There were four guitars, and some smaller instrument cases; a pile of extra sweaters and rain jackets; a Scottish road atlas, dog-eared and stuck with bits of paper; a bag full of used paper coffee cups and biscuit wrappers; three pairs of worn leather boots and two pairs of muddy Wellingtons stuffed with socks; a box full of books, mostly paperback; a pair of cables for jump-starting an engine; a gasoline can and a powerful-looking electric lantern; several lengths of rope; two foam pads and two sleeping-bags, neatly rolled; a scuffed soccer ball and a small camp stove. At first glance the van seemed hopelessly cluttered, but as Charlotte made space for herself, she began to see an order to the clutter.

As they drove out of Cullen, she experienced a thrill of panicky excitement. What was she thinking of? Where was she going, and with whom? What if Graham simply kept driving? She had no idea where Oban was, and no one—except the people in the van—knew where *she* was. She chewed her lower lip, wondering whether she ought to say something, and if so, what? Leaning forward, Ariadne solved her dilemma. "Hey, Graham? Charlotte can't be away very long. She has to meet someone this afternoon, okay?"

"Charlotte?"

"Yeah, Charlotte. Oh, jeez, I'm sorry. This is Charlotte. I forgot to introduce you."

Graham's eyes shifted to Charlotte's face in the rearview mirror. She had the distinct feeling that he was noticing her for the first time. "I'm Graham," he said unnecessarily.

She nodded. "I know. I was at your concert in Edinburgh." She thought he ought to know that she understood at least some of what was going on. "It was really good. I loved the music," she added, thinking how dumb and inadequate that sounded. But Graham's mind was on other things. "Yeah, thanks."

"There," said Nick suddenly. "Try that." Graham swung the van left at a sign that said FINDLATER CASTLE. A gray Volvo and a motorcycle were parked in a small, rutted field. Graham stopped beside the Volvo and pulled out an old plaid blanket, and they carried their provisions down a farm track toward the sea. Findlater Castle was nothing but rugged heaps of mortared stone clinging to the cliff edge. A middle-aged couple was sitting stolidly on folding chairs, reading pieces of newspaper and drinking tea out of plastic mugs. Near the ruins, the couple off the motorcycle, in leathers, was standing entwined, crash helmets on the ground by their feet. Along the cliffs toward Cullen, small figures were strung out on a path. Somehow the presence of other people made Charlotte relax a little. Graham spread his blanket on the prickly turf, avoiding a pile of sheep droppings, and they arranged themselves on and around it. Although they had come to talk, no one seemed anxious to begin; instead they applied themselves with great concentration to lunch.

Nick and Graham had thick ham and cheese sandwiches and a large bag of potato chips as well as the bottle of beer, which Nick offered around. He did not seem offended when Charlotte and Ariadne declined. Charlotte's lemonade went off like a rocket when she opened it, covering her with sticky spray. She mopped herself off while Ariadne hacked clumsy chunks off the lump of cheese with a butter knife she took out of her shoulder bag. Charlotte noticed a TWA logo on the handle. Graham munched his way methodically through his sandwich, apparently deep in thought. Several times Charlotte looked up to find him regarding Ariadne, although she didn't seem to notice. He barely touched his paper cup of beer, while Nick barely touched his sandwich.

Charlotte took out her Swiss Army knife to cut the tomatoes before Ariadne could mangle them. Eliot had given her the knife for her thirteenth birthday. Being Eliot, he had chosen a knife covered with blades and tools, including a little ivory toothpick and a gadget he claimed was for taking stones out of horses' hooves, though Kath snorted when Charlotte showed it to her. Nick's eyes lit with interest and he asked to see it when she'd finished with the tomatoes. She wiped it and handed it over, and he opened it tool by tool. "I always wanted one of these."

"I didn't know that," said Graham, watching him. "I'd've got you one for Christmas."

Ariadne stood up, catching her foot on a fold of the blanket; she recovered her balance and wandered over toward the castle. Nick snapped the miniature scissors back into place and returned the knife. "It's a long way to

Oban, Graham. We'd better stretch our legs a wee bit first."

Graham glanced at Ariadne, then scrambled to his feet and went off after Nick in the opposite direction. Charlotte heard Nick say, "So now what're you going to do?" before they moved out of earshot.

A muscular little breeze drove in off the ocean, plastering Ariadne's skirt to her legs and pushing her hair back as she stood near the cliff edge gazing out to sea. She reminded Charlotte of the ships' figureheads at the National Maritime Museum in Greenwich. For a moment Charlotte considered joining her, but the blanket had been spread in a shallow depression, sheltered, and the sun laid a warm blessing on her, making her drowsy. Left on her own, she lay back and closed her eyes, seeing yellow-orange patterns through the lids. She wished there weren't so many things to worry about. If only she could let her mind blow empty and drift, like the gulls that rose and dipped on cushions of air.

"Um, Charlotte?"

She thought of pretending to be asleep. Actually, she must have been; she had no idea how long she'd been lying there, but she hadn't heard Graham return.

"I need to talk to you about Claudia."

"Ariadne, you mean," she said, her eyes still shut.

"Aye, well, Ariadne, then." The irony was clearly lost on him. With a sigh, she rolled over on her stomach and pushed herself upright, blinking against the glare. Nick was nowhere to be seen, and Ariadne was sitting on a piece of ruin, talking to a tall girl with long, straight blond hair and very short red shorts. Graham sat down heavily. "You know what I thought at first? She's gone after him, that's what she's done. Followed him to London. But Nick said no, even Claudia had more sense than that."

"Mmmm." Charlotte wasn't sure how to respond.

But Graham didn't expect a response. "Nick said she'd go to Aberdeen, that's where we'd find her. And he was right, but by the time we got there she'd left. Well, you know that, of course, don't you? Are you a friend of hers from university?"

"Me? Oh, no. We're not really friends—well, yes, we are, but I haven't known her all that long. Only since Sunday. To speak to, I mean. I saw her at the concert."

"Sunday?" He looked surprised. "Not day before yesterday?"

Charlotte nodded, marveling again at how long such a short time could feel. "I met her on the beach in Aberdeen—we were both out walking. She didn't remember me, but of course she wouldn't, would she? I mean, considering what happened—I remembered her because she sat next to our table while you were singing."

"How could I have been so thick?" he exclaimed. "Nick said she was making up to Ewen. He said she'd be trouble, right from the start he said it. And I should've listened. He's cannier about people than I am, is Nick."

"Ariadne?"

"Ach, no. Deirdre. Claudia's just lost, like most of the rest of us, trying to find her way. But Deirdre—" He pushed at his hair distractedly. "I felt sorry for her, see. We had a gig in Glasgow beginning of May, a weekend at this pub. We'd been the year before and they'd asked us back—we got good audiences. Anyway, it's the last night and Deirdre O'Donnell turns up. I know who she is because I've seen her with Payton Allen, and after the set we get to talking, just her and me. Ewen and Claudia'd gone off somewhere, and I don't know where Nick was. So she tells me she'd been touring the Borders with Payton and he's left her. Just like that, away off and no warning. She says she doesn't know what she's going to do next, she hasn't got enough money to get home on. So I say, why not come back with me and meet the others, Nick and Ewen, see what we can think of. No harm in that." He gave a humorless little laugh. "See what I mean? Thick. There I am thinking maybe she can come along with us for a wee while, just till she gets herself straight. She's got talent, even Nick'll admit that. He didn't like the idea much, I could see. But we talked him round. I never thought she'd do something like this to us." He sat, staring unhappily at his clasped hands.

"Ariadne told me Deirdre left Payton, not the other way around," said Charlotte. "She said he wasn't as good as Ewen."

"Aye. That's what Nick said as well. She'd her eye on Ewen from the start. Me, I'm that dim I really thought she needed help. If I ever get my hands on Ewen, he's the one'll be needing help."

"What'll you do without him?"

"Ach, we'll be okay, Nick and me, whatever we decide. It's Claudia I'm worried about. I'm not sure what to do."

"She doesn't blame you," said Charlotte, wanting to make him feel better. "She told me it wasn't serious with Ewen. She said—"

"Aye, I know what she says. D'you believe it?"

"Well—" Charlotte hedged. "It can't ever be easy to end a relationship, and to do it that way, in front of a crowd of strangers—"

He nodded sadly. "Aye. He's a right bugger, my brother Ewen. So what does she mean to do now, has she told you?"

Carefully, Charlotte said, "She hasn't decided yet. I've been trying to convince her to go home, back to Massachusetts."

"D'you think she will?" He sounded hopeful.

Charlotte shook her head regretfully. "That's what I'd do, but Ariadne doesn't get along with her parents."

"Aye, I thought as much. There's the aunt in Aberdeen?"

"No good. She's leaving Ariadne's uncle and going back to Pennsylvania in a few days."

"I knew there was something wrong there when we stopped. Ach, what a muddle!" He dropped his head in his hands and scrubbed fiercely at what was left of his hair. "I'd go down to London myself and drag Ewen back by the collar, only I think she's better off wi'out him, the good-for-nothing gowk. Well, one thing I'm sure of—she can't knock around on her own." He looked at Charlotte. "I'll put it to you straight. If I asked her, would she come with us, d'you think?"

"To Oban, you mean. Now?" Charlotte's brain whirred.

This was a possibility she hadn't considered. "She might. Yes."

Graham nodded, giving Charlotte a weary smile. She felt the weight of Ariadne's problem lift from her shoulders and realized how much she had dreaded leaving Ariadne by herself. "What about Nick, though. Will he mind?"

"Ach, no. Dinna fash yourself about Nick—he growls a lot but he doesna bite. He knows we canna turn our backs on Claudia. I'll have a wee talk with her."

He heaved himself up and ambled over to Ariadne. The girl in red shorts had left and Ariadne was sitting on the grass, leaning against the stones. Charlotte had a sudden revelation as she watched them. He's in love with her, she thought. Of course. But Ewen was the handsome, flashy one, eclipsing his older brother. Without Ewen to distract her, Ariadne would be able to see how kind and responsible Graham was. He'd take her away and look after her and she'd fall in love with him, and when the baby was born, Graham would adopt it. They'd be a family and live happily ever after.

"We should've gone straight to Oban," said Nick.

Charlotte, enveloped cozily in her fairy tale, jumped. In silence they watched Graham and Ariadne standing close together. They were too far away for Graham's voice to carry, but Ariadne's head was bowed and her arms were drawn tight across her chest.

"Ach, Graham lad, think what you're doing. She's not our problem," said Nick urgently, as if Graham could hear him.

"Ewen's his brother. He feels responsible," said Charlotte, immeasurably relieved.

"But he's not, is he? It's bloody Ewen," replied Nick morosely. "I'll tell you something. I wasna sorry to see the back o' Ewen Robertson, and that's the truth. He was ruining us wi' all that modern crap he wanted to sing. Now he's gone and we've got the chance to start over, Graham and me, just the two of us."

Ariadne raised her head and studied Graham's face. She nodded slowly. They both looked toward Charlotte and Nick, and Ariadne nodded again.

"She's going to have a baby, isn't she," said Nick.

Taken aback, Charlotte said, "How do you know?"

"She's got that look. I guessed as soon as I saw her. She's only herself to blame for being daft enough to get mixed up wi' Ewen. She's not the first, and I could've told her she'd no be the last. He changes like the weather."

Charlotte glanced at him, expecting to see in his face the anger that matched the words, but saw instead a puzzling mixture of sadness and affection. She felt confused, out of her depth somehow.

"Well, he's done it now, the soft-hearted bannock." Nick began to collect the picnic things. He gave the blanket a sharp tug. Charlotte moved, and he folded it efficiently and set off by himself in the direction of the van.

"Guess what, Charlotte?" said Ariadne, her eyes bright. "I'm going to Oban!"

"Oh," said Charlotte. "Good."

"I'm going to, like, keep house for them, and Nick and Graham can try out their new stuff on me."

Nineteen

Graham dropped Charlotte and Ariadne at the hotel and drove on to park in the square, where he and Nick arranged to wait. Now that the question of Ariadne's immediate future was settled, there was no point in wasting time. All three of them were eager to be off. Charlotte helped collect Ariadne's few belongings—mostly bits of damp laundry.

"I was so sure I'd be watching *you* leave," said Ariadne, bunching up a petticoat and stuffing it into her shoulder bag. "I never once thought of going with them, you know? But I have this gut feeling, Charlotte. I think it'll work. And if it doesn't, well, okay. I don't have to stay there. I figure it's worth a try, though, you know?"

"Yes," said Charlotte, sitting on the bed. "Of course it is. I really like him, Ariadne. I feel as if he's someone you can trust—he means what he says."

"Graham? Yeah. He's a lot nicer than Ewen. Too bad

that would never have worked out."

Charlotte seized the opening. "But it isn't too late. You're getting another chance," she pointed out. "I think he's in love with you."

"Graham?" Ariadne paused and looked at Charlotte. "Oh, no."

"Why not? He was worried enough about you to come all the way up here, and when we were talking—"

"Look, Charlotte. It's not like that. I mean, he's this really caring, sensitive person and everything, but—well, it's Nick."

"It's Nick?" Charlotte echoed. "You mean you're in love with *Nick?*"

"Oh, Charlotte—it's Nick and Graham. It's always been Nick and Graham, since before I met them. You didn't guess?"

Charlotte closed her mouth and shook her head. "They don't—I mean, I didn't—"

"Yeah, well, you hardly know them and I've spent a lot of time with them, of course. They don't tell everyone they're gay, but it's not this big secret."

"Will it be all right? I mean for you?"

"I'll be fine. Graham's a real sweetie, just like you said. And Nick's okay, too. He's kind of hard to figure out—he comes across like he's mad at you at first, but really he's just shy. He doesn't connect very easily with people, especially women." She sat down beside Charlotte and took her hand. "I'm going to be all right, Charlotte, I really think I am, you know? I'm not just saying it. They'll give me space to figure out what I want to do. It's what I need."

"Nick knows you're pregnant."

Ariadne nodded. "Then Graham does, too, but he didn't say anything. I was going to tell them on the way to Oban, anyway. I still will. Don't worry, Charlotte. They'll take care of me. You know, make sure I drink lots of milk and don't eat pizza all the time and go to the doctor and everything?" She smiled.

Charlotte was aware that she was being teased gently. Reluctantly, she smiled back. For some reason she felt alarmingly close to tears.

She walked back to the van with Ariadne. Graham and Nick were leaning against it. "Nick thought you'd change your mind," said Graham. Nick scowled.

"Oh, no." Ariadne's chin went up. "You're stuck with me, at least for a while—a wee while. Anyway, you guys need me. I'm going to tell you how fantastic you are, just the two of you." At that Nick's expression softened, only slightly, but Charlotte, who'd been watching him, understood that Ariadne was right: together, they'd take care of her. She needn't worry.

Impulsively Ariadne put her arms around Charlotte. "Oh, Charlotte, I don't know what I'd've done without you! I must have one of those guardian angels. I was really down when I met you. See, it proves that things always work out in the end. You've got to remember that. They'll work out for you, too—I just know it."

"Will you write to me?" said Charlotte, hugging her back. "Tell me all about Ziggy. Promise."

"Yeah, of course I will."

"Here's my address—you won't lose it?"

Nick took the piece of paper out of her hand, folded it and put it in his shirt pocket. "It's safe there," said Graham. "Nick never loses anything." And then, to Charlotte's surprise, he gave her a hug. "You'll be all right yourself, will you?"

She nodded. "Oliver—my friend—will be back soon, and then—" She stopped. And then.

Ariadne, who'd climbed into the front seat of the van, leaned out the window. "Maybe it won't be so bad? I mean, once they see you're all right and everything—"

"Maybe," said Charlotte without conviction.

"Well, good luck. I mean, with Oliver. Oh, Charlotte—I wish—" But whatever she wished was carried off in the van to Oban. Charlotte stood and waved until it disappeared at the end of the street.

Ariadne was gone. The realization came like thunder after distant lightning. She tried to swallow, but her throat closed and she almost choked. For a blank, terrifying moment she couldn't think where she was and how she'd gotten there. She grabbed for the nearest handhold; she'd gone almost a block before she stopped and made herself begin to think. Instinctively she'd headed toward Bayview Cottage, but that was the wrong answer. Oliver would be unreachable. If she tried to explain her panic to him he would withdraw still further and she'd be hurt and angry. Misunderstanding and hurt feelings were luxuries they had no time for.

The hotel was wrong, too; if she went there, she'd have nothing to do but wait and fill herself with dread. She had been using Ariadne as a shield. As long as she was there,

Charlotte could hide behind Ariadne's problems; without her, Charlotte had no protection from her own.

For the first time, Charlotte thought about her parents and wondered how they must have felt when they called London Sunday night. For a whole day they hadn't known where she was. Since she and Oliver had left London, *no* one had known where they were. If they'd gotten into trouble somewhere—

But they hadn't, and that was an unproductive line of thought. She looked at her watch: two-thirty. She had to *do* something, so she chose one of the banks in the square and cashed two fifty-dollar travelers' checks. If she was on the verge of being sent home in disgrace, then it didn't matter how much of her money she spent, and she felt a sudden urgency to find presents to take back with her.

For the next hour and a half she distracted herself by poking through gift shops, examining shelves full of souvenirs. She bought a pair of horn salad tools for Deb and Skip, and a letter opener for George Schuyler. For Pat she chose a tea towel patterned with Scottish thistles, and for Kath a mug decorated with Shetland ponies. In one shop she found a corner full of books and picked out a folksong collection arranged for guitar to send Eliot, and an illustrated book of folktales for Jean. Paul would have to figure out what to do with a paperweight; for Andy and Kath's younger brother, Dan, she got an envelope of British stamps, and for the youngest Schuylers two highland cows. She'd thought of getting Cindy a sheep and Carl a cow, but realized that one of them would only want what the other had. Thinking of everybody filled her with a hot, fierce yearning. In a day or two she'd be seeing them. She'd be safe at home, where she could stop having to concentrate so hard on everything and let other people assume responsibility for the structure of her life.

If only she could just skip over the Paula and Eric part—go straight home to her family and get the worst over quickly. At least Paula and Eric already knew what she and Oliver had done, and she and Oliver didn't have to face the trip back to London with the awful burden of confession hanging over them. They'd been so intent on getting to Cullen to see Captain MacPherson, they hadn't given a thought to the journey south—at least Charlotte hadn't. Oliver probably had, being Oliver, but he hadn't mentioned it.

Thinking about it now, Charlotte realized that it would have been dangerous as well as grim. Dangerous because the focus would have changed; they'd have lost their sense of mission and that would have altered the balance between them in a way she knew she wasn't ready for. Whatever she'd fantasized before leaving Concord, she'd told Ariadne the truth: she wasn't old enough yet.

There was more to it than that; of course there was. The one person she hadn't found a present for anywhere was Andy. She had considered buying him a mug like Kath's, only decorated with sheep and a sheepdog. It was very attractive, but it wasn't right. Andy had nothing to do with sheep. Either she found him the right thing, or she took him nothing; she couldn't just buy him a present that had no meaning. He was too important.

The hotel was quiet. She checked at the desk, not

expecting anything, but, to her surprise, there was a message for her. She recognized the envelope: it was the one she'd left for Oliver that morning. He'd crossed out his name and written hers, and he'd used the back of her note. "Charlotte—it's 12:40. I'm going back at 2:30. Maybe I'll see you somewhere in town. Oliver. P.S.—back for dinner."

She'd missed him. If only she'd known—but what if she had? She couldn't have deserted Ariadne, and she couldn't imagine Oliver going along on the picnic with Nick and Graham. Ach, what a muddle, as Graham had said!

Heavily she went upstairs, washed her face, brushed her hair and rebraided it, tucked herself in, smoothed herself down, and figured she'd done the best she could. It was just after four. She returned to the lobby, where she chose an inconspicuous chair and settled so she could see anyone coming in the front door. Oliver said he'd be back for dinner, which meant he didn't plan to be on hand when his mother and stepfather arrived. It had doubtless occurred to him that if she saw Charlotte first, Paula was likely to have calmed down somewhat by the time she got to him. Charlotte hoped that meant Oliver was not going to be hostile and difficult, but she knew there was no guarantee of that, and Paula certainly had good reason to be upset with him. No, to be fair, she had every reason to be furious.

Charlotte hadn't a clue what part Eric Preston would play in the looming drama: whether he'd remain aloof and uninvolved, or take his wife's side, or try to mediate between Paula and Oliver. Maybe, Charlotte thought with grim humor, she should suggest he take her out to dinner somewhere and leave mother and son to fight it out on their own. If only she dared, but Eric Preston made her nervous, quite apart from everything else.

This was all Oliver's fault, he'd said so from the beginning. She couldn't be held responsible for arriving in London on the wrong date when she hadn't known it was wrong. Certainly she was blameless up to that point, and beyond it—before she realized something fundamental was wrong. But that's where she ran into trouble. When *had* she realized? If she was being absolutely honest, she had to confess she'd guessed before Oliver had told her. She was too smart to be that dumb. And when she'd guessed, that's when her parents and Paula would figure she should have done something. She could have gone to the woman downstairs, Paula's friend Connie, and asked for advice. Or she could have called home and let her parents figure it out. Her father had friends in London and Paula would have been back in a few days. If she'd acted then, the damage would have been minimal; she and Oliver could have patched together some kind of story between them to explain what had happened. The parents would all agree she'd behaved responsibly.

But what of her responsibility to Oliver? He had relied on her to understand the urgency of the situation and to help him. He'd given her a choice: to go to Scotland with him, or to stay in London. He probably thought it was a *real* choice when he offered it. But Charlotte, on reflection, saw that it wasn't. Lots of choices were deceptive that way, apparently straightforward until you thought hard about the consequences. Then you saw there were right answers and there were wrong answers. If Charlotte had picked the wrong answer to this one, she wondered if Oliver would have forgiven her. That was a risk she hadn't been willing to take.

Lost in her thoughts, Charlotte wasn't paying attention to the people who came wandering through the lobby on the way in or out. But when Paula Preston walked through the front door she was instantly alert, as if Paula had tripped an alarm in her head. Her heart began to hammer at her ribs as she watched Paula cross to the reception desk and ring the bell. She wore a pair of fawn slacks and a silky, silver-green shirt, and she looked thinner than Charlotte remembered, her blond hair pulled severely back from her face and secured with a green scarf. She had a leather shoulder bag and a small suitcase, and she seemed to be alone.

Charlotte sat for a moment, gathering herself together, then stood and squared her shoulders self-consciously. "Hello, Mrs. Preston."

Paula turned sharply. "Charlotte?" Her face had lost its soft prettiness since Charlotte had seen her last, and the tendons in her neck were visible. Perhaps it was weariness and strain that showed; she'd only just returned from one trip to face another, unexpected one, fraught with crisis. There was an awkward silence, as if neither of them knew what to say next. Then Paula asked, "Where's Oliver?"

"He'll be here soon." Charlotte made an effort to sound confident.

"Soon?" Paula frowned. "You don't mean he's left you here?"

"Oh, no. I mean, yes, he has, but only just for the afternoon. He's visiting a friend. It's kind of complicated, but I can explain."

"I think Oliver's the one who needs to explain, Charlotte," said Paula dryly.

"He will, but—where's Mr. Preston?"

"He didn't come with me. He couldn't get away."

Charlotte tried to read her expression, but she couldn't tell whether this was good or bad.

"If you'd just sign here, madam?" said the receptionist. Mrs. Findlay's niece must have been having the day off; the man from the bar was behind the desk. "I'll need your address and car registration number. Here's your room key. Will you need help with your bags?"

"No, thank you." Paula copied the number off the Avis key ring, then turned back to Charlotte. Her eyes were green, like Oliver's; Charlotte was suddenly struck by the resemblance between them. She had no idea what Paula was thinking. "It's been a long trip. You wait here while I go and freshen up. Then if Oliver hasn't put in an appearance, you and I will have a talk."

Slowly, Charlotte let her breath out and nodded. She wondered what Oliver would want her to tell Paula, then decided that it didn't matter since he wasn't there.

"Just a pot of tea for me, please, with lemon," said Paula. "Charlotte?"

They were sitting in a corner of the lounge. A nattily

dressed older man sat some distance away, reading a book and eating a large cream cake. The sight of it made Charlotte feel slightly queasy. "Oh, tea's fine," she said. "I'm not hungry." Paula didn't urge her to change her mind. They sat in silence until the waitress, who couldn't have been more than fifteen or sixteen, returned with a tray, which she set on the table in front of Paula.

"Um, milk and sugar, please?" said Charlotte in answer to Paula's query.

Paula squeezed a slice of lemon into her tea, took a sip, and sat back in her chair while Charlotte stirred and stirred hers and wondered despairingly what to say. Looking at the liquid in the cup, she wasn't at all sure she could swallow it; the silence was paralyzing.

At last Paula set her cup and saucer down and said, "Well. Perhaps you can begin by telling me where Oliver is. Who is this friend he's visiting, and why didn't he take you with him?"

"I could have gone, but I didn't want to. We both went yesterday, but the whole point is for Oliver to talk to him—that's why we came. He and Commodore Shattuck were on the same convoy ship during the war. They were very good friends."

"The war was a long time ago, Charlotte. How did Oliver find out about this man?"

"He came to Concord—the first year Oliver was there. We all met him when he visited the Commodore." She paused, feeling unequal to the task of explaining to Oliver's mother about that April nineteenth, when Captain MacPherson had arrived in Concord with his motley troop of Britishers. "Oliver wrote to Captain MacPherson when his great-uncle died, to let him know."

"MacPherson?" Paula's expression was thoughtful. "Oliver's had letters from a MacPherson, I remember seeing them. I asked him once or twice—" She stopped and gave Charlotte a hard look. "Were you planning this all along, the two of you?"

Charlotte cast about for an answer that wouldn't damn Oliver. "Not from the beginning, no. But Captain MacPherson isn't well and Oliver felt it was really important to visit him now—and—well, I agreed."

"Did Oliver tell you that Eric and I weren't going to be in London when you arrived?"

"Um, not exactly."

"Not exactly?"

Charlotte gave up on her tea. "No, he didn't."

Paula nodded. "So when you left Boston you didn't know."

"No," said Charlotte in a small voice.

"And did he tell you when he met you at the airport? I'm assuming he did meet you at Heathrow?"

"Yes, of course he did. He'd promised he would."

Paula was not impressed. "But he didn't tell you then."

"Not right away. But"—she forced herself to meet Paula's eyes—"there wasn't any point, not when I'd just gotten off the plane. I wouldn't have turned around and gotten back on it. How could I?"

"And then he tricked you into coming to this godforsaken place by telling you this person—this friend of his uncle's—is sick." Paula's face was calm, but her eyes glittered.

"No." Charlotte felt her courage seeping back. "He didn't trick me. He asked me if I'd come with him to visit Captain MacPherson, that's all. If I'd said no, we wouldn't have come."

"Oh no, of course not," said Paula with a trace of bitterness. "Oliver knows how to apply pressure in very subtle ways."

Charlotte bit her tongue to keep from asking how he'd learned. Provoking Paula would accomplish nothing.

"I knew he was angry with me, naturally I did. He made no secret of it. But it never occurred to me he'd do this. I told him we weren't canceling your visit, Charlotte, only postponing it a week. We set another date and I rescheduled as much as I could. I'd never have done it if it hadn't been so important. I had to go with Eric, there wasn't a choice. I thought Oliver understood that, but clearly he didn't, or he wasn't listening to me." Her hands were clasped in her lap, the thumb and index finger of her right hand worrying the rings on her left. She gazed fixedly at the man reading. He'd finished his cream cake and was peacefully absorbed, but the intensity of Paula's stare made him look up uneasily. She didn't notice. He closed his book and left.

Making up her mind to face the worst head-on, Charlotte said, "What are you going to do now?"

"About what?" Paula blinked, refocusing.

"Us. Me. What will happen?"

"We'll go back to London tomorrow."

"Then what?"

"What do you think I should do?"

"I expect you'll send me home as soon as possible." In the face of Paula's challenge, Charlotte found she was quite calm.

"Is that what you want?"

That was not the right question. She had no answer ready for it.

Paula didn't wait for one. Instead she said, "You have every reason to be angry with him yourself, Charlotte. I'd certainly understand if you wanted to go straight home. He's used you to get back at me, you do realize that."

At some level she did, and the knowledge was painful, but Paula made it sound simple, and this was so much more complicated. What Charlotte hadn't considered, however, was that what Oliver had done would hurt his mother. She'd known it would make Paula upset and furious, but not that it would hurt her. She didn't want to think about that; it confused everything still further. "But it was all planned," she protested. "I had my passport and my ticket. We'd been planning it for months and months."

"It was only a week, Charlotte. If Oliver had done what he was supposed to, you would be on the plane tonight. I'd changed our reservations in the Cotswolds, reserved theater tickets, gotten everything reorganized. Eric's trip came up suddenly and I had to made a quick decision. We'd hardly seen each other for months and we needed a little time together. I really had no choice—I had to go with him. I never imagined Oliver would do this to me."

"What about my parents?" asked Charlotte, backing

away from what Paula was telling her. "What did they say when you called them?"

"They were glad to know you're safe and that we knew where you were." Paula's tone was ironic. "I spoke to your father and he sounded remarkably calm, considering. I promised you'd phone them tonight—they'd like to hear your voice. You are safe, aren't you?"

Charlotte nodded, thinking of Ariadne, wondering would it have made things better or worse if she'd still been there. Paula seemed to have forgotten all about the friend Charlotte had mentioned—or perhaps she'd never really believed in her existence.

"Suppose," Paula went on, "suppose we were to send you straight home. What do you think that would accomplish?"

Cautiously, Charlotte said, "I'm not sure what you mean."

"You can believe me, I came up here with every intention of doing precisely that. We'd fly back to London and put you on the first possible plane to Boston. You might very well not have left Heathrow. That's what I told Eric I was going to do. But on the way up here I've had time to reconsider. Of course, if that's what you want and what your parents insist on, then that's what we'll do."

Feeling uneasy, Charlotte wondered why what *she* wanted to do had any bearing on what was going to happen. Paula was watching her, gauging her reaction. "You still have a week of your original holiday left."

She was right, although it hardly seemed possible. It felt like months and months ago that Charlotte had sat on her bedroom floor packing and repacking her luggage. . . .

"Well, I propose to let you stay."

"You do? Why?"

"For several reasons. I'm sure my son expects me to send you home immediately. He expects me to punish him. But I doubt very much that he's bothered to consider that it would punish you, too, even though this isn't really your fault. Or not the worst of it. I don't think that's fair. But to be honest with you, Charlotte, I would very much like to surprise Oliver."

Charlotte blinked at her. "You will."

"After Sam died, you know, I thought I had another chance," she went on. "Eric and I were married and I felt as if I had a much more secure foundation for my life. I'd stepped back from the edge. And Oliver was old enough to understand some of the things he couldn't when his father and I split up. I hoped we were both at a place where we could finally make a relationship. I knew it wouldn't be perfect. Oliver and I will never be really close, we've lost too much time. He's almost grown up."

"Do you think letting me stay will change that?" asked Charlotte.

Paula didn't answer right away. After a while she said, "I know that if I send you home, that will only make things worse. It will give him one more reason to hate me. No, I don't believe letting you stay will make much difference to the way he feels about me, but sending you home will. Does that make sense to you?"

It did.

"When he's old enough," Paula went on, "he'll leave. I

know that. He's just waiting. And when he does leave it will be a relief for both of us, but I can't tell you how much I will miss him. I'll always regret what we didn't have. All I can hope for, Charlotte, is that maybe once in a while, just briefly, he'll come back." The words floated in the air between them like cigarette smoke, gradually dispersing. Charlotte bent her head, studying her hands. Absently she noticed that she'd broken a fingernail somehow. With a brittle chink, Paula set down her cup and said, "But it's your choice, of course. If you don't want to stay, you can say so and I'll understand."

For a moment Charlotte was tempted. She had already adjusted her mind to the idea of being sent home; Paula's unexpected proposition required an abrupt shift of gears. Charlotte couldn't avoid the conviction that this whole adventure had gone on long enough. She was tired of feeling squeezed between Paula and Oliver. If she stayed in London, no matter how well everybody behaved, the week ahead would be as strenuous as the last one: filled with tensions, self-conscious politeness, carefully disguised suspicion. If she went home, she'd be able to let go of it all, reflect in peace about what had happened, and make up her own mind about it.

With a resigned little sigh, Charlotte raised her head to find Paula watching her with an intensity that belied her calm. Paula was giving her another non-choice. "It's all right," said Charlotte. "I'll stay."